I0654443

# Queen of the Quantum Realm
## Book 1 of the Nanosia Series
### Rhonda Denise Johnson

# Table of Contents

ISBN

978-1-958248-00-3

# Table of Contents

# Acknowledgements

Thanks goes to Dr. Alexander Karl Knochel of Heidelberg. The German physicist who authenticated the names and behaviors of elementary particles so that I could flesh them out in this novel.

Much thanks is due to Lisa Gilliam who fought the never ending battle of proofreading.

Thanks goes to Katie Weiland for her online treasure chest Helping Writers Become Authors

Thanks as well to Theophilus Nortey of Ghana for his art work.

The Nanosia Fantasy Series is truly an international effort.

# Chapter 1

"Plague! The purple plague!"

Jawan froze as a surge of panicked town folks rushed toward him.

He tried to reason out what was going on, but his heart raced as he picked up the hysteria of fifty wild-eyed faces, coming closer at a speed that only fear could drive them.

The summer sun shone down with indifferent brightness as farmers pushed slowpokes out of their way with pitchforks and shopkeepers puffed along, trying to avoid the pitchforks. Children of all shapes and sizes ran ahead of women in long dresses ill-suited for running, much less escaping.

"Fools!" an old man screamed. "You can't outrun the plague!"

But he might as well have asked a whirlwind to stop and think its actions through. A grocer abandoned his vegetable cart and darted down a side street. Tomatoes leaped into the air and stained the cobblestones blood-red as the horde raced on, heedless of anything in its way.

The only intelligible sounds Jawan heard over the staccato of pounding feet were piercing cries:

"The plague!"

*No!* Not here. The plague was something that happened to other people, in other unfortunate places.

"It's here!" came a scream, slaying his only sustaining, but false, security. The purple plague had found its slow, malignant way to Hadley Town.

"Plague!"

The single-minded mantra echoed through his head and up the street, and Jawan envisioned his own body squashed underfoot like a tomato if he didn't run. They were coming fast, young boys like himself and men. So close. *Run!* His frozen legs ignored him.

Like spooked horses, they'd gallop right over him. On this narrow street, Jawan saw only one way they could go—past shuttered shops, over startled pigeons, toward him.

*Move, legs!* He screamed at his comatose body to move. He started running—just another spooked horse. Fear was guiding him. He had to stop and think where he was going. Stop?! *No!* Run and think. He could think while he ran. He had to get out of their path before they trampled him.

An alley that smelled of rotting garbage even from ten feet away offered his only escape. Holding his breath, he dashed into the mouth of the alley, crashing through garbage and castaways. He heard the shrill terror of the crowd as they swarmed past the alley, but he didn't look back. The mob and the plague some of them might even be carrying were behind him—gone another way.

But like the man warned, they couldn't escape that dreaded disease no one could see. He had to tell his master. Myrlo, the great earth mage, would know how to stop this.

If only he could reach Myrlo before the mob spread their panic all over the town. They went another way and would not chase him down this alley. Still, he couldn't stop. He had to reach his master.

The other end of the alley seemed a long way off, and Jawan thought he'd never breathe fresh air again. As the mob's clamor faded into the distance, he heard glass crunch under his feet, and the sharp edges of discarded furniture scratched his limbs. But he paid it no mind. The stench and decay only made him long for the stuffy rooms of his master's castle, and the stuffier books he had to study as an apprentice of earth magic.

Finally, Jawan emerged from the alley and raced down one of Hadley Town's narrow little streets. Front doors and a little less garbage distinguished the street from the alley. As shanty after shanty sped behind him, he wondered if his master sent him on these trips to the market only to show him how different the lives of other people were from his own.

No thick stone walls, turrets, and battlements protected these people. Instead, they lived in rickety wooden hovels. The most prosperous among them might have had a house made of mud bricks. But Jawan knew that wouldn't keep out the winter chill or the plague.

He stumbled over some children playing a game on the sidewalk.

"Where you going?" a boy with ruddy cheeks and ragged curls asked as Jawan muttered an apology and kept going.

Jawan knew they would stare after him, a boy not much older than they were—young enough to play with them, but old enough to give them something.

Oblivious to their poverty, they chased one another around, just like Jawan used to play in the mud outside a house just like these. The children didn't know, as he hadn't known, the wrongness of a yard not covered by lush grass, or that their beds were supposed to be more than sacks filled with straw, as his had been.

A nagging stitch in his side made him slow to a lope. He worried that he wouldn't reach his master in time, but he had to slow down. He certainly wouldn't be in time if he collapsed in the street. Though he wanted to stop altogether and sit down somewhere, he kept up a steady jog. Then he heard someone call his name.

"Hey, Jawan."

Jawan looked up from his musings and saw his friend Sipal. So, while his mind fled the crowd, intent on reaching Myrlo, his feet had taken him down a street he knew well.

Sipal's usually cheerful eyes darted around. He'd obviously come out to clear debris from his front yard but was holding his rake like he might have to club somebody with it.

"Slow down," Sipal squealed, not lowering his rake. "What's going on? What was all that yelling? What're you running from?"

*He'd heard it?* Jawan gulped. Of course, he'd heard it. And he'd go down there to the market, walking right into what the mob had been running away from, if Jawan didn't think of a way to stop him.

Jawan paused, the word *plague* on the tip of his tongue. Should he tell him? No, he might as well run down the street like those terrified people shouting and carrying panic throughout the whole town. No, he'd better tell his master first.

Jawan glanced over his shoulder as if expecting someone to come up behind him.

"I l-lost them," he said with a belated gasp.

Sipal frowned. "Lost who?"

That's what Jawan liked about Sipal. He didn't make fun of Jawan's stutter but kept on like it was perfectly normal and not worth noticing.

"Th-thugs from the Dripping Daggers gang."

"They were chasing you?!" Sipal's big green eyes grew even bigger.

"Well, n-no. Something's going on down near the market, and I guess they just wanted me to go away."

"They're always up to something," Sipal said, embarrassment reddening his cheeks as he lowered his rake to the ground. "But never so loud. They were screaming."

"I th-think there might be a gang war brewing. From what I heard, one of them got played."

"Played?"

"Y-you know, somebody played a trick on him, and now the whole gang is mad. I barely escaped with my life. You'd better stay away from the market until this trouble settles."

Jawan knew he was overdoing it, but if it worked . . . Then he remembered his mission.

"W-well, listen, I need to go tell my master something. But stay away from the market for a while—unless you want to run into one of the Steps or the Daggers."

"Oh, no! No way. You don't have to tell me twice to stay away from those lads. Not like I can pull an avalanche down on them." Sipal frowned at this thought. "I wish I had magic and could be an apprentice. Your life is so exciting."

Jawan shrugged and took off. As he ran, he gave himself a mental thump on the head. Something happening down at the market? Well. It wasn't a complete lie. There was something going on down there, and he had seen some gang thugs somewhere, just not at the market today. And they were always planning something. At least this would keep Sipal away from danger.

His feet fell on smooth streets, repaired by his master's earth magic. He detoured around piles of refuse and slick puddles, wondering if the town folks expected his master to keep the streets clean as well. But some problems Myrlo couldn't, wouldn't, repair. He could do nothing about the hearts of the people. They thought having magic performed for them as no more consequential than falling rain.

Despite this, Jawan couldn't imagine his master not helping the people. Without the earth mage's ministrations, many of which the people weren't even aware, life in the town would be wiped out by the Earth's overpowering vicissitudes.

He reached a corner where he knew he had to turn. The red daggers painted on the doors farther down that street marked the territory of the Dripping Daggers gang.

The king's soldiers, sworn to keep law and order on the streets, made themselves scarce for anything short of an out-and-out insurrection. And they did nothing about the gangs. If Jawan entered gang territory, he'd be on his own. So, he turned left on Cobblers Alley and took the long way around to his master's castle.

Just ahead of him, a blind man in rags begged for alms on the corner.

Before Jawan crossed the street to drop something in the man's cup, members of the Dreaded Steps gang approached the man.

They were out of their territory. Probably on their way to start something with the Dripping Daggers. Jawan tried to keep running. He had to get to his master, and he didn't want to tangle with those lads. But something about the way the thugs snickered and elbowed each other as they eyed the beggar made him stop.

"Alms for the poor," the beggar cried out.

"Shut up," one of the thugs sneered, throwing a rock at the man. "I'm tired of hearing a mouse squeaking."

"What's he got in the cup?" another Step asked.

Jawan started toward the bullies, then stopped. What was he thinking? The Dreaded Steps weren't people you could talk out of mischief. But by the time he considered his options, their deeds against the blind man would be done.

His master warned him not to use magic, especially not in public. He was just an apprentice, after all, and something could go wrong. His master wanted him to use spells to direct and fine-tune his raw magic. Spells! He had to talk right to use spells, but that, his master assured him, would give him the control that wasn't always there in his innate magic.

Jawan had no spells, but he knew he couldn't win a fistfight against three big beefy thugs. He'd get hurt, maybe killed, and the thugs would still have their way with the beggar.

Taking his master's "especially" to mean there were exceptions, Jawan located his target and backed into the shadow of a nearby tree. The Steps hadn't seen him and wouldn't know what hit them. Using earth magic, he picked up a rock near the blind man and threw it back at the thug.

Wincing from the blow, the thug whirled on the beggar. "Why, you dirty rag doll. Hit me, will you?"

He raised his foot to kick the man. But Jawan rolled the pebbles under his other foot, tumbling him to the ground. The other two Steps started to close in on the blind man, but Jawan concentrated his magic on all the stones in sight. The stones rose unsteadily, shaking this way and that, as if they weren't sure what they were doing in the air. He gritted his teeth and focused as each stone hurled itself at the thugs until they were all laid out on the ground.

They weren't dead, but they'd need a physician for sure. These superstitious creeps would accept that they couldn't explain some mysteries and shouldn't mess with some people—like supposedly blind beggars who could aim rocks at their heads with painful accuracy.

Jawan turned to run. How much time had he lost now? But before he could take a step, he heard the old man beckon him.

"Young lad."

Jawan walked to the man as if compelled. He had to go home, but his feet were not his. They kept walking toward that voice, carefully avoiding the bodies reposed on the ground.

"Y-yes, sir?"

The man looked right at him, though Jawan couldn't imagine that his milky white eyes saw him.

"Thank you for helping a tired old man."

Jawan blinked his own eyes. "What? Thank me for what? I didn't do anything."

The old man's face crinkled into a mischievous smile. "Did something you aren't supposed to, huh? Don't worry. I won't tell."

Jawan was dumbfounded. How did this blind man know? Even if he had eyesight, how could he know Jawan's secrets?

"H-how did you know? How could you even know what happened?"

"You'd be surprised what I know. Others see only with their eyes. I see with the whole Earth."

"Th-the Earth?"

"That's how I knew you, mage of my mother."

"I'm n-not a mage. I'm just an apprentice."

Jawan could have sworn the man's colorless orbs regarded him even more keenly.

"Ah, lad. You don't know yourself. You don't see what I see. If you did, you would not stutter, for you would have confidence in yourself."

"C-confidence? I don't understand."

"No. I guess you don't. But you will. You are a poor boy who does not know the world, but, boy, you will marry a queen."

Jawan felt his legs released from the beggar's spell and took that as a dismissal. He raced back to his master's castle, wondering what had just happened to him. If the man had magic, he could have disposed of the thugs himself. He'd known what was going on but had let Jawan take care of it. Who was he?

Marry a queen? Jawan tried to dismiss this as the ramblings of an old man who hadn't had enough to eat. But what had he meant by confidence? Jawan mused. *Was that the answer?*

He passed the last dingy hovels on the outskirts of the town and made his way down a path flanked by wildflowers and weeds. That reminded him that he still didn't have the plants his master needed for his magic potions. He'd have none now. If only Myrlo could use these wildflowers and weeds. But he needed the exotic plants the merchants brought from afar.

There was no help for it. No telling what he might find at the market—or what might find him. Better to go back to his master empty-handed than with a nasty little gift. He shrugged and sighed. One way or the other, he'd have to bear the bad news that the plague had come this far north. With that task ahead of him, Jawan slowed down, allowing gravity and inertia to prolong each step.

He tiptoed into his master's laboratory, though he needn't have bothered. Myrlo was already there.

Jawan paused at the door, sweat coating his hands where the package his master sent him to get should have been. With anyone else, he could have taken this time to calm himself, but Myrlo, the great earth magician, knew everything that moved around his castle. He could fine-tune his focus or stretch it out with diminishing results.

"What has frightened you, boy?" Myrlo asked without moving his eye from his nanoscope.

There was no help for it. Jawan stepped forward, empty hands clasped behind his back.

"Th-the plague is here. I heard the town folks screaming . . . and I ran."

Jawan tried to get his tongue to move as fast as his thoughts, but it tripped all over itself, stuttering the words out as his mind raced on to the next five thoughts. It made him sound and feel stupid.

"Yes, I know. It's what I've been studying," Myrlo said impatiently, as if he didn't want to talk about it.

Jawan stared at his master. *He knew?* In his long, dark earth-colored robe, in the depths of his forest-green eyes, Myrlo knew!

"Y-you knew it was here?"

"I knew . . . well, there've been reports."

Of course, he would know. Myrlo knew everything, even if he didn't tell Jawan everything. That was the way of magicians, to conceal more than they revealed. But still, Jawan sensed his master's unease.

"W-why are you studying it? Why not just make it go away?"

"And how am I to do that?" Myrlo raised his head from his nanoscope only to show his irritation. "I don't have a magic wand. I work with the elements, not against them, and I can't do anything until I know what I'm dealing with, and that takes study."

Jawan's heart slumped inside him. He'd been so sure the powerful earth master would rise to obliterate the problem.

"P-people will die, master."

"Yes, I've heard the rumors from other towns. People with the plague are given up for dead. There's nothing I can do."

Jawan squealed in frustration. "But there must be something we can do."

Myrlo clucked his tongue, and Jawan gulped. He'd never spoken so boldly to his master before. Not in eight years. Though the stern-faced mage in the dark robe no longer terrified him, Jawan always kept his objections to himself. Some masters would whip their apprentices for merely raising an eyebrow at them. His master had never raised a hand at him. Still, Jawan shuddered, thinking maybe he needed to check himself before he went too far.

But suppose someone he knew came down with the plague? One of his friends? He didn't want to believe his master didn't care about the people, but he found it just as incredible that Myrlo, the great earth mage, didn't know what to do. Jawan had seen him perform awesome feats of magic and couldn't understand why a plague should be beyond his ability.

Didn't disease come from the earth? It was something that was supposed to exist, just not inside people's bodies. He started to open his mouth, sure that logic and reason were on his side. But Myrlo had turned back to his nanoscope, clearly out of patience with a discussion he'd rather avoid.

Jawan tried anyway. "Th-there's got to be something we can do."

"*We* aren't going to do anything right now. I will continue my studies, and you, young man, will focus on yours. Are you ready for the coming exam?"

"N-not quite," Jawan admitted. "But I will be."

"*Will be* is not the same as *am*. Saving lives is an honorable pursuit, but you will save a lot more if you focus on moving past apprenticeship."

Jawan wondered at these dismissive words. An honorable pursuit? As if saving lives were an extracurricular activity, or a hobby—something to do in his spare time. *Honorable pursuit.* This didn't sound like Myrlo at all, and that troubled Jawan.

"You should be in the library right now instead of worrying over matters you are ill-prepared to deal with. I'm not even sure what I can do. Be off with you."

"Y-yes, sir."

***

Jawan heaved open the massive doors of his master's vast library and walked past rows and rows of books that held the secrets of the Earth. Books like *Master of Spells*. He wanted to touch the spines. Just touch them. But once, as a small and curious child, he'd merely brushed the surface, and a spark ran through his fingers and up his arm.

Fascinated, he'd pulled the book from its shelf. The spark increased until it became painful. These books weren't just about magic, they embodied magic.

The memory still made him shudder. He walked on past until he came to a recess where Myrlo kept a special section of shelves containing the books for Jawan to learn what he needed to know as an apprentice. And these were the only ones that didn't try to electrocute him when he touched them.

"Jawan."

He stopped, wondering who could be calling him. There should be no one else in the library. He shrugged and dismissed it as the rustling of his slippered feet on the stone floor.

The upcoming exam would test him on quantum physics and the elements controlled by the five mages. He pulled down the books he needed to read: *A Comprehensive Study of Bosons and Fermions, Pair Production as a Means to Create Matter, Mastering the Elements, Synergy of the Elements.*

"Jawan."

He swerved around to see who had called him in this empty chamber but saw no one.

He opened *A Comprehensive Study of Bosons and Fermions* and turned to where he'd left off:

Magical Science: Matter and Antimatter

Positrons are antimatter. They are identical to electrons except they are positively charged while electrons are negatively charged. See Figure C to transform a positron into an electron using W bosons.

"Jawan, we know you hear us calling."

He stiffened and focused all his energy on Figure C. It showed a W boson colliding with a positron, changing it into a neutrino. Then another W boson collided with the neutrino, changing it into an electron. He read on:

> "A neutrino is a form of dark matter, not to be confused with antimatter. They can become hot dark matter when their velocity approaches the speed of light."

Jawan closed his eyes and pictured a sphere of dark matter dancing to his own choreography. Irrational, he knew. Dark matter wasn't visible. But he could imagine it. Just like he could imagine himself moving mountains by his will alone. He'd never seen even Myrlo move a mountain, but he liked to think big.

"We'll dance too, Jawan. If you dare open our pages."

Jawan looked around. That wasn't rustling slippers or paper. The voices were coming from Myrlo's forbidden books.

If he dared open their pages. He remembered the pain.

"When you were a little kid, yes. But what about now?"

Jawan stiffened again. Did they know his thoughts? He lived in a world of magic. His master performed wondrous feats that no ordinary human could, but to have his mind invaded by books he wasn't even allowed to read . . .

The voice taunted him. "And do you still believe you can't read us, just like you couldn't when you were a little runt?"

This was too much. Jawan sat up, staring toward the magic books. No, this was magic. This was real. The books knew him and had something to tell him.

What? When he was a little kid. After eight years, did he have no more power? He still couldn't utter a decent spell.

"And you never will, reading those baby books."

Picking up one page with languid fingers, he glared at it, remembering once again what it meant. There were no spells in the books Myrlo let him read.

He sighed. Despite his academic successes, Jawan longed to practice real magic. Though Myrlo made sure his apprentice understood the responsibilities that went with the power, Jawan couldn't wait for the day he'd acquire the highest honor of magicians. He'd be able to go to those secret meetings.

"They won't be secret anymore. All the secrets lie within our pages. Just waiting for you. If you dare."

Rising from his seat, Jawan walked toward the forbidden stacks. He could at least find the book that was talking to him. Hold it in his hands and learn its secrets. There had to be something to those books, else why would they be protected with magic? And why could there be only one master of each element?

"Only one earth mage. Learn our secrets, and you can be that one."

*Earth mage?* That meant Myrlo would have to die. Jawan gulped and hurried back to his seat. He put the sphere of dark matter down in his mind like a toy he no longer wanted to play with. How could he play when he coveted a position that could only be his after his master died? He didn't want that.

Myrlo had been the earth mage as long as Jawan could remember, and he couldn't imagine the Earth without him. Truth be told, Jawan knew the planet would be in big trouble if its stability depended on his limited knowledge.

Magic books? Humph! They'd told him what he'd desperately wanted to hear. Maybe one day he would overcome stuttering and move up to a journeyman. But to be the kind of master the Earth needed he'd first have to master himself.

There was no help for it. From the bottom of a well-established hierarchy, Jawan turned his focus on moving from apprentice to journeyman. Journeyman. He liked the sound of that. Journeyman—especially the man part.

Jawan sighed. Who was he kidding? Eight years of stuttering every time he opened his mouth. Eight years and still studying for tests that he should have taken long ago if his master meant to make him a journeyman.

All this jumbled in his mind with the realization that nothing would stop the mob spreading panic all over town. He'd raced back, believing that Myrlo the Great would take care of everything, but instead . . .

The library closed in around him, not with dingy brick walls but with endless rows of books from which he'd never escape.

Maybe his master knew that he'd never be a journeyman and just didn't want to break the bad news. Jawan had invested so much and excelled in all his lessons. If only he could write his way out of apprenticeship. But one day he would have to utter a spell. If he stuttered, he might accidentally call up a gigantic mudslide or make a mountain collapse. This must be what his master feared.

His friend Loby liked to boast about being the fire master's journeyman. Jawan could hope, he could wish, but he feared he'd always be a lifelong apprentice, fit to be sent to the market or to fetch for his master, but little else.

# Chapter 2

Myrlo watched Jawan head for the library to study.

The stillness of the laboratory suddenly enveloped Myrlo like a shroud. The room was full of things—his nanoscope, a microscope, racks of culture dishes holding samples of earth, rock, plant, and animal. Still, when Jawan left the room, it was empty. Water dripped in the sink, and birds rustled under the eaves. But still, it was quiet.

Maybe he shouldn't have let the boy grow on him like this. Jawan could be a journeyman with all his scholastic success, but he had to stop stuttering or he would never move past academics and take on the practical aspects of magic.

That was a tremendous burden by itself, but it wasn't the only worry bedeviling Myrlo's mind. Jawan's report meant news of the purple plague now ran loose in the streets of Hadley Town.

Myrlo blamed the authorities' mismanagement. If they had just kept it in quiet quarantine while he and the other elemental mages searched for a cure. Now the pressure was immense.

He turned back to his nanoscope, hoping something he hadn't seen before would dispel his worries.

The nanoscope went deeper than a microscope, allowing him to see the whirling subatomic particles—bosons and fermions—from a known virus that caused symptoms similar to the plague.

That was all he had to work with, and maybe he'd find something. But just when he saw something unusual, the particles sank out of view, replaced by the one fermion he'd hoped never to see again.

He groaned. He knew where this fermion was—in Nanosia. It was a different world. A world that wanted something from him that he couldn't give.

"Pym."

That was what she'd called herself, so he'd thought of her as a her and a she. His magic senses heard her calling him.

"Yes, it's me. Good to see you. Will you come and help us this time?"

"I'm trying to work."

Frowning, he wished he could just look away, but he needed her to go away so he could see the other particles.

"But you must come, Big One. We need you so desperately."

"I cannot help you. I have nothing to give you."

Pym twirled and offered what might have been a nanoscopic bow.

"The prophecy said you will help us. You must fulfill the prophecy."

"Prophecy? Is this about some religious nonsense?"

"It's not nonsense. The prophet is real. His prophecy is real, and you must . . ."

"Enough! Whatever you believe, it has nothing to do with me, so it must be about someone else. Now will you please . . .?"

"If not you, then who?"

"You'll have to ask your prophet. Now please . . ."

"He is not with us. Come, Big One. Come."

"I will not. Let me get back to my work."

"What do I care about your work if you won't help us?"

"I'll say it once again. Leave and let the other fermions and bosons come out."

"I won't! So there!"

Myrlo threw up his hands and backed away from the nanoscope in frustration. He'd find no answers in Nanosia today.

Without that task to occupy him, his mind floated back to Jawan. He rose to his feet and paced the floor. Something he didn't want to think about—something Jawan didn't even suspect—tugged at Myrlo's mind.

Answers? Is that what Jawan needed? An answer?

He shook his head. As master, he was responsible for giving the boy what he needed. And whether Myrlo found an answer or not, he knew he'd still have to face one dreadful task. He'd have to tell Jawan the truth. The boy's astute mind would eventually see the holes in what his master felt safe telling him, and his youthful imagination would devise every horrid scenario except the truth.

Myrlo could have done it just now, when the boy came to him with news about the plague. But he'd let that perfect opportunity slip by because—? No valid reasons stuck with him.

He slammed his fist into the long wooden table, wanting to bury his cowardly heart in the deepest avalanche.

All he needed to do was open his mouth and say . . . but he couldn't. He could open the Earth and swallow a town, but he couldn't open his mouth and swallow Jawan's heart. The words just would not come.

He felt the weight of responsibility as he remembered how Jawan's father brought the boy to him eight years ago. Caught in the midst of a nasty seismic episode, Myrlo had scant time when the young peddler came to him, claiming his child showed a gift for earth magic.

This kind of imposition happened more frequently than the mage had time to deal with. He felt a little guilty for making the man wait, since his claim turned out to be true. But that was a small regret compared to now.

Myrlo felt like a cold-hearted fiend as he recalled Jawan's little face buried in his mother's skirts.

"It will be all right, son," his father said.

"I'll come to visit often," his mother promised.

But Myrlo shook his forbidding head.

"No, you must not."

Jawan's parents were taken aback.

"Excuse me?" his father asked.

"There will be no contact with his old life until he has finished his studies. Training as a mage is intense, and there must be no visits, letters, or gifts to distract him."

Jawan began to cry as his parents reluctantly left him with his new master.

His mother reached to comfort him one last time, but under Myrlo's grim presence, she could only hug him and wipe his tears quickly before she and her husband hurried away.

"M-ma!" the little boy wailed. And for the first time in his life, Jawan began to stutter.

Guilt wrung Myrlo's heart into a twisted rag. Had he caused Jawan to stutter? The one thing the boy needed was the first thing Myrlo forbade him. Jawan hadn't seen his parents in eight years, and now, he'd never see them again.

Though he forbade the boy to see his parents, Myrlo himself kept a close eye on them. According to Myrlo's plan, after the lengthy but temporary separation, mother and father would be invited to attend his graduation and welcome their son as a journeyman. They'd entrusted their only child with Myrlo. They deserved to know they'd done the best for their son.

To ensure this, Myrlo kept them especially safe. He multiplied the produce of their garden to put them one step ahead of the tax collectors, and he kept the wooden walls of their house in good health.

This he did without Jawan's knowledge. The boy would be just as distracted from his studies if he were constantly asking about his parents every time Myrlo went to see them.

Worried that the father might be waylaid or taken ill on his travels and need help, Myrlo hired a trusted townsman to track the father as he sold his wares from town to town.

Myrlo often did favors for Godar and had learned to trust him.

As a peddler, the father came in contact with a lot of people. He picked up news and gossip and carried it from town to town. But one day, as ill luck dictated, he picked up something else.

Staring at his memories in the cold and empty laboratory, Myrlo recalled the day Godar had come to him with distressing news.

"I couldn't even go near the home. I didn't dare."

Those were his words.

As he approached the street where Jawan's parents lived, he stopped. To his bewilderment on that otherwise normal day, everything stopped at that street. People and horses, wagons and sound bustled all around but didn't go into that street.

"It was the oddest sight," Godar told Myrlo.

Godar had seen people on that street before, always people coming and going on foot, children playing, and women gossiping across their rickety fences. But on that day, everyone turned down a side street well before they reached the block where Jawan's parents lived.

"I looked down the street really good, trying to see what was going on. My eyes fell on that poor boy's folks' house, and I knew."

Godar couldn't mistake the purple boards covering the doors and windows of the house. He knew the father would never again go about his rounds. The house was quarantined.

Myrlo sighed. After so many weeks, he still shied away from telling Jawan about his parents. He had to do it. Otherwise, on some unwelcome day, in some unwelcome way, the truth would come out, and the longer Myrlo waited, the harder it would be for him to control how it came out. He was, in fact, putting off an unpleasant task only to create an ugly situation.

He rose slowly to his feet and headed for the library.

# Chapter 3

Jawan stared at the book in front of him. The words swam across the page, not making sense. Nothing made sense. How could he make himself care about quarks and leptons when his parents were all but gone?

"W-when did it happen?"

Jawan braced himself for the answer. He wanted to know, but he didn't want to know. Didn't want it to be real. And any answer would make it real.

"A month ago."

"A m-month?" Astonishment widened Jawan's eyes. "You've known for a month and never told me?"

Secrecy was the way of mages. But this?! Could his master be keeping other secrets from him? His suspicion mounted as he looked back on the conversations they'd had over the past month. The smiles and encouragements. All the time he'd thought his life was going fine, and all the time his master had known this terrible secret and kept it from him.

"Jawan, I'm so sorry. I should have told you. I wish I could help."

"R-right."

Jawan stared at the aisle that led to Myrlo's magic books, remembering how they had called him. He stared at the library's high vaulted ceiling, the stone floor. He stared at his study books.

"Look at me." Myrlo wanted him to understand. "We've been trying. I told you we . . ."

"M-master, this isn't about helping the town. These are my mother and father."

"I know that, but . . ."

"You've got to help them. They're shut in. They can't even come out for food. How long will they survive?"

Jawan looked away from his master, focusing yet not focusing on the incomprehensible book in front of him. They both knew the answer. His parents would die. What else could they do? No physician would come near people who caught the purple plague.

Until now, people in town only whispered about a horrible disease happening to other people far away. Nobody knew where it came from. But last year people started breaking out with purple splotches that turned their whole body into one big bruise. They stayed this way for a few days before breaking into hundreds of bloody sores. No one ever survived.

Myrlo bit his lip.

"I'm sorry, Jawan. Believe me, I wish there were something I could do."

But Jawan didn't want to hear that. Eight years of not seeing his family. And now he would never see them again—nor would anyone.

Jawan's chest heaved with the thought. Nor would anyone. Other towns didn't even bury people in a quarantined house. It would probably be the same in Hadley. The authorities torched the houses after they figured the people inside had time to die. A priest would pray over any ashes that retained a vaguely human shape. If his parents had been quarantined a month ago, they were probably already gone.

"Y-you just don't want to! You just don't care!"

Myrlo said nothing but turned his gaze past Jawan at the stacks of books behind him.

That was it. Jawan's next breath refused to come. He couldn't breathe in the same room with this monster who couldn't even look his apprentice in the eye. Jawan's chair clattered to the floor as he bounded out of the library, leaving Myrlo still staring helplessly at nothing.

His pounding feet echoed against the stones as he raced down the corridors, under the portcullis, and into the castle's courtyard. There he caught his breath but didn't stop running.

Was he running toward the plague that he'd only hours earlier been running away from? He didn't care. His mother and father were as good as dead, and no one would bury them. What did he care about his own safety?

He kept running until he reached the forest. Thick foliage blocked out the sun, enveloping him in darkness that matched his thoughts. He couldn't seem to run fast enough to escape this darkness.

Leaves rustled above him, and he looked up in time to see a hawk emerge from its nest. It squawked and took to the air. Jawan wished that he could fly away, escaping the Earth over which his master was lord.

The path he was on led to the town and its people, its noise, and its business. None of which Jawan wanted to deal with. He ran on until he reached a goat path.

Underbrush slowed his pace, and branches reaching across the path scratched his face. His heel sank into a hole the wrong way, and his ankle twisted as he fell to the ground. Gasping, he pulled himself up on a tree trunk and ran on until the path opened up on a lake.

Sunlight dazzled his eyes as he emerged from the dark forest. Squirrels and field mice scurried out of his way as he approached the water. He looked down at his reflection. It was smooth and bright.

That made him wince. Town folk whispered about the purple blotches that marred the faces of those with the plague. There were none on his face. He couldn't be his mother's child. As he envisioned his father's purple cheeks, a pang of guilt and sorrow tightened Jawan's heart.

Then he felt rage. Rage at Myrlo and then at himself. Rage for being alive in a world where his parents were not.

He picked up a stone and hurled it at the face that had no purple blotches. The stone sank into the water where his mouth was. His face expanded in ripples. Distorted now, the face was no longer smooth and bright. His hairline expanded to the far edges of the lake and disappeared. But Jawan's dark thoughts didn't disappear.

Why couldn't he expand into nothingness? An image—an illusion carried away by water.

Jawan closed his eyes and gritted his teeth until he felt it. Every atom in his body broke apart and expanded. Ripples of atoms floated past the sun into the darkness of space. They kept expanding until each was an infinity of light-years from the others.

Then they imploded into black holes, alone without mother or father—each in the center of its own nothingness.

But the darkness remained within Jawan's heart, as if it, too, were a black hole from which the light of grief couldn't escape.

He opened his eyes. The sun still shone on the water. The daylight mocked him. The single light reflecting off the water beckoned him. He plunged.

Bubbles floated up from his mouth as he sank deeper and deeper. He didn't close his mouth or his eyes. He wanted to sink to the center of the Earth—so deep that even the Great Myrlo couldn't reach him.

But it was a lake, not the sea. It couldn't swallow him up as he wanted. His head bumped against the floor of the lake, and he grabbed for something to anchor himself. He wanted to stay there. He gurgled as his lungs filled with water and they burned.

"You will live."

"What?"

"You must live."

Jawan looked around but didn't see anyone. Only a silver fish brushing against his face. It shone like the moon, and silver light trailed in its wake as it swam away.

Jawan followed the fish to the shallows of the lake. It could go no farther, but he pulled himself up onto the shore. His eyes squeezed shut as water poured from his mouth and nose. When he could breathe, he gasped. Coughing, he raised himself on his hands and knees, but collapsed onto his stomach as his limbs gave way.

He opened his eyes and regarded the dark earth beneath his head. He wanted to hate it. He wanted to hate the soil and the grass, the trees and the animals that found succor in the world that Myrlo loved. He wanted to hate Myrlo, the villain who kept dark secrets and found better work to do than find a cure for his dying parents.

But though hatred stalked around in his heart, it found no place there. And Jawan knew that if he let go of hatred, the darkness would go with it.

"I'm s-sorry," he whispered between gulps of air.

*So sorry.* What would that mean for him if he accepted the idea that this man couldn't be trusted? He cringed when he realized that he'd just thought of Myrlo, not as his master, but as this man.

And he still remembered how, when he was six years old, this man took him on as an apprentice after his parents noticed his magical talent.

A wistful smile tugged at Jawan's lips as he envisioned himself building a castle with the soft brown mud that covered his backyard after it rained. He was determined to build the same castle he dreamed about after his father described one in a bedtime tale. Jawan needed only that vivid oral description to visualize what a castle would look like.

The castle in his father's story had a drawbridge that soldiers raised to keep enemies out, or lowered to let merchants in. Jawan wanted the drawbridge on his mud castle to go up and down so badly that he just made it happen. When his father saw this, he knew his son had the gift of an earth mage.

Jawan felt both awed and afraid the first time Myrlo peered at him. The mage gave no sign that Jawan had anything worth his time.

"What can the boy do?" Myrlo asked his father.

"He makes things move."

"Is that so?" Clearly, the magician had no intention of selling his approval cheaply. "What sort of things? Move them how?"

Jawan's father cast around for something that would impress a mage. Myrlo's sitting room lacked mud, but surely there must be something in here from the Earth. This was the Earth mage's castle. His eyes fell on a wooden bowl of fruits and nuts.

"Jawan, show the mage how you can make the acorn take off its cap."

Little Jawan had followed his father's finger to the acorn with its pointy hat. As Myrlo watched, Jawan closed his eyes and without any gestures or incantations directed magical energy at the acorn. It shuddered and twirled as if to unscrew the cap. After a breathless moment, the cap came off.

"That's something!" said Jawan's father.

"Pop!" said Jawan.

"Yes, that's a start. He has something I can work with."

Soon, Jawan stood mouth agape before the imposing master. Myrlo towered above the little boy, and his long white beard and long dark earth brown robe made him look otherworldly. Jawan clung to his mother.

But instead of her comforting skirts. Jawan found himself grasping earth, trying to hold back the memories that hurt.

He clenched his fist and wondered what painful memories would he have had if Myrlo hadn't come to him? Myrlo gave him an education that his father would never have been able to afford.

As he wondered, he felt something brush his face that was not earth or grass. He shuddered as a wizened hand emerged from the sleeves of a dark robe and touched him.

"The Earth told me you were in pain, and I came," Myrlo whispered.

"M-master."

Myrlo helped Jawan to his feet. Though his legs wobbled, they held as Myrlo led him back to the castle.

The castle was cool after the heat of the sun. They climbed the stairs to Jawan's room, a bare space with bed, table, and chair. Nails on the wall held his few clothes.

"You are weary. You must lie down."

Jawan looked toward his bed, then shook his head.

"N-no, I'm okay. Loby and Zap are supposed to come soon to work on our studies, so I have to go to the laboratory."

"You will not enter my laboratory in those filthy clothes," Myrlo said, brushing a bedraggled lock of hair out of Jawan's eye.

Jawan tensed. Was this something his own father would have done? He looked up into the stern affection of Myrlo's eyes and couldn't hate this man. But neither could he forget that another man was once his father.

When Myrlo left the room, Jawan peeled off his damp clothes and washed himself in the basin of water that sat on his table. He pulled down a tunic and britches from a nail and put them on. Then he went down to the laboratory.

His master looked up with concern when Jawan entered. Jawan felt there was still a pint of water in his lungs, but he did his best not to falter. Making his way to the long wooden table, he fell rather than sat down and, despite all efforts, had to lay down his head.

"You left because you blame me for not telling you about your parents."

"N-no," Jawan croaked. "I mean, yes. You should have told me."

"Listen," Myrlo whispered. "I know this is difficult, but you must bear up."

*Bear up?* That's it?

"I g-guess we won't talk about it anymore. No more mention of the plague."

"Oh, no, this isn't finished. In fact, I must be off to the conclave soon. The mages will be talking of nothing else."

"A c-conclave?" Jawan raised his head. "Can I go?"

Myrlo frowned at him. "Of course not. Why do you keep asking?"

"B-but this is about the plague—my parents. This is different."

"How so? Apprentices are never allowed at these most high meetings. This is no different."

Myrlo got that far-off look Jawan knew well when his master was thinking deeply about something. Then suddenly, the earth mage gasped.

"Fascinating!"

"W-what is it?"

"Nothing. I was just remembering something I'd seen in the nanoscope. I must mention it at the conclave."

"Y-you saw it? The plague?!"

"I wish. But no, I can get no closer to the victims than the physicians. I don't have a sample. But I saw something, at least, I think it was something—a clue . . ."

"W-what was it?"

Myrlo furrowed his brows and straightened his posture, as if he suddenly remembered he was speaking to his apprentice.

"It's not anything that you would understand."

*No,* Jawan thought, *nothing a mere apprentice would possibly understand.* He'd always wanted to use the nanoscope. It was more powerful than the microscope his master allowed him to use to study plants.

He wondered if Myrlo would make an exception now with the plague. Maybe Jawan would find something. But if he asked, the answer would just be another denial. He'd had enough of them for one day.

Myrlo turned to survey the lab. With a look of satisfaction, he headed for the door.

"I must go. Fetch my cloak and the green case."

Seeing his master off to these high meetings occupied an increasing amount of Jawan's time lately. They must be close to accomplishing something, but whenever Myrlo came home, he never had that bright gleam in his eyes he got whenever he was on the verge of something. In fact, he always seemed more troubled, like a man whose dreams left him more tired upon waking than he'd been when he'd gone to sleep.

Jawan sighed. He had work to do, and Myrlo expected him to do it. His master hadn't said a word about what was expected. They both knew, and Jawan wouldn't disappoint him.

\*\*\*

After Myrlo departed, Jawan sat down at the high, black marble table that held the tired, old microscope and other stuff his master thought suitable for an apprentice. *Baby stuff.*

He was supposed to draw pictures of plant cells and write an essay about how they differed from animal cells. That was what he was determined to do. He shook thoughts of what he wasn't allowed to do out of his head and turned the microscope on.

A bright light snapped on, illuminating the platform where he'd place the plant culture. He stuck his finger on the platform and put his eye to the lens. How different the world would seem if we could see people's cells instead of their solid bodies.

His head popped up when he heard a knock on the lintel of the open lab door and his friends Loby and Zap sauntered in.

"Hey, mouse," Loby greeted.

Some of the more callous masters experimented on their apprentices like mice. So, he and his friends formed a secret league of apprentice solidarity—The Sacred Order of Mice—and called each other mouse.

The three boys stood with their forefingers interlocked:

"Though fire and rain assail us
Though earthquake and storm impale us
We are mice!"

"Solid," Loby said as they shook hands. He turned to Jawan. "Does Master Myrlo need any fire cubes? I'll have to whip up some."

Loby insisted that since he was a journeyman, he should be the leader. Jawan and Zap humored him, unless he told them to do something they didn't want to do.

"H-he's not here," Jawan replied.

Like Sipal, these guys didn't laugh when Jawan stuttered. They carried on like the way he talked was just the way he talked. Jawan knew better, but he appreciated that they didn't make a big deal of it.

Zap set his notebook on the long wooden table that ran down the center of the lab. "What are we supposed to be doing?" he asked, turning a chair around and straddling it backward.

Loby leaned over and traced the grain of wood along the tabletop. "Don't know what you poor apprentices are supposed to be doing, but I've finished all my schoolwork."

"Lucky you, Lord Journeyman," Zap retorted. "Some of us have to work for our keep."

Jawan wouldn't let himself be envious of his friend Loby, but he wished he were a journeyman. He wished he could say he was finished with lessons and studying. Still, Loby had been his friend since they were all little apprentices, and he never let his promotion go to his head.

Zap turned to Jawan sitting at the microscope. "What are we looking at today, Jawan?"

"P-plant cultures." Water rose in Jawan's throat with the effort of speech, making him gurgle. He jumped up and ran to the sink, where a gallon of lake water poured out of his mouth.

"You okay?" Zap asked.

"Y-yea. Just a little water," Jawan said, returning to his seat.

"Just a little water?" Zap looked like he would throw up himself. "How can you stand it? Why would you even go near water?"

Loby shook his head. "And that coming from the water mage's apprentice."

"Uh, I-I'm okay." Jawan turned the microscope on. "Like I said, we'll be looking at plants."

"What a challenge." Loby smirked. "I wish we could look at plague cultures."

Jawan gulped. *Do they know the plague is here in the town?* He shook his head. *No,* he reasoned. *Loby was just making a general statement.*

"Plague cultures?" Zap yelped. "That's got to be disgusting."

But Loby looked interested. "Maybe if we had some cultures, we could find a cure. I'd become Journeyman of the Year. Just one step away from being a master."

Loby cocked his head, but Jawan shook his. "F-far be it from you to think about that." It embarrassed him that he couldn't even utter a decent quip without stuttering. "We all know how fond you are of the fire master. You wouldn't want to replace him."

"Wouldn't you rather look at plague cultures, Jawan?" Loby asked.

Jawan felt the words on the tip of his mind, ready to spill out: *My parents have the plague*. But his mouth would not open. Instead, he kept his words impersonal. "I s-saw it out on the street. You want to see plague structures, step outside."

That wasn't what he'd meant to say. Not like that. They flinched at his revelation. *Too late now,* he thought.

"The plague is here?"

"You saw it?"

Jawan knew he still had to be careful, even if Myrlo couldn't do anything. People had to know, but if their first reaction was hysteria, that would do no good.

Loby shook his head. "How could something like the plague be here and we not know about it?"

"People won't even whisper about it, much less talk about it," Zap said.

"Our m-masters know about it. That's what the big meeting is all about," Jawan said, hoping to reassure them that everything was under control.

"They knew and didn't tell us?" Zap gasped.

Jawan gulped. That wasn't the sedative he'd hoped for. "I m-mean, they have everything under control. They're studying it and . . ."

"If they have it under control,, why do they need to study it?" Loby wanted to know.

"M-maybe they'll have a cure tonight."

Jawan knew this wasn't likely, but he had to fish for something—anything to keep them from panicking.

"If only we had some plague cultures," Zap said. "Maybe we'd be able to find something."

Loby slid his eyes over to the nanoscope. "We sure wouldn't find anything in a microscope. Nothing they don't already know. If we want to find something, there's the glass for us." He pointed to the nanoscope.

Jawan suddenly felt a fit of obedience to authority. "N-no!"

If Myrlo wouldn't let his own apprentice mess with the nanoscope, Jawan knew it was off-limits to these guys.

"Come on, mouse." Loby said *mouse* with significance. "Why not? We might find something that will save lives. Maybe our own lives."

Jawan shook his head.

"Aw, you're just scared," Loby chided. "Being a mouse doesn't mean acting like a chicken."

"L-look, you get to go home. I'll be the one who has to stay here and face Myrlo."

Jawan hated how he sounded. There was just no way to sound strong and forceful with a stutter. Everything came out whiney—like pleading. And he sure wasn't pleading.

Zap opened his notebook, as if to signal a change of subject.

"Well, we still have to do the assignment, and we sure won't be able to turn in anything we found in the nanoscope, so maybe we should just get to work."

*Good old Zap,* Jawan sighed.

He retrieved a plant culture from the wall racks where they were kept and placed it on the microscope. "Y-you can go first," he told Zap. "It's sea grass, so we can both look at it."

Zap bent his eye to the lens. "It's purple!"

"What?!" Loby and Jawan said together.

Loby jumped up, pushing Zap out of the way, and peered into the microscope. "Let me see. I never heard of pur . . ." He groaned. "It's green."

Zap laughed.

"He's just clowning. I wish we did have something purple."

Jawan sighed, wondering if Loby would always return to that subject. And Zap wasn't helping this time.

"Maybe we could get . . ."

"No," Loby objected. "We'd just as soon put our own hands under the nanoscope as get near a plague victim."

"Well, what are the masters studying if they don't have a plague culture?"

"S-something. They've got something. Let's just finish our assignment."

Zap peered into the microscope again, then took a piece of paper from his notebook and began to draw. "You know, I always thought chlorophyll was just like a juice that gave plants their green color. But it's actually a molecule."

"Wonderful," Loby growled.

"Y-yes, it is."

Zap gave Jawan a piece of paper and stepped aside so he could look into the microscope.

"So, you're not going to look at anything you're not supposed to?" Loby snapped.

"N-no."

"So much for solidarity. Suppose somebody dies of the plague because you're too scared to . . ."

"Sh-shut up!"

Loby smirked and scrutinized Jawan's drawing.

"That's not how it looks."

The drawing was precise. Jawan knew it wasn't the drawing Loby criticized. His work was not finished, but he was. He just couldn't do any more.

"If y-you've nothing to do, you can leave before you get cabin fever."

"Let me finish this last drawing," Zap said.

Loby plopped into a chair, giving the nanoscope a fierce longing stare.

When Zap finished his drawing, he put it into his notebook. "You know, this is usually where we sit around planning how we're going to take over the world and solve all its problems."

"Yeah, when we were all mice. But some of us don't want to deal with real problems. Some of us want to remain babies," Loby had the nerve to sneer like he'd put Jawan in his place.

"S-some of us don't know when to shut up."

"I got no reason to stay here with a baby."

"N-nothing standing between you and the door."

Zap looked at Jawan and Loby, then shrugged. He gathered his notebook, smiled at Jawan, and headed for the door. "See you later," he said cheerfully.

But Loby just left.

Jawan slumped into a chair. *Baby?* he thought. *Chicken? Am I?* Babies did what they were supposed to do. *NO!*

What was his master afraid of? Jawan knew what he'd see in the nanoscope: fermions, bosons, quarks, neutrinos—all the tiny particles that his textbooks told him made up matter. But the microscope lens wasn't strong enough to reveal those elementary particles.

He glanced at the nanoscope, but saw instead Myrlo's green eyes, stern and disappointed, and he saw the loss of something more precious than his life.

Jawan wanted to stare at the floor, but his eyes kept snapping back to the nanoscope. After seeing it in that same spot for two years, why was he pulled to it now—pulled as if it were a magnet and his eyes were balls of iron.

What was he thinking?! He'd just all but lost his two best friends over this nanoscope. They'd kill him if he turned around and looked into it himself—if his master left anything for them to kill.

Maybe now wasn't the time. Maybe if he waited and studied his lessons the way Myrlo wanted, his chance would come. It just had to. But Jawan had little faith in Myrlo's assurances that his chance to be a journeyman would come—way down some distant road that Jawan couldn't see.

No, if he wanted to be a great magician, he couldn't wait for chance to mosey along. He'd have to go to chance.

Loby didn't know what he was talking about. Jawan was a mouse, and he wasn't going to sit back and let the unknown remain unknown. It was too late for his parents. But there were still so many people that could be saved if he just had the knowledge. He had the will, and now nothing would keep him from the knowledge.

Nothing? He got up. He sat back down. He got up again and sat down again. *Nothing.* He got up and walked over to it. He'd just look at it was all. He'd just touch it. *Famous last words.*

# Chapter 4

Loby and Zap trudged down the road that led from Master Myrlo's castle like they'd just been told there'd be no party.

"He's no fun," Loby complained.

"Can't blame him for not wanting to get in trouble when we probably won't even be there to get him out."

"Still, a nanoscope! Imagine what we might have seen. I can't even imagine."

"Me neither," Zap agreed. "But maybe it won't be worth angering a master."

"Aw, mine is always angry. Don't you want to know what they're hiding?"

"What makes you think they're hiding something?"

"Things are happening, Zap. I can feel it around my castle, and I bet that nanoscope will tell us something our masters don't want us to know."

Zap shrugged, then he shuddered at the edge of the forest. He stopped.

"Why are you stopping?" Loby asked, annoyed.

"Oh, nothing. I just . . . It's getting dark . . ."

"You're afraid of the dark?"

"No, I . . ."

Zap's words were swallowed up in a grimace of horror as he stared at the first forbidding trees of the forest.

Loby rolled his eyes and pushed past Zap into the trees. It was always dark in the forest, even during the day. The night just made it more so. For a moment, he despised its sameness, as unchanging as his friend's ever-green fears. He'd have to change that. Zap had always been a little scaredy-cat, but he had to grow out of that, and Jawan too. "There's nothing here in the dark that's not here in the day. Come on."

"Are you sure? Nothing looks the same. Nothing sounds the same."

Loby's keen gray eyes detected movement in the darkness. Moonlight made its way through the trees to reveal a piglet scurrying for cover as the boys approached. He picked up a stone and threw it. The piglet screamed at the same time Zap yelped. Then all was quiet. As still as death.

Loby's long strides brought him quickly to the spot where the piglet lay. He reached down and picked it up. It was small, just large enough to roast over a little fire. They'd have a little fun after all. He smirked at the relief evident on Zap's face.

"Don't worry, Zap. I won't let the goblins eat you."

"It could have been a goblin." Zap stared at the ground, embarrassed.

"I'm hungry," Loby announced. "I think I'll have roast piglet tonight."

"Doesn't your master feed you?"

"Sometimes. But tonight, I think I'll fend for myself."

"You'll burn the forest down."

"Not here, dummy." Loby smirked, flipping the piglet over his shoulder. He continued down the path that led to his castle, and Zap followed. "We'll go to my master's cellar."

"Oh, no." Zap shuddered.

"Why not? It's all stone. Fireproof."

"The stones may be fireproof, but I'm not. If your master catches us . . ."

"Look, haven't you ever done anything your master didn't want you to do?"

"No," Zap assured him.

"Baby. I'll bet there's a whole lot he won't let you do. I know mine is like that."

The path grew darker as the canopy of trees blocked out the starlight. An owl stood sentry on a nearby tree branch. Its eyes betrayed its presence like two low-burning campfires in the night.

"They're all so secretive," Loby continued. "Why don't they at least tell us why, instead of just saying no? You've got to be a mouse, Zap." He touched his index and middle finger to his nose in the official salute of the Order of Mice. "Find out what those secrets are."

He'd make mice out of Zap and Jawan. He hadn't started the order just to sit around and complain about their masters' petty abuses. Something big was afoot. And the Sacred Order of Mice would find out what was what.

But Zap was far from there. "I think my master would kill me if I did something he'd told me not to do."

"Nah."

"They can do that, you know. There's no law against it. And they have so much power."

*Hoo! Hoo! Hoo!*

Zap jumped.

"What was that?!" he squeaked.

"An owl." Loby laughed.

"It's not funny. My master could make all the water in my body evaporate."

"That's crazy."

"A crazy way to die."

Loby picked up a dead branch from beside the path and started swiping the ground behind them as they walked.

"What are you doing?"

"Erasing our tracks, so the Mage Monsters can't follow us."

"Oh, shut up," Zap snapped, but he kept looking over his shoulder the rest of the way.

"Your master couldn't be as creepy as the fire mage," Loby said. "But I'm always doing stuff he doesn't want me to do. I'm just smart enough not to get caught."

They passed out of the last of the trees and followed the path toward their own masters' castles. But when Zap started down the path to his castle, Loby stopped him.

"I can't eat a whole roast piglet alone. Come with me. We'll have a party."

"With you? Yeah, you're smart enough to make sure I'm there to get you out of trouble."

"You?"

"Come on," Zap sighed, heading toward Loby's castle.

As they approached the fire mage's castle, heat from the flames licking the castle's walls pricked Loby's skin. They passed under the portcullis and down a hall of heated stones. They tiptoed, but their soft leather soles seemed to boom down the hall before them.

Just as they were about to pass by, the attic door creaked open. The two boys froze. Loby knew who it was. Itch. That ungifted zombie his master found somewhere.

The attic held Lord Elveston's observatory. And in his observatory, Lord Elveston kept his precious camera. Loby couldn't understand why his master let Itch handle the camera. Loby was never even allowed in the locked observatory with the cursed thing.

And for all he knew, cursed might be just what that camera was. It had a sinister aspect. His few glances of it left him feeling more than a little spooked, as if he were looking at something with evil properties, meant only for evil.

He felt the piglet slip off his shoulder behind him just as Itch's rasping voice snarled, "What are you looking at?"

Loby turned to shield Zap, but the skittish apprentice was already back in the shadows where Itch couldn't see him.

"Nothing. Just going to my room."

"Itch." Lord Elveston's voice echoed through the halls of his castle. It carried the quiet menace of one who expected to be obeyed. Itch could be anywhere in the castle, and his master could demand his presence.

Itch pressed a button on the magic summoning device he wore on a thong around his neck, snarled at Loby, and disappeared. Loby started forward but hadn't taken three steps before Zap joined him.

"That was close." Zap sighed.

"So, you're the one who's going to keep me out of trouble?"

"That's what the Order of Mice is for."

"Come on," Loby said, heading for the cellar. He snapped his fingers, and a small flame flickered on his index finger. He took down two torches from the stair wall, lit them, and gave one to Zap. There was still just enough light to create creepy shadows on the stones, but it kept them from stumbling when they reached the last step. Loby knew it was the last step. He'd counted them.

They placed their torches in sconces along the wall and looked around the bare room.

"What's in there?" Zap asked, pointing to a row of heavy oak doors.

"Things my master won't tell me." Loby shrugged.

He broke into kindling the branch he'd used to tease Zap and laid it on the floor.

"We're going to get in trouble," Zap warned.

Loby ignored him, setting fire to the sticks. He jumped back as the flames shot up from the floor.

"Now what?" Zap asked.

"Wait."

Loby got up and walked to a door at the far end of the room. The door for storing kitchen utensils would not be locked. He went in and opened a box.

"I thought you didn't know what was in there," Zap said from the doorway.

"I also said I do a lot of things I'm not supposed to do, like knowing where to find a knife in my master's cellar."

But it was the wrong box. He sighed and closed it, careful to leave it just as he'd found it.

"Maybe it's in one of the smaller boxes," Zap suggested, but didn't come in to look.

Loby found the knife and two long sticks and went back to the fire. He gutted the piglet and let its entrails burn. He cut the meat in pieces and skewered them on the sticks.

"It's like camping out," Loby said, holding his stick over the flames. "All we need is a ghost story."

"I don't need a ghost story right now. If your master catches us . . ."

"He won't."

The fire crackled, and the smell of pork filled the cellar.

"Your master's going to smell that, you know."

Loby lifted his head. "And what are you going to do? Run and hide? There aren't any mouse holes down here."

Zap's eyes darted around. He shuddered like he had suddenly realized where he was.

"Why did I let you talk me into coming here?"

"Because I need you to keep me out of trouble. My master won't come down here."

"You don't know where I will go."

Zap gulped, and Loby turned slowly to face his master.

Lord Elveston loomed over them like a tower of doom. Though there was no wind, his black robe billowed among the flickering shadows. Loby didn't dare look into his fiery eyes, but he knew they were livid.

Loby felt a stream of rage welling up to choke his fear. Why was his master so upset over a little fire? Wasn't like the flames were out of his control and threatening to burn the castle down. Zap condensed the air over the fire into water to douse it. The half-cooked pieces of meat fell onto the wet sticks.

Loby started to meet his master's eyes, but his anger was no match for the fury of the fire mage.

"You will never be more than a journeyman. Twelve years of your idiocy. How much more can I tolerate?"

He turned to Zap. The boy flinched. "Aren't you Lacus's boy? I will speak to your master. Doubtless, you'll get off with some light punishment." He looked at Zap with enough menace to frighten the dead. "But when I have my way, such foolishness will be over. Go."

Zap's legs trembled in their sockets, but he shot out of the cellar faster than Loby thought possible.

Then he was left alone with his master. Lord Elveston's eyes crackled and danced like fire. They were fire, and they sizzled into Loby like branding irons. For all his defiant talk to Zap and Jawan, Loby shrank into a quivering mouse in his master's formidable presence.

He quivered even more when it dawned on him that his master had said "when" not "if" he had his way.

"Where have you been?" Lord Elveston snapped.

Loby tried to open his mouth to answer but could neither open his mouth nor close his eyes to the inferno that burned in Lord Elveston.

His master saved him the trouble. "Fraternizing with apprentices. And the water apprentice at that. Have you no sense, boy?"

He put such an emphasis on the word *boy* that Loby knew his master meant it as an insult.

"Since you like fire so much, maybe I should let you have a taste of the real thing."

"Sir?" Loby gulped.

His master grabbed him by the ear and dragged him out of the cellar, down the hall, and to his laboratory.

"Master, please."

Through the blur of pain, Loby saw Itch hunched over the central table, tinkering with the controls of an ugly black box. Loby wondered what that box could be—sitting there for the past year. He resented the fact that Itch knew secrets that he himself didn't. As if the big zombie were the journeyman and Loby just happened to live there.

But Loby barely registered Itch's smirk as his master dragged him to the top of the stairs that led to the firepit. He gasped when he realized where he was going.

"Why are you resisting?" Lord Elveston taunted. "Now you get to go somewhere you've never been allowed to go."

Sweat trickled down Loby's back as he tried to pull away. The firepit was the one place Loby never wanted to go. No one but the fire master was allowed to go down there.

"You will remain there until I am satisfied you've had enough playing with fire."

Itch was apparently enjoying this. "Master, will you let him out before you go to the conclave tonight?"

"If I feel satisfied."

"No, please, master. I'm sorry. I . . ."

"What's the matter, boy? Don't you have enough magic to protect yourself from a little heat? You are useless and will never be a fire master. Itch is of more use to me than you."

Itch didn't have a drop of magical talent. Yet, the fire master valued him more than he did Loby, his own journeyman, whom he'd trained as an apprentice.

Itch smirked as Lord Elveston shoved Loby down the stairs and slammed the door. Loby stumbled down the stairs, down, down, endlessly down into a pit lit only by the fire.

Losing all sense of up and down, Loby tried to hold onto something. But there was nothing to hold onto. It was a long way down, and he had time to bang every part of his body on the jagged edges of the steps.

When he reached the bottom, his momentum kept him rolling toward the fire. No way did he have enough magic to guard himself if he fell into that bottomless pit that drew fire up from the bowels of the Earth.

He tried to stretch his arms and legs so that he'd stop rolling. This slowed but didn't stop his progress. *Nothing to hold onto.*

Red, yellow, orange, and black flames licked the ceiling and obscured the edges of the pit. He tried to recoil. He wanted to stop. In his ears, the inferno roared, and beneath it all was a sizzling sound that he could only imagine as his own body crackling like fresh venison on the grill.

He saw Crisp, Lord Elveston's pet salamander, watching him with interest. Stupid beast. Did it think he'd come to play with it?

Loby rolled once more, inches from the edge of the fire and still too close for coziness.

Unable to stand, Loby crept as far up the stairs as he could to get away from the fire. All he could do was wait there until his master was satisfied.

# Chapter 5

Myrlo dismounted his horse behind the isolated castle that held the secret conclave of mages. His brow, usually smooth, was knit with the task before him.

His black hair fluttered as it caught the tail end of some distant storm. Though the other mages came through the portal, as the earth mage, he preferred to travel through his element. He drew power and comfort through his horse, an earth creature, as it raced along the ground.

Touching the horse's flank sent it among the trees where it would not be seen and raise suspicions. The people of Hadley Town thought the castle was haunted and would wonder what anyone with a horse was doing.

Not that the mages were *personae non grata* among the people. But their meetings had to be kept secret to avoid the contempt that often accompanies familiarity.

The people kept their distance from the forbidding castle. Anyone looking in Myrlo's direction would not see his black cloak as separate from the dark night. They might see his disembodied face, if they had exceptionally good eyesight, and run screaming to report to their neighbors that they'd seen a ghost.

So Myrlo wasn't concerned when he trod across the grass and cobblestones to the hidden entrance. His concern was how much progress the other mages had made in finding the source and cure for the plague. Jawan's news that the plague was now in Hadley meant they had no more time. Something had to be done.

He stopped to savor the roses beside the door before entering.

The other four elemental mages were already seated when Myrlo entered and took his seat. They all watched and listened as the conclave chamber transformed into a theater displaying each mage's elemental power. This was their customary way to start each meeting.

The air mage stood and bowed to his fellows.

"I am Volvo, mage of the air and the wind."

A great wind roared through the room, upsetting the papers each mage had meticulously prepared for the meeting. A gentle breeze blew through the nearby mountain forest and animated the clothes a maiden had hung on a line. It swirled away to the sea where it drove the ships of men.

Then Volvo grew bored with his gentle ways and tore at the ships. He yanked the clothes basket from the maiden's clasp and bent the mountain trees to the ground.

The other mages saw all this. They heard the wind and felt its power but didn't stir. When Volvo subsided and took his seat, the water mage arose.

"I am Lacus, mage of the waters."

The oceans and rivers of the Earth surged, and a great wall of water surrounded the conclave. The mages saw fish and mermaids in the water. A small boat sailed atop it, and a young boy skipped stones across its surface.

Then the wall of water joined with Volvo, twirling in a maelstrom that sunk great warships. The Earth mage opened a fissure in the floor of the sea into which Lacus's eternal vortex poured. Yet, its power was never diminished.

Then Lacus sat and Myrlo stood.

"I am Myrlo, mage of the Earth and all that live upon it."

Horses ran across the meadows, and goats climbed among the mountains of the Earth. Myrlo cradled Lacus and planted his trees and flowers wherever the waters flowed.

But great pressure weighed down his heart, and Myrlo shook to relieve it. Men lost their footing, and their flimsy dwellings collapsed. He opened pores in his skin to release steam and liquid rock. Top-heavy mountains slid into valleys.

Myrlo sat. The fire mage rose to his feet. As chair of the conclave, he sat on what amounted to a little throne in the center of the meeting table. Myrlo and Lacus sat on his right side, and Volvo and Quintessuma, the mage of ether, sat on his left.

"I am Lord Elveston Peruro, master of fire, giving heat and light to the creatures on the Earth."

The other mages tolerated his pomposity with varying degrees of patience. Whether they held him in awe or disdain, he was one of the mages, so they gave him due respect.

As they watched, an old man sat reading by the light of a blazing hearth. Vagabonds warmed their hands over a makeshift furnace. Elveston lent his lightning bolts to Volvo to purify the air and his heat to Myrlo to melt the rocks that clogged the Earth's pores. A long hall of revelers drank and cheered as their women roasted a pig on a spit.

It was a merry scene—until a fire consumed an entire forest on the side of a mountain, then devoured the blacksmith's livelihood.

Satisfied, Lord Elveston resumed his throne, and Quintessuma rose to her feet.

Quintessuma felt an affinity with Elveston, for unlike the other three mages who ruled over matter, she and the fire mage ruled over energy. They had no weight and took up no space, but they both knew the material world would be a cold, dead place without them.

"I am Quintessuma, mage of the ether—the fifth element and spirit of the universe."

Then the mages felt a presence, unseen, but there. Everywhere. This presence kept all the planets in their courses around the sun and nestled the Earth in her special embrace. She soothed men with sweet dreams and comforted lovers with pleasant thoughts. When each man's time on Earth ended, she gathered the soul into her eternity.

But Quintessuma had another side. She let comets and asteroids slam into planets. She altered the spin and orbit of the Earth when Myrlo shook. She sent men nightmares and magnified needless worries in the minds of lovers.

Myrlo stroked his white beard, contemplating this display of powers. It never failed to astonish him the great powers over which they were masters. He knew from the grave expressions at the table that, with the exception of Elveston, they all held their powers as a sacred trust.

He was reminded of the frailty they shared with the rest of humanity when Cintella, the serving girl, entered with mugs of ale and platters of sweet meats. Eating was not optional for them. With the same two hands and ten fingers they had, she placed a mug and a platter in front of each mage.

The mugs were filled to the brim, but she took care not to spill any on their papers. Myrlo was thus reminded that the mages also had a duty not to allow the destructive forces of nature to wipe away precious life.

"Thank you, Cintella," he said.

She dropped a wordless curtsy and disappeared back into the kitchen.

There would always be death and destruction, he knew, but something must always remain—some seed from which life could spring again.

"The meeting is called to order." Lord Elveston cleared his throat. "What is today's first business?"

Myrlo fidgeted in his seat. In his mind, only one topic was worth talking about tonight. But Volvo was the first speaker at these meetings, so Myrlo could only hope the air mage shared his concerns.

Volvo drew one of his scattered papers in front of him and peered at it briefly before speaking.

"What will we do about the plague?"

Myrlo sighed with relief, but Elveston frowned.

"The plague? Leave it alone. It will run its course."

"But how long will that course be?" Lacus asked. "How many will die in the meantime?"

Elveston waved his hand, as if brushing aside a pesky insect.

"Men die every day. What is that to us masters of elements that men can't even begin to understand? Let humans take care of their own affairs. We have loftier business."

Myrlo banged his fist on the table. "We have a responsibility to the beings of this planet."

"Of this universe," agreed Quintessuma.

"What responsibility?" Elveston retorted. "We don't owe anything to those decaying hordes of humanity, as if it were they who gave us these powers in the first place."

Myrlo shook his head with impatience. "It's not about us owing humanity anything. Our own innate goodness gave us this responsibility."

Elveston rolled his eyes. "Hogwash."

Quintessuma looked surprised. "I explore the spirits of men. They are open books to me—including yours . . ."

Elveston winced.

Quintessuma went on. "We mages have no greater business than caring for our fellows with whom we share this planet. We must use our powers to find a cure for the plague."

Lord Elveston leaned back in his throne and shrugged. "What can you do?" he challenged. "Can you spirit the plague away? Can Lacus draw it down into a vortex never to be seen again? Can Volvo blow it away, or can I burn it away? And what could Myrlo possibly do? Bury it in a mudslide? You talk about responsibility? Who made you responsible for something over which you have no power?"

The other mages were at a loss about how to answer him. They stared off into space, as if they might find an answer there.

What could they do? It wasn't as if they hadn't tried. They'd mixed potions and run experiments. Myrlo, especially, had searched the plant kingdom for some antidote there but was still following possible leads. He'd been so excited earlier by what he'd glimpsed in the nanoscope a moment before Pym disrupted him. But he knew it wasn't the answer to Elveston's withering question.

With so much power at their disposal, why couldn't they perform the one feat that needed to be done? And that was just it. They didn't know what needed to be done. If they knew, then maybe they could do it.

Myrlo looked at his papers. They held no answers. They were just reports of where the plague had spread. He didn't think they needed the reports now since they all knew how urgent this was. All save Elveston. They probably each had their own reports, including Elveston.

The citizens from other towns sent these reports to Myrlo seeking his aid. Authorities quarantined entire households, and the people were panicked. They left the reports outside the portcullis because the authorities feared that an infected person might go to the mage and that would be the end of all hope.

Quintessuma sighed. "What can we do that we haven't already tried?"

Myrlo slapped the table. "I know something we haven't tried."

"What, pray tell?" Volvo asked.

Myrlo took hold of his idea like it was a gift from the Earth itself. "We've all tried to work on this task individually. Why don't we work together? We do our best work together. No element functions alone."

All but Elveston warmed to this idea, nodding, and glancing at one another for affirmation.

So, they were surprised when Elveston roared, "No!"

"Why, Elveston," Quintessuma asked. "How can you object to such a wonderful plan?"

"It might work," Lacus agreed.

"It will work," insisted Myrlo.

"No. No. No. You must leave this alone. In fact, I'm on the verge of a cure myself."

The other mages looked doubtful.

Quintessuma raised the question they were all asking. "But you've been acting like you didn't think it was our concern to find a cure. Now you tell us that you almost have one?"

"I do," Elveston assured them. "I've been working on it for some time now. It has to do with my camera. A very sensitive device, involving sensitive technology that doesn't work well with magic, so I haven't sought you out about it."

Myrlo raised more than an eyebrow at this condescending nonsense. "We're all familiar with sensitive technology."

Elveston's patronizing tone wasn't lost on the other mages either.

Quintessuma shook her head. "That's no excuse for keeping secrets from your fellow mages. You know our guild doesn't work that way."

"You must tell us. What exactly does this camera do?" Volvo said.

"Yes," Lacus agreed. "What are you going to do, take pictures of the purple plague? That sounds helpful."

"We demand that you disclose this to us," Myrlo insisted.

"Yes," they all agreed.

"Demand?" Elveston hissed. "What gave you the audacity to think you could demand aught of me?"

"The articles of the guild of mages," Quintessuma repeated. "Must I invoke them, or will you tell us what we have every right to know?"

Elveston turned away, but not before Myrlo saw flames flare up in his eyes. "I can't do that."

Myrlo thought he saw beads of sweat trickling down Elveston's neck. How could the fire mage be hot—or nervous?

"I can't," Elveston repeated. "Now, if you will all just please be patient."

"Why?" Lacus asked.

"You see the need. Why should we wait on you when we have a perfectly good plan we can put into effect?" Myrlo asked.

"Your plan is still inchoate. My camera is all but ready to do its work."

"Its work?" Myrlo sneered. "My boy's parents were quarantined last month. Last month! Do you hear me? This has been going on for months. How long are we supposed to wait? Tell me, how much longer?"

Elveston looked pleased to see Myrlo's outburst. "Now, now. There's no need to lose control. Calm yourself down and let's talk reasonably."

"Reasonably?" Myrlo muttered. Elveston was putting him in the place of an apprentice. This was what Jawan must feel like when Myrlo kept secrets from him. But this was different. Jawan was an apprentice. Myrlo was a mage and wouldn't stand for such patronizing. "You think you're above the rest of us today."

"You can't erupt your volcanoes without me, Myrlo. So, calm down."

Elveston began to straighten his papers—*rather nervously*, Myrlo thought. The edges began to curl under the fire mage's hot fingers.

They all looked at him as unfinished business, but he focused on his papers and avoided their eyes. Finally, he gave up and sighed. "I've given you my reasons and don't know what else I can tell you."

"Tell us what you're doing with your camera and what it has to do with the plague," Myrlo demanded.

"We've been over this before. I've given you all the answers I'm going to. Now, since there is no other business on the table tonight, the meeting is adjourned."

"Adjourned?" Lacus exclaimed.

The mages stared at Elveston in astonishment.

"We're not finished with this business," Myrlo assured him.

"I am. The meeting is officially adjourned. You can all go home."

"You know what this means, Elveston?" Quintessuma asked. "You do know what steps you are forcing me to take?"

Lord Elveston sniffed. "It doesn't matter to me. I know what I'm doing, and by the time you go through the process of invoking the articles, there will be no more plague."

"That's not the point . . ." she started to say, but Elveston waved her silent.

Myrlo rose to his feet. Since he was already seated next to Elveston, this move was unmistakably confrontational. "You may think that all you have to do is end this night's meeting. But this issue goes beyond this meeting.

People are dying, and we mages are not going to sit idle and watch. We will do something, with or without you."

"Oh, you will?" Elveston smirked. "Okay. Good luck."

Myrlo fumed. "I see now that you don't care about the people. Sensitive technology? On the verge? All humanity could be wiped out, and you wouldn't care."

Elveston said nothing.

All the other mages stepped through the portal. Myrlo stood back to regard Elveston with one last baleful glare before departing.

# Chapter 6

Lord Elveston smiled, though fire smoldered in his eyes. Myrlo might be suspicious, but it was the suspicion of ad hominem. He knew nothing of Elveston's plans.

His footsteps echoed throughout the stone chamber as he strode to the portal and passed through to just outside his castle where he could admire the tongues of flame licking up the stone walls. By day, the flame turned to blackened scorch marks. But at night, they put on a lovely fire show. Elveston loved stone for its ability to withstand the flames better than wood and flesh. But even stone melted to lava when the fire was hot enough.

Affectionate tendrils of heat caressed his cheeks as he strode through his empty castle. He had no apprentice, just his servant Itch and that worthless journeyman Loby. Elveston kept the boy around because the other mages expected him to teach some rascal to take his place when he died. Only he didn't plan to die. They had no idea. Still, he kept Loby so he wouldn't have to waste time dodging questions.

Elveston went straight to his laboratory to perform the ritual that kept the fire within him from consuming his mortal flesh. Itch, anticipating his master's desire, hauled in a barrel full of hickory wood chips. With zombie-like strength Itch rolled the barrel off his back and set it at Elveston's feet.

It would take a zombie to lift that much matter. Elveston knew he couldn't do it. That's why he had Itch because matter was so heavy. Fire had no weight—no mass. Fire was pure energy with no limitations at all.

Itch stood back as Elveston opened the firepit door. Even that big burly hulk couldn't stand the flames. A pity. Itch could help Elveston carry out his plans but would never be a part of them.

Nor could Itch or any unprotected mortal . . . He remembered his journeyman. *Worthless, overgrown urchin. I'd better let the boy out before he burns to a crisp.* Elveston smiled thinking of Crisp, his pet salamander.

"Wait here," he told Itch and opened the door to the pit. Glancing down, he found Loby in a fetal position on the top step. "You may rise, boy." Elveston made no effort to help.

Loby groaned but didn't move.

"Then stay there." Elveston started to close the door, but Loby reached out a hand.

"No, master. Please."

With what seemed like his last bit of strength, Loby rose to his knees, then, leaning against the wall for support, he eased up to his feet and staggered but managed to step through the door and into the laboratory.

Itch sneered at Loby and went off to perform some task. Elveston noticed Loby taking furtive glances at the device on his central worktable. A device the journeyman was strictly forbidden to touch. Why was he looking at it?

"Have you prepared the fire cubes for Master Myrlo and Master Lacus?" Elveston asked. "They're going to need a lot of heat this year. Volcanoes and hurricanes and such."

"Yes, sir."

Elveston walked over and caressed the side of the device, then turned to regard Loby. "I could have sworn I'd left this on the side table."

He watched Loby's face for any sign of nervousness. Ordinary humans betrayed themselves so easily. Any unexpected information or question they weren't prepared to answer sent them quivering like pines in a forest fire.

But Loby hadn't reached journeyman status by being an ordinary human. The boy had some measure of power, and catching him took a great deal of cunning. So, Elveston watched him even more for signs—any signs—of insubordination.

"No, sir. It's been there since you put it there."

Elveston needed Loby out of the way. "You prepared the fire cubes. Have you delivered them?"

"No, sir."

"Then I suggest you do so."

Even Loby's eyes seemed to let out a breath of relief as he scrambled for the cart of fire cubes under the long table and pulled it out of the laboratory.

Elveston turned back to the firepit, opened the door, and savored the staccato rhythm of crackling flames. Only he heard the music. He eased the barrel down the narrow steps, dropping it one step at a time.

"What have you brought me?" Fuego's voice echoed through the chamber as shadows danced among fiery reds, yellows, oranges, and purples.

Elveston paused at the foot of the stairs and bowed his head as if in a holy moment. He couldn't just answer the fire spirit as if it were a mortal like himself. But he had to answer. He thought some holy thought, then spoke. "Hickory wood chips. They will smell delicious when they burn."

"Smell? A mortal word. You do this for yourself. Selfish as all matter is selfish."

Elveston cursed his body. "Yes, master. I am made of matter for now."

"For now. You languish in the misery of the massive world. But if you do as I have instructed, the day will come when you will be like me—a ruler where there is no matter. Nothing to smell, just pure energy. I'll be glad, for then I'll no longer have to talk to you. You'll possess all knowledge, and no one will have to say anything to you."

Elveston longed for that day. He opened the barrel and stood within tossing distance of the pit. Fuego might protect his flesh if he stood closer, but fire overflowed the lip of the pit, and Elveston couldn't know where the stone ended and the pit began until he fell in. He doubted Fuego would fish him out if he proved to be such a fool.

Hickory aroma wafted up from the barrel. He picked up the first wood chip and kissed it. With his sharp canine, he punctured the forefinger on his right hand and placed three drops of blood on the chip. Holding the chip aloft, he closed his eyes and chanted.

"To the one who brings the heat,
To the one who brings the light,
To the one who needs neither of these
I bring this sacred offering."

He tossed the chip into the pit, then tossed the rest of them in by handfuls. Somewhere within the roaring inferno, Elveston thought he heard a sigh.

"Is that all? That is hardly enough to whet my appetite."

Elveston didn't understand. Why did the spirit of fire need matter? The plan was to destroy matter. In a universe of pure energy, what would Fuego eat? "Why do you need matter?"

"I don't need matter to exist, but to be seen by your material eyes in this material world I must be fed matter."

Yes, in this material world with his material eyes. The heat and light of the sun traveled through miles of vacuum space, yet between the sun and the earth's material atmosphere all was cold darkness. The heat and light were there but undetectable by physical senses.

Elveston's heart leapt at the thought—without matter, he wouldn't need matter. Fuego had the answer to all his questions. All he had to do was ask them. "I have material eyes in a material body. How will I survive a universe of pure energy?"

"*In* a physical body, yes. But you are not that body. You, Elveston, are the fire burning within your physical shell. You are sentient energy, just as your body is sentient matter."

"Then everyone will survive."

The fire flickered and grew dim. "No. The essence of man will be conflated into the universal essence, and they will cease to exist as individuals. That is the ultimate goal of the universe, to unite all its trillions of pieces into one monolithic singularity. This is the way it was in the beginning. This is the way it shall be in the end."

Puzzlement knitted Elveston's brow. "Youtold me I would be lord and ruler of this world of pure energy. Now you tell me I'll just be an undifferentiated part of the universe."

The flames roared and licked at Elveston's feet. He jumped back, appalled that he had spoken so boldly to his master.

"You will remember your place, or I will remind you of it. You can still feel pain just as other men do. But you are different. You will survive, but not as Elveston. As Fuego!"

Elveston shuddered. He would become his master. He wouldn't be the lord of an empty lifeless world but of a universal megalith.

Fuego calmed down, and its flames retreated to the lip of the pit. "I sense that you are happy, child. Then why have you made no progress? You are in the position to bring about the destruction of the material universe. Yet, these walls remain around me. There are as many atoms in the universe now as there were before."

This was the part Elveston dreaded. How could he tell such a formidable master that his efforts failed? Would Fuego abandon him? Choose someone else? He would do that anyway if Elveston stalled indefinitely. And it would be indefinite, for Elveston had no idea what to do to make his device work. Ask. "I'm on the verge of making my device work. I have the concept, but something is making it not do what I want it to do."

"You are using positrons. They are unstable creatures."

"Should I be using something else? But that would mean developing an entirely new concept."

"Keep the positrons. But you need more of them to make them stable. Your plan is sound. The whole purpose is for the positrons and electrons to annihilate one another when they come into contact. But there are far more electrons than positrons. Even if all the positrons connect with electrons and are annihilated, trillions more electrons will still be here, and you will not be any closer to wiping out the material world."

"How do I get more positrons? Every time my device creates a positron, an electron is created with it."

"Where would you find any elementary particle?"

Elveston knew. But he'd hoped there'd be a less involved way than scavenging for positrons in the Quantum Realm. That was work for a servant to do, but sending Itch to Nanosia was out of the question. Itch didn't even need to know Nanosia existed. Elveston had to think of something. He *would* think of something. "Once I get them, how do I stabilize them?"

"That you will have to discover. I offer you the rulership of the entire universe. Prove yourself worthy by doing something on your own."

Yes, it was a little thing. Matter couldn't be created, but it could be manipulated. It could change its form. He'd find out how to do this whether the secret be in the realm of light or the region of dark matter where light never ventured. "I'll find out."

A warm glow surrounded Elveston. If only he could take such pleasure in his own servants. If Itch weren't so slow and Loby weren't so mischievous. They weren't worthy to survive. Nor would they. He would rule the universe. Alone? No. There was one other that he had to have by his side. There'd be no point without the queen of the Quantum Realm. "There is one other who must survive with me."

The conflagration that was Fuego flared. Elveston couldn't tell if those were shadows or scorch marks on the ceiling. Had he overstepped his place again?

The flames simmered down, but Fuego's voice told Elveston to tread carefully. "Must? There is nothing that I *must* do for you, material one. I chose you, but I can choose another. It may take me a thousand years, but I have a thousand years. You do not. Who do you wish to survive?"

"Queen Quanta. The queen of the Quantum Realm."

"A queen? What makes you think a queen will bow to your rule?"

"She will rule with me."

Elveston wasn't sure if he heard a crackle or a cackle.

"She is the queen of the basic elements of matter. And you expect her to agree to rule a universe where there is no matter?"

"She'll do it. I'll make her do it."

"Force her to be a ruler? You are nothing if not ambitious."

"Queen Quanta is no fool. If the only way to survive is to be with me, she'll want to survive."

"It's not totally up to you. I am the one who can make her survive, even as I am the one who can make you survive. She must do as you do and come to the firepit to offer her spirit to me. And if I approve of her, she will survive."

*If he approves.* Elveston sucked his teeth. He was Lord Elveston. How can anyone not approve of what he has already accepted? He reminded himself that this was Fuego, the spirit of fire. He could do what he pleased. Still, Queen Quanta was stunningly beautiful. A monarch to surpass all monarchs. She was his equal. But what did that mean to someone like Fuego? He wasn't a One. Fuego was . . . Elveston had nothing in his store of words to describe the being he called Fuego.

"She is the queen of matter. That alone is reason for me to reject her survival."

Elveston caught the flaw in this argument. Dared he tell the fire spirit that it was wrong? "There are bosons in her realm. They are the carriers of energy. Both electrons and photons bow to her."

"That may work in her favor. Bring her to me, and we will see what we will see."

*Bring her to him?* Far easier said than done.

He returned to his laboratory and summoned Itch.

"Yes, master?"

"I have a task for you, Itch."

"A task, master?"

Elveston rolled his eyes, then wondered at himself. Itch had never been quick. Why was Elveston impatient with him now as if more were expected? After a session with Fuego, Elveston figured he'd be impatient with the slowness of lightning. He shrugged. Itch's mind might be slow, but given time, he figured things out. "Go to my library. Search for information on positrons—how can they be created and stabilized."

Elveston watched Itch's hulking form head toward the library, then turned his mind to the task of bringing Queen Quanta to the firepit. That was impossible enough. Queen Quanta didn't even know Elveston's world existed. Would bringing her here leave her in such shock that she'd bow down to Fuego for sheer astonishment? Then a thought occurred to him. Cintella. The serving girl at the mages' conclave. He could put the queen's essence in her. Make them one, then bring Cintella to Fuego. She'd be frightened at first, but with care Elveston would bring her around. Whatever Cintella did, Queen Quanta would also do. He'd still have to win the queen's favor, but at least her survival would already be assured. All he needed now was some excuse to hold another conclave with the mages so he'd have an excuse to be where she was. A moment's thought and he knew just what to do.

# Chapter 7

Jawan perused the cultures his master kept, looking for a label that would give him a clue.

*"Earth Specimen 3."*

*"Stomach Mites."*

*"Charcoal."*

Nothing useful. Nothing that caught his eye.

*"New Study."*

That had to be it. Why would his master give this culture such a cryptic name unless it contained something so secret . . .? He slid the culture off its rack and removed the lid. In the dish, it looked like someone had spread a glob of spit in it. But in that glob of spit lay secrets his master knew and Jawan would soon find out.

Placing it under the nanoscope, he gulped. There were no magic books here, tempting him into the world of the forbidden. He was acting on his own.

He was doing the right thing. He shook his head. This was the only thing to do. He saw Myrlo's discouraged face whenever he came home from one of his meetings and knew he had to do it because no one else would.

Behind his master's downcast face, Jawan heard Loby's voice taunting him. To make it worse, Jawan's own mind put words in Loby's mouth. "If you chicken out, you'll be responsible for the deaths of everyone who dies, while you tell yourself what an obedient little apprentice you are. Chicken."

Jawan wasn't going to chicken out. He was a mouse. And who knew, maybe as an apprentice, he might see something too obvious for the trained masters to see. He might see a clue—a cure for the plague.

Now he had a problem. Two switches protruded from the sides of the nanoscope. Which one turned it on, and which one blew it up? A closer inspection of the switches revealed no markings to tell him. *Reason?* Most people were right-handed, so it made sense to put the on switch on the right. He flipped the switch on the right, and the nanoscope came to life.

He put both eyes to the stereoscopic lenses of the nanoscope. This was it! He recognized the elementary particles from drawings he'd seen—quarks, electrons, and bosons—so many bosons. But now he saw them in three dimensions, spinning like little tops. They were little tornadoes moving in one direction, as if pulled by some nano force.

As he watched this show, all the fermions, and the bosons, too, spun away in an endless stream. Except one lone quantum that took center stage in Jawan's vision. He couldn't say why, but he felt like it was looking at him. Jawan blinked. This wasn't happening. He was imagining this—wasn't he?

If an elementary particle could look up and see him, what would it see? If eyes the size of the moon looked down on the Earth, Jawan imagined he'd be scared out of his skin.

But he didn't sense fear coming from this fermion. He recognized this quantum as a fermion. There was something going on. Just looking at this one fermion was interesting, but it wasn't telling him anything. If only he were small enough to enter that world and find out where the other particles had gone.

He blinked again. The fermion was beckoning him. He felt it. *How?* This had to be his imagination. He imagined the thing crooking its little forefinger to urge him down and into that little world. This had to be his imagination. Quanta are not people. They don't have forefingers. And they have no awareness of people in Jawan's world.

If only he could.

A boson spun into view, and Jawan thought he might see some action. Bosons were containers for energy. They made things happen. Before he could even wonder what might happen, the fermion danced around the boson, and the boson came hurtling up the tubes of the nanoscope—straight at his eyes!

Astonishingly, although the boson was moving toward him, it was still standing next to the fermion. Jawan caught his breath at this first glimpse of quanta's uncanny ability to be in two places at once.

He tried to back away as the boson careened toward his eyes, but he couldn't. He pulled, but something was pulling back. Bracing his hands on the edge of the table, Jawan struggled to back away. He panicked. The force he struggled against felt like gravity. The same gravity that pressed his backside against the stool. It was pulling him into the nanoscope!

*Oh no!* Too late, he realized that it wasn't an ordinary boson. This was a graviton. *It can't be!* There's no proof they exist. They're just hypothetical.

But exist or not, this one was pulling him—pulling him down. He felt himself shrinking, exponentially, until he was one-billionths his normal size. He'd become a nano-sized Jawan.

The graviton surrounded him, pulling him inexorably toward its center. Jawan took this moment to wonder if this was what Myrlo had feared. He'd known something that Jawan hadn't known, and now Jawan was about to find out what and why.

The gravity of his own world lost its hold on him as he plunged into the atmosphere of this nano world. He was falling through some sky, and his fermion jumped and spun.

Jawan ran his hands over his body. He felt his hair and wriggled his nose. Ten fingers. Check. Two legs and ten toes. Check. Check. He was still himself. He still had arms. What he didn't have were wings, and whatever surface the fermion stood on loomed closer by the nanosecond.

Instead of crashing into the hard surface of the culture dish, Jawan sank below the ocean-sized glob Myrlo had smeared onto the dish.

He hadn't had wings. But now he needed gills, and he didn't have those either. It felt more like foam than water, and he had to get to the top before his lungs burst. What would his master say if he looked into the nanoscope and saw Jawan's lifeless body floating around? He let the thought energize his legs and kicked himself up.

"Gee, I thought you were lost." The fermion seemed more amused than concerned.

Jawan blinked and took in gulping breaths.

"What?" He gasped.

"I knew there was something different about you. Wondered why the eyes were brown instead of green this time. He comes and goes regularly. Guess it was too much to hope I'd finally hooked that emerald in the sky."

Jawan just stared, trying to make sense of the words. Realizing that no response from him was expected, he concentrated on trying to breathe and let the fermion continue.

"That green-eyed disappointment was powerful enough to break away from the graviton before we got it all the way here. Said he couldn't stay. Said he wasn't our savior. Hope you won't say the same thing. Doesn't matter. Now that you're here, we're keeping you."

That kind of got through to Jawan's fuzzy brain.

"What?!"

"You're the Big One. Our prophecy said you would come, so what else can you be?"

"Prophecy?"

Still trying to get his bearing, Jawan couldn't focus on what the fermion was saying. It stood on the surface of the smear in which he dog-paddled. Then it dawned on him that he hadn't stuttered. He had to find out what was going on.

"Where is this place?"

"Nanosia. Why don't you know? The other one knew about planet Nanosia."

The fermion looked at him as if to say, "No sense at all."

*The other one?* Had his master been here? Who else had green eyes? So, this world was what Myrlo hadn't wanted him to see? But why?

He was in this world. He could find out stuff about the plague even a nanoscope couldn't show his master from outside.

The fermion scowled and reached down to pull Jawan to his feet. He stood beside it. He thought of it as an *it* now. This sexless entity smiled at him as the other fermions and bosons swirled back into view. The bosons seemed to herd the other elementary particles toward wherever they were going.

"Follow the crowd. But don't join," the fermion said, pulling Jawan close to it.

"Huh?"

"You've got to stay close to me. Real close. I don't want to lose you. That would be terrible."

"Why?"

"Because you just got here. Wouldn't want you to leave so soon, after all I've done to . . . well, never mind. You're here."

And it marched on, as if that were the end of that.

"Who are you? Where are we going? Why should I follow you? How come I'm not stuttering?"

"One question at a time please. Stuttering? I don't know. What is that? But anyway, I'm Pym."

"That name means nothing to me."

Pym sounded like a girl's name. Did he have to start thinking of it as a *she*?

"But it means something to me," *she* said, clucking her tongue with what sounded like indignation. "We're going to see the queen."

"Queen?"

"Queen Quanta, Sovereign of the Quantum Realm."

"Wait a minute. The quantum realm is just a term in physics. It's just when things are really small. It's not a place you can go to."

"Maybe not in your big world. But here Queen Quanta rules. Now stick close to me."

"Why should I?"

"Well, stay out here and let the Negatron get you. But I didn't bring you here for that. You're sticking with me."

"A negatron is just an electron. They're all over the place. You make it sound like the boogieman."

"Don't know what a boogieman is. If you have the boogieman in the Big World, we have the Negatron in Nanosia. And it's nothing like an electron. See that darkness over there?"

Jawan looked where Pym pointed. In what must have been the horizon on this smear, he saw a darkness that swallowed the light. Just looking at it threatened to devour his stamina and leave an empty cavern of dread. He gulped.

"That's the Realm of Chaos, where Antipan rules and the Negatron lurks." She paused for effect and lowered her voice. "I feel something strange is going on in the Quantum Realm. Maybe on all Nanosia. Antipan always has something to do with strange things."

"Everything here seems strange to me, and I haven't even met Antipan."

"Hope that you don't. He's evil, but I believe in the prophecy of the Big One."

Jawan stared at her. "You have prophecy in a place like this?"

"What other place to have a prophecy about the one who can defeat Antipan, since he is here?"

"I thought prophecy is connected to some kind of religion. I didn't expect religion in the nano world. And you actually believe in it?"

"Absolutely." Pym beamed. "I not only believe it, but I've seen the Big One. Though it was the wrong Big One. It was a Big One, nonetheless."

"The green eye in the sky you were talking about?"

"Exactly! He told me he can't come here to help us because he has some plague or something in his own world he has to deal with."

Jawan frowned at this. He knew how his master was dealing with the purple plague. This dilly fermion might not know anything about it, but he'd find some clue and show his master that he was good for something other than going to the market.

"That reminds me," he said. "I was looking through the nanoscope hoping to find a clue to curing the purple plague. Hopefully, I'll learn something here. Maybe this Antipan is the clue I'm looking for."

"Maybe, but I'm not concerned about your problems. The prophecy said you'd save us from *our* problems. You didn't just come here. I summoned you, and since you're here, you will help us. The prophecy says you will."

Jawan stopped. This was too much. Did she really think . . .? "I don't know about any prophecy. And I don't have to adhere to your religious beliefs." He shook his head at the nerve of this *thing*. "And why should I help you if you're not interested in helping me?"

"Because otherwise, you will be on your own. I know more about the dangers here than you do."

"Now, wait a minute . . ."

"You don't even know what Antipan or the Negatron look like. You could walk right up to them to ask for directions."

She had a point.

Pym grabbed his arm.

"Come on. We don't have time to stand here gawking. They will come, and that will be the end of us. Stick close to me."

As if he had a choice with the fermion holding him like a firm ion. They trotted along on the flank of the crowd, close enough for the bosons to ignore them, but still separate enough to go their own way without a hassle.

His books told him all about elementary particles—quanta. But Quantum Realm? This was crazy. Not science. Nothing he could document on the assignments his master gave him. But maybe he'd get knowledge far more important than that. Who knew what he'd find? But the only way he'd find out was to go along with this herd, then he'd find out soon enough. *Famous last words.*

A portal made of carbon opened in the smear, and all the fermions and bosons poured down into it. Jawan could see nothing on the other side of the portal. Just darkness.

"We're going down there?" He gasped.

"Of course. That's the nanotube that leads into the Quantum Realm. All the elementary particles have to go through there so Nano can inspect them for treachery. He's always on the lookout for treachery."

"Nano?"

"Queen Quanta's right-hand man and guardian of the realm. Nothing enters without his inspection." She paused, glanced over her shoulder, and whispered, "Though rumor says something peculiar is happening in the queen's court."

"You said that already."

"I'll say it again. It's what you're here for, Big One. The prophet knew what would happen, and you have to be prepared. Now get ready for Nano."

Jawan hesitated. "I don't know if I'm ready to pass an inspection."

She looked at him and frowned, then shrugged. "You should have no trouble getting through. If he says anything to you, keep quiet and let me do the talking."

When they stepped into the nanotube, Jawan felt immediately lost. He spread his arms, trying to steady himself. Pym, the bosons, and the other fermions swirled around in this place that had no floor or ceiling or walls. The particles were already spinning, and that made it even harder to focus.

Focus? He tried to focus on the tube itself. Its graphene sheets were bound together by—he couldn't recall what mortar held them together. Trying to make visual sense of this endless, spiraling vortex made him dizzy. He had no sense of up or down. His eyes told him nothing. He couldn't escape the confusion. He could only flow with it.

His ears ringing, his mind whirling, Jawan tumbled out of the nanotube. He sank to his knees, trying to reorient himself and catch his breath.

When he looked up, he saw a little man standing beside a barrier. On his head, the man wore a silver hat emblazoned with a big, blue number nine.

The elementary particles bottlenecked at the barrier while Nano checked them out.

"Your spin is right. We need your kind. Enter."

So, each fermion passed the barrier as the bosons ushered them on. But when Jawan approached the barrier, Nano put out a hand to stop him.

"Irregular. Irregular. You are irregular. Why do you not spin? Why have you no orbit? There's no particle in the universe that does not move. You are irregular."

Pym stepped in front of Jawan, who despite Nano's accusation, was moving—shaking with fright. But shaking and spinning were two different things.

"He's with me," Pym declared.

Jawan didn't know where she got the confidence, but he hoped being with her meant something.

"With you, Pym?" Nano sneered. "As if that improves his properties."

"You've got to let him see the queen. He's from the Big World."

Everyone within earshot gasped.

"The Big World," they whispered.

"The Big World?" they questioned.

"The Big World," they confirmed.

The nine bosons surrounding Nano choked on the words as they each took a turn repeating them like a mantra.

To Jawan's horror, Nano frowned and abruptly ordered the bosons around him, "Take them!"

"What are we to do with them?"

"Take them to the queen."

"The queen," they whispered.

"The queen?" they questioned.

"The queen," they confirmed.

The nine bosons surrounded Jawan and Pym.

"If you all come with us, who will guard the gate?" Jawan asked.

"What does it mean: Who will guard the gate?"

"He doesn't know how things work here," Pym explained.

"Work here?" Jawan turned and looked. The nine bosons shimmered. They ushered Pym and Jawan forward. Yet, when he looked back, nine bosons still flanked Nano. He'd have to get used to the same particle being in two places at once. He had a feeling he'd have to get used to a lot of things. All the stuff he'd learned, all the stuff his master had taught him, he was witnessing firsthand.

If only he could tell Myrlo what he was seeing. Myrlo! What had he said about time in quantum physics? Did it pass at the same rate? While he meandered about the queen's court, would his master come back and find him gone? How long would he be gone? How long had he been gone already? A second? A year? He was going to be in so much trouble when he got back—if they were planning to let him go back. He didn't know.

# Chapter 8

Jawan trudged through the trackless mists of Nanosia in silence, not looking at Pym. She'd brought him into this mess. She'd told him to let her do the talking, but she had nothing to say now, and he just didn't want to look at her.

Instead, he looked at the big beefy bosons herding them to the queen. Pym had wanted to go there, but she was clearly no favorite of Nano's.

He glanced at her. She walked with sure steps as if all were going according to her plans. Neither she nor these bosons cared about his plans. Should he follow her? Again, like he had a choice. He had none, so he just let the bosons rush him toward whatever doom or glory awaited him.

Fermions and bosons rushed around him. He looked for a fixed point. If he ever tried to escape, any landmarks might help. But all he saw was nothingness. He was inside a smear on a culture dish. What had he expected to see? Grass? Trees? A road?

He saw none of that. They were elementary particles, and nothing was smaller than they were. His feet touched the same quasi-material that made up the surface of the smear.

All around his little party, fermions went about their business—spinning and orbiting yet always sure of their direction. Something about them was different. Something that his master wouldn't see. If he could think. If he . . .

He blinked. This had to be his imagination, but they looked humanoid. The electrons and protons in his study books were spherical. They weren't supposed to have arms and legs like these. He shrugged. They weren't supposed to talk, and he wasn't supposed to be small enough to walk through a nanotube and think of bosons as big and beefy.

Pym clasped his arm to bring his attention back to their journey. He looked at her and shuddered. Her eyes glowed with the confidence of a martyr facing her execution.

He didn't plan to be with her when it happened. That was no way to find a clue to the purple plague. So far, he saw nothing that even suggested a clue, but his master wouldn't have been studying this culture if he didn't think there was something here. Something Jawan had to find.

Their boson escort kept them marching straight on some invisible road. A crowd lined up on either side, creating a path for them to follow—watching and pointing at Jawan and his entourage, as if they were in a parade. Obviously, word had gotten around about the Big One from the Big World, and everyone wanted to see.

In the general hubbub, Jawan caught comments here and there.

"Could that be him?"

"The Big One we've been waiting for?"

"He doesn't look like much to me."

"There is no Big One. That's just a myth."

Jawan saw a girl near the front of the crowd. But for the bosons, he could have touched her. He just knew in some inexplicable way that it was a girl, and he was madly attracted to her but couldn't have said why.

He realized it was the same feeling of attraction that held the graphene sheets together in the nanotube. What was it? He still couldn't think of the name, but he liked it. He liked her and craned his neck to catch her eye. When he did, he smiled at her. She smiled back, and he knew which direction up was by the way his heart jumped.

"Move it!" the boson behind him barked.

"I was just trying to see what's going on."

No need to tell them about the girl. The boson pushed him, and he took two or three stumbling steps to keep his balance.

"That's none of your concern. Keep moving."

Jawan wanted to slug this thing that was neither a *him* nor a *her*. He hated being treated like a kid. Bad enough in the Big World. But here? Looks like they'd show some respect for their so-called Big One. Was Pym the only true believer? But the bosons towered over him—pure energy. No telling what they might do to him. He kept moving.

In the distance, he saw a structure so brilliant it had to be made of diamonds. It had to be the queen's castle. They made their way to it., but guards outside the entrance stopped them.

"The queen does not wish to be disturbed."

The boson captain strode up to within two feet of the guards. *Plucky,* Jawan thought. The guard was an even bigger boson, but Jawan's boson acted like he had all the authority. Maybe he did.

"She'll want to see this," he said. "We have orders from Nano himself to escort it to the queen."

The boson pointed to Jawan, who was getting tired of being called an *it*.

The guard took a step back but remained firm. "Since when do Nano's orders take precedence over the queen's?"

"It comes to us from the Big World. Let us through."

While the guards stood there astonished, Jawan's bosons pushed through. He was astonished himself to realize he could see the individual quarks and electrons that made up the castle walls. *Of course.* He was as small as an elementary particle, so only from a distance could he tell that all together they were the elements of a diamond.

Though he was as small as the fermions staring at him, their open-mouthed gawking made him want to be even smaller. They passed under a jagged portcullis, and Jawan caught his breath.

In Myrlo's castle, the tops of the columns faded into the darkness of the high vaulted ceiling. But here, everything shone, revealing the brilliant colors thrown across the ceiling by each column's many faceted diamonds. These vibrant lights twinkled to the sound of music emanating from the end of the hall.

The beauty made him slow his steps almost to a halt. Everything was illuminated by the light of chandeliers made of pure photons hanging from strings of flux tubes.

Jawan's party marched toward the music and passed through a mist into a space that had no size. Bosons led the electrons in a dance—spinning and orbiting. Everything in Nanosia spun and orbited like the Earth around the sun. No wonder Nano thought he was strange. But this orbit wasn't a circle. It was a sphere. They danced in three-dimensional space undefined by floor or gravity.

In the center sat what could only be Queen Quanta. Protons and neutrons danced around her. She wore a crown of sparkling quarks that orbited her head while the other fermions orbited her throne. Jawan grew dizzy gaping at all the spinning and twirling.

To his surprise, Nano stood beside the queen—on her right side, of course. So, like the bosons, Nano could be in more than one place at a time.

The queen glared at them. "Who are you? What are you that dare to enter our presence unannounced when we expressly forbade any disturbance?" she thundered.

"Your Majesty, we can explain," stammered the boson captain.

Nano glared at Jawan and whispered into the queen's ear. She nodded and gave Jawan a baleful glance. Then she turned to the captain.

"Of course, you can explain," she snapped. "But when we give an order, we don't want explanations. We want obedience."

"But Your Majesty, I'm here to present . . ."

"Enough! One more word from you, and you will be taken to the dungeon. Now be gone."

Without another word, the bosons all bowed to the queen and ushered Jawan out of the castle. Pym just followed, not sure what to do. They paused in the courtyard and looked at Jawan in a way that made him want to disappear.

"What are we to do with it?" the bosons asked one another.

"We can't let it wander around free. Who knows what mischief it may cause?"

Jawan bristled at this insult. "I'm tired of being called an *it*. I'm a boy."

"What is a boy?" they questioned.

"Never mind," he sighed. "And stop talking about me like I'm not here. Ask me what I want."

The bosons looked at each other like Jawan couldn't have said anything more preposterous.

The captain suppressed a chortle. "Ask you what you want? Whatever for? You're going to do what we want anyway."

"Don't be so sure," Jawan warned.

"Well, we know where to put you if you don't," the captain warned back.

"Where to *put* me?"

Pym nudged closer to Jawan. "Don't antagonize them. You don't want them to be angry at you."

Jawan remembered the queen saying something about a dungeon. He tried to imagine what a dungeon would look like in Nanosia. Then the boson captain got his attention.

"We will take it to The Room."

"The Room!" Pym gasped.

"Is that a bad place?" Jawan asked.

Pym looked at him. She turned on the bosons. "You can't put him in The Room. He's our savior. He was sent according to the prophecy. We will be counted as unworthy of salvation if we mistreat the Big One."

Jawan wanted to protest that he hadn't come to save anybody but decided to let it stand if it would keep him from being mistreated.

The bosons looked at Pym.

"What business have you here?" the captain scoffed. "Be gone immediately."

"But I brought him here. I wanted to . . ."

"Your reasons are of no consequence. Be gone."

The bosons closed ranks between Pym and Jawan. Their eyes glowed, and she trembled. She looked at Jawan as if to say, "Sorry," and hurried away.

The bosons marched Jawan in another direction. No parade of onlookers followed their progress now. Curiosity had given way to the mundane affairs of elementary particle life.

Jawan still wondered about that. What was this world like? What could he learn that would help his understanding of the purple plague when he got back home? *When he got back home?* That *when* seemed more like an *if.* He sighed as the bosons led him along.

He looked at his feet. Again, he walked on no street. Just a suggestion of place and organization that the natives understood—if he didn't.

Finally, they came to a door. The boson holding his arm opened the door and ushered him in.

"You will remain here until we decide what to do with you permanently."

"Permanently?!"

"And that is for the queen to decide."

They left, closing the door behind them. Jawan saw that the door was made of spinning quarks. Maybe they could talk. Maybe they'd be on his side.

"Will you let me out?"

"You must stay," came an answer from all around The Room. "You must stay. We cannot move without the bosons. This is The Room, and you must stay."

"Look, I'm just a kid, and I need to go home."

"What is a kid? You want to leave, but we can't let you out. The bosons are our energy. Without them we cannot move."

Jawan groaned. He was stuck at the mercy of something that, for all he knew, had no mercy. What would they do to him? He thought of all the worms and crickets he'd dissected to see how they worked. Were these people . . . these particles curious enough to dissect him?

He knew he was letting his imagination run wild, but the rules for what made sense at home didn't apply here. There was no way to even imagine what might happen in this world.

Still, he was here, and he wasn't going to sit around regretting the curiosity that brought him here. He had to find out why Myrlo was looking here for a clue to the plague. Nothing else mattered. Not Pym. Not the bosons. Not even the queen. And he had to find out what about this place made him stop stuttering. If he knew what it was, maybe he could make it permanent. His stuttering wasn't connected to the purple plague, but maybe one clue would lead to the other. He couldn't do it stuck in this room. He had to get out. But how?

He walked to the door. There was a barred window just above eye level. His nano body couldn't fit through a nano window, but if he stood on his toes, at least he could see outside. He looked out and gasped. Coming right toward him was an army of dozens of bosons. They wore the livery he'd seen in the queen's court, and they marched like an army of zombies intent on one purpose—coming to get him.

They halted ten yards from the door while six of them detached from the main force and came toward him. One of the bosons yanked the door open and motioned for Jawan to come out.

"You are wanted by the queen, and she is quite agitated."

Jawan gulped. "What does she want with me?"

"I am not privy to the queen's motives, nor do I question her desires—especially not when she's agitated. That is never a good sign."

Flanking Jawan, three on each side, they herded him to the waiting army. *All this for one kid?* Jawan remembered how the queen had glared at him when Nano whispered in her ear. Nano who thought he was irregular. So, after kicking him out of her court the queen now wanted to make sure he wouldn't get away. Nice to be wanted by a queen—if she weren't agitated.

# Chapter 9

Queen Quanta clapped her hands as the quanta danced around her throne. Fermions and bosons spun and orbited in a majestic choreography of matter and energy. Quarks in many flavors—some up and some down. Some top and some bottom. Some so charming and others downright strange. The queen laughed at the leptons. Driven by caprice, they couldn't decide whether to stay or leave. But some were quite stable.

"It's marvelous!" she exclaimed.

Nano stood by her side and only grunted. "There are so many electrons leaving."

"Electrons do that. They come and go. Why are you upset?"

"I'm not upset. I just . . ."

"Hush, Nano. You're as bad as those pesky bosons who came in here with that thing. But nothing will disturb my delight today."

She wished he could just enjoy the dance as she did. Why should beauty and duty be mutually exclusive? And yet, something was wrong. More and more of the fermions seemed weak, and there were fewer of them than she remembered.

Something caught her attention. Something that had been there, unnoticed, for a long time. Here and there around her throne—gamma rays. As many gamma rays as there were missing fermions.

"Your Majesty! Your Majesty!"

A royal page approached her throne, pushing his way through the orbiting quanta. He halted abruptly and prostrated himself before her.

"We hope you have a very good reason for interrupting our dance," the queen warned.

"Yes, Your Majesty. The ambassadors from Atomidon and Cenozonia are at the gate and beg audience with Your Majesty."

Nano and the queen exchanged glances.

"And when has Lord Jevon ever begged for anything?" the queen retorted, waving her hand. "See them in."

The page rose, bowed, and hurried out. Queen Quanta gestured for the dancers to disperse as the ambassadors approached her throne. They were nothing like the fermions and bosons of her kingdom. Estenbaum of Atomidon stood in the center of his own orbiting electrons. Twin serpents entwined Heeston of Cenozonia like a double helix.

"Long live the queen!" cried Estenbaum.

"Long may she reign!" cried Heeston.

"Yes, yes," said the queen. "What brings you here?"

She dreaded the sight of them. They'd come a long way, and with no imminent festivities to plan, that could only mean they'd come to bring bad news. She had enough troubles trying to figure out what was going on in her own court. Ill tidings from abroad were all she needed. Well, she couldn't help them, whatever it was.

"We come to tell of danger brewing in the east. Antipan is mobilizing his forces. We don't know what he's planning, but photons are missing and there's a proliferation of gamma rays and neutrinos causing instability in the courts of Atomidon and sickness in the land of Cenozonia."

Queen Quanta stiffened. *Gamma rays?* Was this a problem throughout Nanosia? No. It was just a coincidence. That's all. This was still their problem. "Surely you can't expect to run kingdoms that never see trouble. Can't you handle your own problems without worrying us?"

The ambassadors glanced at one another, not sure how to proceed.

Then Heeston said, "We came to you because this trouble with elementary particles has to have started in the Quantum Realm."

The queen sucked her teeth and turned to Nano. "What do you know about this?"

"I've seen no imbalance coming through my nanotubes. I don't know how this could be. Everything comes to Nanosia through my nanotubes. I didn't miss anything. I surely would have noticed this."

"But you did notice the missing electrons?" the queen asked.

"I . . . Yes, Your Majesty."

"And I've seen the gamma rays here in my court."

Nano shifted his weight, obviously trying to stay composed. "Your Majesty . . ." he stammered.

Heeston eyed Nano closely. "Are you sure there's no other way to enter Nanosia? Only your nanotubes?"

Nano gave an indignant harrumph. "I'm sure."

The queen turned to Heeston. "Then it must have begun somewhere else. Did you come all this way to present us with problems that aren't ours?"

"No, Your Majesty. We've come to seek a power that only you can wield. Only you can bring the Big One down from the Big World, and only he can stop Antipan."

Nano stepped forward. "The Big One? Why, that's just a rumor. A myth someone came up with."

The queen nodded. "We've never seen the Big One and have no power to conjure what probably doesn't exist."

One of her courtiers came forward, trembling and wringing his hands. He prostrated himself before the throne.

The queen looked down at him, annoyed by his presumptuous interruption—and yet, glad of it. "Do you interrupt matters of state with your petty concerns?"

"No, Your Majesty. If I may speak."

"Speak then."

The courtier cleared his throat and spoke. "Your Majesty, the Big One was here."

"Here?" the queen and the ambassadors said in unison.

"We saw nothing very big here, today, sirrah," said the queen.

The courtier shrugged but didn't rise. "No, Your Majesty. It was quite small, but it was from the Big World. The bosons said so."

"Then where is it, if it were here?"

"Begging your pardon, Your Majesty, but you sent it away and wouldn't see it at all because of the dance. You wanted nothing to disturb you from the dance."

Nano shook his head disapprovingly, but the ambassadors gasped. They couldn't very well be outraged at the queen in her own court, but they were clearly astonished.

"You sent the Big One away?" asked Heeston, as close to shrieking as diplomacy allowed.

"For a dance?" asked Estenbaum.

"Nano told us it was just an irregular particle, and we will not be disturbed."

"Of course, Your Majesty must not be disturbed. Forgive us," Heeston said. "But now that you see the Big One is real and it is in your realm . . ."

"Unless it has departed," the queen interrupted.

The courtier, still prostrate, spoke up. "No, Your Majesty. They took it to The Room."

"The Room? Oh, no," Heeston gasped. "Worse comes to worst. Your Majesty, you must release it at once."

Nano jumped up. "No! This is ridiculous. The particle we detained was highly irregular. It had neither spin nor orbit. What makes you think such a one could destroy Antipan?"

Queen Quanta wasn't sure what Nano had against the Big One. Maybe it was only his natural incredulity. But she knew she had to assert her authority as queen.

"I *must*, sirrah?"

Heeston winced and rearranged his serpents. "I beg Your Majesty's pardon. What I mean is . . . it must be done. If our kingdoms are to survive the machinations of Antipan, we need the Big One, and you are the one who can bring him back."

"And are you sure this Big One can help us?" the queen asked doubtfully.

"Your Majesty," Nano sighed. "We know nothing about this so-called Big One. It'll only make things more disordered. For all we know, it may be the cause of the present disorder."

Heeston just rolled his eyes and continued. "It's the one, Your Majesty. The only one."

"Very well."

The queen determined that the only way to find out what's what was to bring the Big One forth and see what it was about. Ignoring Nano's tacit disapproval, she summoned a boson and sent him to mobilize an escort of three dozen elite bosons.

A collective gasp followed by silence fell over the court. A menacing silence that made Queen Quanta look up to see what caused it. While her guards stood motionless, the cause of all Nanosia's woes strode toward the throne.

"Antipan, what are you doing here?"

He didn't stop or bow before her. He was the king of the Realm of Chaos, after all, and couldn't be expected to prostrate himself. But he could have done something to acknowledge her royalty even as an equal. He just mounted the first steps of her throne's dais and kissed her hand. "My queen, I come to honor you with my presence."

"Your presence does not honor us. Though your departure will."

She snatched her hand back, but not before he pricked her skin with his sharp teeth. She stared at her hand dumbfounded as droplets of blood welled up.

"Your pardon, Your Majesty." He took out a handkerchief and dabbed at the blood. "Here, allow me."

"Get out!"

Her guards trembled on a precarious edge. Caught between their dread of Antipan and their care for their queen's distress, they didn't know what to do. The queen's distress won out, and they came forward.

But Antipan waved them away. "Her Majesty is well. See, there is no wound. I will leave now."

And to everyone's utter astonishment, he left.

"Why was he here?"

"What did he want?"

Questions without answers buzzed around the throne room. Queen Quanta looked at the back of her hand. A small white spot was all the evidence that Antipan had been there.

# Chapter 10

Jawan thought his worst fears waited for him in the queen's court as the bosons marched him away. She'd thrown him out before. What would she do to him now that she was agitated? Would she execute him? He couldn't die down here where his master would never know what had happened to him. This was as bad as it could get.

What was he doing? Thinking things couldn't get worse would bring a jinx on him for sure. He bit his lip.

The six bosons who fetched him out of The Room stuck to him like static electricity. Maybe that's what it was. He could feel their energy sizzling on standby, but ready to fry him if he gave them the slightest reason. The other bosons marched in formation. Their single-minded cadence unnerved him.

"Why does the queen want to see me now?" he asked the boson clinging to his right side.

But his captors ignored him. Hemmed in on all sides, Jawan had no choice but to march in step. They formed a parade without spectators.

The diamond castle loomed up before them, its brilliance growing dimmer as the party drew near. The awe Jawan had felt the first time he'd seen it was replaced by the feeling that it was all a mockery. He saw the quarks imprisoned in the castle's walls and forced to shine for the pleasure of those who imprisoned them. Maybe they'd imprison him that way. He shuddered.

They marched under the portcullis. It seemed closer than Jawan remembered. Its jagged edges more menacing. He hardly noticed the hall's beauty as they passed into the queen's presence. As they approached her throne, all but two of his boson escorts dispersed.

He wasn't sure of court protocol but thought he should bow or something. Just when he was about to bow, the two bosons flanking him prostrated themselves and dragged him down with them. His arms sank beneath the floor that was not a floor. The mist he'd been walking on moments before licked around his face, but the rest of his body remained level with the surface, if it could be called a surface.

He felt ridiculous lying on his belly like a worm. He wanted to get up but thought he was already in enough trouble. He shrugged. *Why not?* If they were already going to execute him, what difference would it make what he did now? He just didn't know if they were planning to execute him. It could be a self-fulfilling prophecy, so he stayed put.

"The Big One will rise," ordered the queen. "You are to help us, and it wouldn't do to have you groveling like a commoner."

*Help them?What the* . . . Jawan pulled his arms out of the mist, but his eyes didn't send the message that his legs had anything solid to stand on. When he faltered, the bosons yanked him to his feet. He stared at the queen. "Help you?"

Queen Quanta's smile was as brilliant as her castle.

"Yes, the land is threatened by great evil, and it is said that you alone can rid us of this threat."

So, they weren't going to execute him. They wanted him to help them. *A kid?* Jawan felt emboldened by this new turn of events. As fear faded, anger grew. "Why should I help you after the way you've treated me?"

The court gave a collective gasp. Nano smirked and shot the queen a vindicated look.

"Treated it?" the courtiers murmured. "Is it mad?"

The queen stared at Jawan, but he refused to flinch. He was aware that she was the queen, and they could still execute him, but he didn't care. He was too mad and just didn't care.

"Treated you?" the queen asked.

"I didn't ask to come here. That stupid fermion brought me here, and you put me in jail like I'd done something wrong."

Nano, ever quick to see an irregularity, jumped up. "See what I mean, Your Majesty? This thing can do nothing for us." Turning to Jawan, he quipped. "You weren't in jail. You were in The Room."

"Whatever you call it. I couldn't get out, so it was jail."

The queen turned red. "You obstinate thing!"

Indignation drove Jawan on. "You put me in jail and then drag me here expecting me to help you? Fat chance."

"Enough!" the queen shrieked. "You were right all along, Nano. To the dungeon with this insolent knave."

*Uh-oh.* Jawan glanced at the angry faces all around him. Alien faces. Humanoid, but not human, and they were indignant now. Not The Room, but the dungeon. Why couldn't he have just kept his mouth shut?

"Your Majesty, you can't do this!" cried an even more alien-looking creature that had its own little band of electrons orbiting around it.

"You can't put the Big One in the dungeon!" cried another creature wrapped in two snakes.

"We can and we will!"

"Oh, woe to us," Jawan's two lone supporters whimpered.

Out of the corner of his eye, he saw Nano's look of satisfaction as a score of bosons surrounded him and all but dragged him out of the queen's presence.

They entered a stairwell and went down flight after flight until the walls became dank and slimy in the dim glow of sickly photons. He could see that even the slime was made up of quarks—old despairing quarks, damaged quarks, and even dead quarks. Then Jawan began to despair.

They threw him into a cell at the far end of a long hall and slammed the door. There were no photons and therefore, no light.

He felt around until he bumped his shins on what turned out to be a small cot. He lay down but refused to close his eyes and give in to the despair.

As he stared into the darkness, he realized that he still felt angry. No way would he help them after this. They'd bring him out and he'd keep defying them. Dignity and self-respect demanded that he defy them.

But then, they'd just put him back here, and dignity wouldn't help him get out. How would he ever learn anything useful? How would he ever see his friends and master again? His master might even dispose of the culture he was in and never know he was in it.

# Chapter 11

Cintella heard the fire mage calling her name. She knew it was his unmistakable voice but had no idea what he wanted with her. He'd called an impromptu conclave so close on the heels of the mage's last conclave that it had to be an emergency. As usual, she came to serve. Everything seemed normal until now.

She'd known the conclave was over when she heard the portal chime each time one of the other mages left. Only the fire mage would still be out front. And now he was calling her. She'd be silly to think the whole thing was about her, but why was he calling her? He'd never done so before.

When she'd first taken the job as serving girl, her friends at the Red Ale pub told her how it was with serving wenches. All she'd had to do was look around the pub at the leers of drunken men who pinched whatever soft thing was within arm's reach.

Still, she'd always thought the mages were somehow holy and above all that. They wouldn't even look at her, she'd told herself. But something about the way the fire mage was saying her name made her pause before drying her hands on a dishrag and going to him.

"Yes, sir?"

The earth mage, who never took the portal, was still there looking at Lord Elveston with utter dislike. "This was a waste of time." Myrlo hissed, then stomped out the door. Whatever that was about, Cintella decided was none of her business.

Lord Elveston kept his glazing, assessing eyes on her. She couldn't tell if this was more than usual for a fire mage since she never looked the mages in the eye.

"Is anyone escorting you to your cottage?" he asked. His voice was as deep as the fire that burned within him.

"No, sir. I need no escort."

Why was he asking this? She'd been working for them for months. Why was he suddenly concerned about how she'd get home?

"I think you do. It's dreadfully dark out there, and you've a long way to go."

"Not that far. Just through the trees and down the road."

"Through the trees? You don't stick to the path?"

He was holding a sheaf of papers, and his gaze grew pensive. His black robe seemed to hold the secrets of the universe—the secrets of fire.

"No, sir. I'm not afraid. I know every tree by name."

"Even so, since we're both going that way, do you have any objection to my walking with you?"

This man wouldn't be put off by subtle means. Maybe she had nothing to fear from him. Maybe this was a night when rascals really were out there, and she'd be glad of his company. She never knew, so she just shrugged.

"I guess not." Then she remembered: "Just let me tidy up a few things in the kitchen."

"Yes, do what must be done. But don't tarry. The night grows late."

"Yes, sir."

She hurried into the kitchen and dumped the dishwater out the side door. Then she dried and wiped everything that needed drying and wiping. She folded her apron into her pocket and took one last look before rejoining the fire mage.

He smiled when he saw her. It surprised Cintella that the fire mage could smile. *Think of that.*

They walked in silence for a while. He held her arm *affectionately*, she thought. It just felt that way—warm and reassuring. She relaxed.

But when they'd gone twenty paces into the trees, he suddenly whirled her around to face him. She felt the heat of his breath mingling with hers, and it was far from reassuring. What had she been thinking? Why had she let her guard down just because she'd thought he was a holy man?

"Sir, please."

"Please? Yes. I will please you. Anything you want, my queen. Ask and it is yours. My servant, Itch, shall serve you as well."

She squirmed and tried to back away. She realized with horror that although he wasn't grasping her tightly but with confidence, she couldn't get away, as if he held her by some other power than brute force. To her further horror, tears rolled down her cheeks. "I'm not your queen, and I don't know what made you think I'm yours in any way, shape, form, or fashion. And I certainly don't want anything called Itch serving me."

"You don't know who you are—who you can be. You will rule with me as queen, and I will be your king." He took out a handkerchief.

She didn't want this monster wiping her tears away. She didn't want . . . She gasped when she saw what looked like blood on the handkerchief.

When she opened her mouth to protest, he swabbed the underside of her tongue with the blood. "There. Don't cry. Soon, you will have nothing to cry about and will forget the art of shedding tears."

*Art?!* This was a game for him. She kicked him with all her strength. She hadn't really expected such a feeble gesture to have any effect on the great fire mage. She couldn't hurt him, but she could defy him.

To her surprise, he let her run, as if in sport, as if he could catch her any time and take her at his leisure but had more pressing business at present.

"Run, my queen," he called, confirming her thoughts. "I will have you."

She dared not look behind her—dared not look into those eyes again. Was he pursuing her? Why wouldn't he after such a horrid scene? Cintella kept running, listening for any footfall that wasn't the crunch of her own feet in the forest undergrowth. She heard nothing but ran with all she was worth until she reached her cottage.

Rasping for breath, she slowed before she reached the door to the two rooms she shared with her grandmother. Wouldn't do to go in out of breath and have to explain the fire mage's behavior. So, she leaned on the door lintel trying to compose herself before entering.

Even two rooms seemed too big and empty now that her father was gone. She kept a picture of him hanging by a nail near her bed. He'd been a cooper. The best in the town—in the kingdom. His barrels were watertight and sturdy, trusted by merchants, innkeepers, and pirates to keep whatever was put into them safe across land and sea.

She missed her father. Missed his laughter and the songs he used to sing to her. She also missed having a little money left over at the end of the year. Nowadays, she had year left over at the end of the money.

She no longer went to the fairs where his barrels still held pickles, ale, and apples. Yes, his handiwork had outlived him, but his skill hadn't. She couldn't make barrels like her father. Even if she could, no one would trust barrels made by a woman.

So, she worked as a serving girl for the mages. That was one step up from being a scullery maid or drudge in the kitchens where some of her friends worked. Those girls looked twenty years older than they were.

After the fire mage's behavior, she wondered if she really was better off. Would it be better to take a pinch and be done with it? No. Those girls were never done with it.

"Cintella, is that you?" her grandmother called from the other room.

Her grandmother's strong voice was a comfort to Cintella. The woman had been the only mother she'd ever known, since her real mother hadn't survived childbirth.

The old woman was well along in her seventies, yet her voice carried throughout their home, giving life to walls, table, and cupboard. This reassured Cintella that her gram would be around for a while. After losing her father a few months ago, she just couldn't think of losing her gram. Alone in the world? No, she wouldn't think of it.

"Yes, it's me," Cintella called, hanging her cloak on a nail by the door.

She set a kettle to boil on the iron stove her father had bought and began to chop vegetables.

Her grandmother shuffled out of the other room and peered into the kettle, then at the vegetables on the sideboard.

"No meat tonight?"

"I only take what they leave," Cintella explained. "I never even asked them if I could. But tonight, they left nothing."

Cintella knew the question wasn't about meat. With no teeth, her gram hadn't been able to eat meat since before Cintella had been born. The woman was asking if their situation had changed, even a little.

"But there were plenty of ripe vegetables from the garden," Cintella said, trying to sound cheerful.

"Humph."

Then she asked the obligatory question that never failed to sour Cintella's mood.

"Did you meet any nice lads today? I hope so."

Cintella mustered as much politeness as was due to her grandmother.

"No, ma'am. I saw no one."

"You're not getting any younger, you know."

"Yes, ma'am . . . I mean no, ma'am."

"You don't want to grow old and waste your looks as a serving girl all your life . . . Watch what you're doing!"

In her effort to keep calm when she really wanted to explode, Cintella had nearly chopped off her finger. Then she grasped for something to save the moment.

"Well, the fire mage walked me home." Cintella bit her lip. Why hadn't she bitten her tongue? That was the last thing she wanted to tell her grandmother.

"The fire mage! Child! Stay away from them. He's no prospect for you."

Did her gram think she was seriously considering the fire mage, or any mage, as a prospect?

"Yes, ma'am, I know that."

Her grandmother grabbed her shoulder, and for the second time that night, Cintella was turned around and forced to face someone who had their own plans for her life.

"No, child! You don't know. You have no idea what kind of men those mages are. They may promise you the world, but all you'll get is a life of slavery to a man with a lot more power than you. That's what he wants—a slave. Stay away from him."

Cintella wasn't sure. A part of her saw a hidden promise in Lord Elveston—a promise no other chap could make or keep. She couldn't tell her grandmother that, so she nodded. Then her grandmother released her and returned to the other room, muttering about people with more power than any human should have.

Cintella put the chopped vegetables in the kettle. It was just her body going through familiar motions, but her mind was elsewhere.

*Slave?* Is that what he wanted? How could she stop him if it was? What did he mean by calling her his queen? He'd told her she didn't know who she was. What did the fire mage know about her that she didn't know?

She saw a vision of herself as a small child, sitting by the iron stove and listening as her grandmother told her about her family.

They'd come from a land far away. So far away that no map in the kingdom bore its name.

Hers had been a royal family with great wealth and military might. Her grandmother's whole face had come to life as she told Cintella of footmen in fine livery and maids . . . oh, the maids! There'd been a maid to make the bed in the morning, and another to pull the covers down for the night.

The family belonged to a powerful and very old dynasty. But they had enemies. Just when they'd thought their place in the world was secure and their enemies were nothing more than an occasional nuisance, an army that stretched from east to west assaulted their borderlands.

"Long live the king," their most loyal courtiers cried as they pushed the family into the castle's secret passageway.

This saved them from sure slaughter but left them as exiles, bereft of wealth, kin, and country.

They'd wandered here and there, doing odd jobs and farm work to sustain themselves, until they came at last to the kingdom of the mages.

Cintella had never tired of these stories that took her mind off her present deprivation with tales of wealth and gallantry in her family's past. She'd often dream that she herself was a queen with stars for a crown and the universe prostrate at her feet. There was a strange man in her dreams, a man with a strange name. She couldn't remember the name, but it wasn't Elveston.

Yet, as she grew into womanhood, she began to think maybe that's all they were—fanciful tales to ease a child's experience of poverty.

Or were they? Who could say what the mages knew? The fire mage may have been telling her the truth—or at least, a half-truth. Maybe she was a queen, but that didn't mean she was *his* queen, and it didn't mean he could be trusted as a friend.

# Chapter 12

Elveston smiled as Cintella ran away. He could have chased her and taken her right then, but he didn't want to use force—just yet. To make her his—to make her give herself fully to the fire, she must be willing. Despite her initial fright, she'd be thinking about his gentle touch the rest of the night. No, he wouldn't chase her. She would come to him.

She didn't yet know who she was, but in time he would reveal this to her, she would accept the fire, and Fuego would accept her. She'd be one with Queen Quanta.Andwith her as his queen,he would be great. The greatest mage in all the universe.

The other mages thought they were his equals. He smirked at this.

That Myrlo, the insolent mage of the dirt. With his fire, Elveston could burn Myrlo to a single ash.

He could dry up Lacus until the water mage was nothing more than a mist in the wind.

And Volvo? The wind master had reason to think there was an even contest in power. But Elveston certainly had the upper hand, and he would use it before the air mage even knew he had an enemy.

The fire mage was certain that he could even destroy Quintessuma. Hers was an element of energy, like his. But she had scruples, where he had none. She would hesitate to act just long enough for him to crush her.

He took the nearest portal to his castle. The mages had set portals all over the kingdom for easy transport from anywhere to anywhere. All he had to do was step through and think about where he wanted to go.

When he stepped out of the portal, he was in his laboratory. The timekeeper above his workstation told him he'd been gone for three hours.

Elveston turned to the device that held all his dreams and plans. If only he could make it work. He stroked its smooth surface affectionately. Next to his precious camera, this device was his prize. *The camera!* The fools in their little conclave had no idea what he planned to do with his camera. Stop the plague? Indeed, it would stop, but not in the way they had in mind.

Actually, this device was the second one he'd built after he'd sent the first one to Nanosia so his servant Gelic could carry out his plans there. Nanosia had an inexhaustible supply of the photons he needed to carry out his plans. Of course, Nano might get suspicious about the imbalance of elementary particles, but he'd never suspect what Elveston was doing. Even if Gelic were caught, which was unlikely, Elveston lived in a world that Nano didn't even believe in, so Gelic's story would seem ridiculous.

Gelic had been an accidental creation that turned out to be useful. With the device, Elveston had made his first batch of electron-positron pairs using high energy photons and was about to collect them into a cylinder for use in his camera when, to his dismay, the electrons and positrons were attracted to one another like opposite ends of a magnet—like helplessly smitten lovers. The result was disastrous.

Upon contact, each pair was annihilated and replaced by gamma rays, for which Elveston had no use.

He detested gamma rays, the natural byproduct of radioactive decay. He didn't need to produce his own. No matter. He would learn to control gamma rays and subdue them. Then in his new world, gamma rays would be the slaves of his elite creation—pure energy. The bosons would rule in a universe devoid of filthy matter. And he, as pure fire, would be their lord.

Loby broke into his musings. "Master, the fire cubes are ready—at least the ones I made for Master Myrlo. Shall I take them to him?"

"Yes, of course, silly boy. What else would you do with them?"

Elveston's patience was short with the boy right then. It was short with anything that drew his attention away from his plans to the trivialities of the material world. He didn't even note Loby's departure.

He peered into the machine, vexed that he did not know if Gelic was doing as he'd been instructed. The fire mage would not rest until he found out what Gelic was doing. He'd not come so far by trusting others.

When he'd made that first batch of electron-positron pairs, all but one positron had mated with their matching electrons and become gamma rays. This one positron seemed to be aware of what had happened to the others and was, to all appearances, running from its mate, which was pursuing it like an unwanted soulmate.

Elveston had laughed watching them race around under the nanoscope attached to his device.

Then suddenly, there was a pop—an electronic whoosh, and before him stood what appeared to be a man. And what a perfect archetype of man it was. Tall and well proportioned—what Elveston assumed most women would call handsome. He peered into the device, but the positron he'd seen there was gone, and its forlorn mate wandered around aimlessly.

"Hello, I'm Gelic," the man said, sitting on the table that held the device and crossing his elegant legs. "I guess that will be my name. It's a nice name. Don't you think?"

Elveston hadn't risen as a powerful mage by allowing unusual circumstances to astonish him. At least, not long enough to lose his composure. "You are the positron."

"That I am."

At first, Elveston wasn't sure he had any use for a positron that he couldn't fit into a cylinder or his camera. Then he got an idea. This was the servant he needed. To carry it out, he'd have to win its confidence. What did the positron want?

"You look so much like a human. You even have clothes. How could this be when you were just created a few moments ago?"

"Created? I don't know that word. Before becoming a positron, I was a photon. I've lived a googol of years, even before there was any such thing as years. Just particles moving in inchoate time. I've had long enough to study the universe and all that is in it."

Now Elveston was taken aback. How could he carry out his plan without the positron discovering what was what? Surely, it couldn't know everything. But Elveston had no way to determine what it did know. Still, the mage knew his own mind, and the positron couldn't possibly know the future. Gelic's smug merriment faded in the silence, and Elveston thought he saw an opening. "You look sad."

And indeed, the positron did look sad. Could a mere elementary particle have emotions, or was this just a simulation of human facial expressions it had picked up over the eons?

"I'm all alone," the positron lamented. "Those other positrons were like family to me. I was just beginning to think I was in a happy place when they became enthralled by those nasty electrons. I hate electrons. Those electrons robbed me of everything that was lovely in that place. So, I came to this place. But I'm still alone."

"No, my friend. You're not alone. I'll be here for you."

"You're not a positron. You're a human. There's not a positron in your body. But you do smell strongly of electrons. They're on your skin. Stand back, please."

Enough. The positron was mistaking compassion for frailty.

"Yes, these electrons are under my control, and you must be as well, or I will order them to mate with you and you will become the most gruesome gamma ray."

"Oh, really?"

Elveston heated his body to release the millions of electrons that he could spare without destroying the atoms in his body. They flew toward the positron. It shrieked and dived under the table. "Okay, I believe you."

"You had best."

Elveston knew that he'd have to instill a combination of fear and gratitude if he wanted the positron to carry out his will. So, he dispersed the electrons and adopted a reassuring voice. "But I'm not a bad guy." Then he stepped back and gestured for Gelic to come out from under the table.

The positron hesitated, but as he was in an uncomfortable, not to mention undignified, position, he eased himself out and sat on a chair as far from the mage as he could get.

Elveston nodded. "In fact, if you follow my instructions, you'll have an even bigger family of positrons with all the time in the world to get to know them."

"Your instructions?"

"To the letter. It's crucial that you do exactly as I tell you. You will be working with sensitive technology, and if you're careless, the results will be unpredictable—perhaps disastrous. Do you understand?"

"Yes, I'm listening."

"You will go to Nanosia and take this device with you. You will go to the Quantum Realm and set up shop. There you will take photons, like you once were, and draw them into this device."

"As I was drawn in?"

"No, you were not. Your case was quite different. Anyway, make sure the energy level in the device is sufficient to transform the photons into electron-positron pairs . . ."

Gelic's eyes bulged in alarm. *"Electrons?!"*

Elveston raised a reassuring hand. "Don't worry. Just keep them separate from the positrons, and the positrons will be your new family."

Gelic nearly leaped from his chair. "A family of positrons! My own!"

"For eternity. When there are no more years and the planets have spun away from their darkened suns, you and your positron family will still frolic through the universe."

It was a lie, but it was working nicely. The positron was ecstatic and would do as Elveston wanted.

Elveston relished the positron's excitement but knew he had to make it follow instructions exactly.

"It is good you are excited about what is about to take place. Your alacrity will excite the positrons you will bring into existence."

"Yes!"

"But listen carefully to my instructions. One slip and all might be ruined."

He directed Gelic's attention to the device on the table. "This is a particle collider. I call it Posiplus. You will take it with you to Nanosia. Set it up somewhere away from the castle of Queen Quanta. It wouldn't do for her soldiers to discover what you're doing."

"Is it against a law?"

"Not against any law of nature. Otherwise, it wouldn't work. But the Nanosians won't like it. It upsets their control of things. But why do they need to control everything? Why allow them to keep you from happiness just because they're a little squeamish?"

"I shouldn't. I won't."

"Certainly not. And be especially wary of Nano. He won't look like much, but it is he who controls the operations in the Quantum Realm. Not a particle moves in or out of that realm without his inspection. If he discovers you, he will be most displeased."

"Then how will I get in?"

Elveston smiled. "By a way that he does not know."

Sitting up and uncrossing his legs, Gelic smiled back. "Sounds intriguing, but how will I know him to stay away from him?"

"His favorite number is nine. Has something to do with ten to the negative ninth power or some such insignificant thing. He wears a silver hat with the number nine inscribed on the crown. You can't miss him."

Gelic looked puzzled. "I thought missing him is what I want to do."

Elveston wondered if the positron was being sarcastic or if it really didn't catch that colloquialism. Either way, that might prove to be useful information.

"Yes. Well, you do. Now listen. The technology housed within the Posiplus is very delicate. Handle it as if it were a bubble ready to burst at the slightest touch. It won't but handle it that way. When you are ready to start, push this lever."

Gelic leaned forward to see the indicated lever.

"Periodically check this gauge, which will tell you the level of energy being applied. It must reach one point two million electron volts . . ."

The positron jumped to his feet. "Why do you keep talking about electrons?! I don't like this."

Elveston saw he'd have to avoid that word. He waved Gelic back into his seat. "That's just a word. There won't be any electrons at this point."

"At what point then?"

The positron was certainly averse to the very idea of electrons. Elveston knew he had to take its mind off that.

"That's not really important. If you follow my instructions, you won't have to worry."

Gelic relaxed, so Elveston continued. "When the photons transform to positrons, you will keep them safely until I come for them. Do you understand what you must do?"

"It's quite simple, actually. No problem."

"You must not take this lightly. If you don't do it correctly, there will be consequences."

Elveston brushed the surface of his skin to remind the positron of the electrons at his command.

"I understand." Gelic assured him, suddenly sounding very serious. "I will do as you instructed."

But as he ushered Gelic and the Posiplus through the portal that day, Elveston caught a gleam in its eye that he didn't trust.

That was a year ago. Gelic had since found a way to keep the positrons and electrons separate, so Elveston was now able to transfer positrons to his camera. But that was not enough. To Elveston's consternation, instead of being annihilated when he took their picture, people contracted the purple plague.

He hadn't lied to the other mages. Finding a way to stop the plague was as much his concern as theirs—though for quite different reasons and for vastly different results.

And those results were all that mattered. He still wondered what Gelic had done to keep the electrons and positrons apart. But as long as it was happening, the plan would go forth. Gelic provided what he needed for the Posiplus. It was time to deal with the camera. He rang for Itch.

The servant appeared almost instantly. The bell activated a summoning page that allowed Itch to step from wherever he was into the presence of Elveston wherever he was on the planet.

"What have you discovered, Itch?"

Elveston had been studying positron properties for years and had the camera almost to where he wanted it. But, like Fuego said, the positrons were as unstable as their electron counterparts. This instability kept him from his ultimate goal of annihilation.

The positrons in the camera were supposed to collide with the electrons in the subject's body, annihilating the subject. Elveston would then reduce the energy of the resulting gamma rays to transform them into purer forms of energy. The only problem was the instability of the positrons merely caused a biochemical reaction.

Elveston needed to find a way to stabilize the positrons. Hopefully, Itch had found something that might reveal this secret.

"Master, the secret we want "may be in the Ageto scroll."

"*May* be?"

Itch looked uncomfortable at the mere thought of saying something his master didn't want to hear. After all, Elveston could toast him to cinders with a mere thought. So, he quickly amended his statement. "That's what I found, master."

"And where is this Ageto scroll?"

"In some place called Nanosia, master. It sounds far away. I can find out where it is."

"No! I know where it is." He didn't see the need to send his servant to Nanosia. The less people knew, the more faithful they tended to be. When his project was complete and all the parts came together, there'd be no planet, no Nanosia, and no Itch. Elveston could only let Itch help him to a point. Itch wasn't the brightest flame one could put on a candle, but he could read. He was slow, but he figured things out after a while.

Well, Elveston would need to go to Nanosia sooner or later to check on Gelic. Why not sooner?

"Itch . . ."

"Yes, master."

Elveston enjoyed being called master. It sounded so much more heartfelt coming from Itch than from Loby, who said it as an obligation.

"I've no choice but to go off to Nanosia. It is vital that I have that scroll. And I will have it. While I am gone, I want you to keep an eye on the other elemental mages. They're going to try something to spy on me. If you see anything suspicious, contact me at once."

He handed Itch the summoning bell.

When he had checked everything, Elveston stepped through the portal in his laboratory into Nanosia.

# Chapter 13

Myrlo, tired and vexed, trotted his horse into the stable and brushed down its coat. He summoned more oats into its trough and turned to enter his castle.

Even before he got close, he sensed that something wasn't right. Something wasn't there that should be there. Focusing on this absence, he realized that it was Jawan. The boy was not there. Myrlo knew of no business his apprentice might have outside the castle this time of night.

He prepared to go in and find out what was what, when he felt a summons from Quintessuma. The mages seldom summoned one another unless there was trouble. He'd have to answer this. Jawan would have to wait.

Though the stones were there, Quintessuma's true castle couldn't be seen by the naked eye. Like her element, it existed in the spaces between matter. Probably, every body of matter in the universe consisted mostly of ether-filled space. But Quintessuma's castle was thus even more so.

Myrlo marveled at the energies that held the atoms together, giving it a solid look and keeping him from falling through the floor.

"Is there trouble? Has Elveston hatched some mischief?" he asked Quintessuma as he stepped through her portal. He didn't like them, but a summons of this sort left no time for horses.

Quintessuma shook her head. "This is about Elveston, but we don't know yet if he caused the mischief."

Myrlo was about to say something when chimes sounded from the portal. Quintessuma turned to greet the new arrivals. "Good, the others are here."

She smiled as Volvo and Lacus approached.

Myrlo wanted to say what he'd planned to say, but Quintessuma made a show of ushering them all into the conference chamber, and he had no choice but to follow.

Although the small round table was cozier than the crescent-shaped table at their regular conclave, which made it clear that Elveston—Lord Elveston Peruro—was the center of authority, none of the mages seemed at ease that night. The meeting itself was irregular. An emergency meeting to which the fire mage hadn't been made privy. This gave everyone an idea of what the meeting would be about.

So Myrlo felt free to speak. "I don't trust him."

Volvo and Lacus nodded in agreement, their eyes betraying their own private reasons for not trusting the fire mage, but Quintessuma shook her head.

"I don't know if it's a matter of trust. We have no actual proof that he is doing anything questionable . . ."

"But . . ." Myrlo started to object.

"None whatsoever," Quintessuma continued. "Myrlo, you seem to have some special need to believe that Elveston is a villain."

"He is!"

"And what proof can you present to support this claim?"

Myrlo had no empirical proof. Nothing that he could demonstrate. Just his own internal earth sense. But Quintessuma should be sensing something as well. The heart of man was well within the ether domain. Why was she acting as if there were nothing but what lay on the surface?

"Why don't you trust my sense?" he asked. "Why don't you trust your own sense of what Elveston is about?"

Quintessuma sighed. "Again, this isn't about trust. What we sense must be backed up by solid evidence. Otherwise, it's just credulity."

"You're ready enough to give Elveston fiat credulity," Myrlo countered.

"No, you're wrong there. In fact, I called this meeting to discuss what we need to do about the plague. Elveston wants us to wait for him to finish fiddling with his camera. But we can't do that. People are dying. Whether he be a villain or not, we just can't wait for him."

"What can we do?" Volvo asked. "I've sent the wind into every crevice. Wherever air could go, I went, but I found no clue to a cure."

"And where the wind couldn't go, I sent water," Lacus said. "I've charged every drop of water, from the oceans to the aquifers of the Earth, to reveal what they know. But they know nothing."

Myrlo felt the impotence of his rage against the fire mage as he related how he'd searched the deepest secrets of the Earth but had found neither plant nor mineral that might help.

Quintessuma slid her hands across the surface of the table. "I've had no better success than you."

"Where have we not looked?" Myrlo asked, though he knew the answer and knew the other mages didn't want to think about it, especially not Quintessuma.

Volvo shifted in his seat. Lacus studied the table. Quintessuma sniffed.

Myrlo wouldn't let their silence stand. "We haven't looked into the castles of the mages. And since there is only one mage who isn't here—who was not invited . . ." He glanced pointedly at Quintessuma. "We know whose castle is likely to turn up an answer."

"*No!*" Quintessuma cried.

Volvo shook his head.

"It is forbidden."

Quintessuma held the earth mage's gaze. "Myrlo, in my long memory, I can't recall any mage even suggesting that we violate elemental protocol by spying on other mages in their own domains."

"But that might be exactly where the plague is coming from. We may be looking all over the Earth, in every place except the right place. Why should we not look in Elveston's castle if that's where it is?"

"Myrlo! Listen to what you're saying." Volvo gasped. "Do you actually think the plague is coming from Elveston? That's a serious charge."

"A very serious charge to make with no proof whatsoever," Quintessuma agreed. "We don't know that it's there. Should we break protocol for something that *might* be?"

Myrlo scowled.

"Regardless," Quintessuma continued. "The point is that Elveston may be many things, including your precious villain, but he is a mage. He has taken the mage's oath. He wouldn't betray that."

"Are you sure?" Myrlo asked.

"Look." Quintessuma slapped her palm on the table. "What could the fire mage possibly gain by betraying the world on which he himself must live?"

Volvo cleared his throat, apparently in an effort to clear the air. "You know the one thing we said we should try that we haven't? We said we should work together. Our combined efforts may uncover something we can't accomplish individually."

But Lacus looked doubtful. "We're shooting in the dark, you know. We don't even know what's causing the plague. Where did it come from? What does the agent look like? Are we dealing with magic or some mundane pathogen? What's the point of pooling our efforts when we don't know where to focus them?"

Quintessuma smiled. "That's a valid point. Now we're getting somewhere. How do we find out what agent is causing the plague?"

"We need a sample," Volvo said. "Myrlo, you have a microscope. We could put a sample in a culture and study it until we discover what it is."

"How do we get a sample?" Lacus asked.

"We'd have to take it from one of the victims," Volvo said.

Myrlo could tell that the other mages shared his lack of alacrity at the thought of coming into contact with one of the victims. Despite their desire to do something about the plague, they knew that they could easily become one of its victims. "I can't see it happening. The authorities will not allow us to get near those who are afflicted. We can't expect them to open one of the quarantined houses."

The mages stared at the table as if watching their brilliant idea slip into oblivion. Myrlo grasped at a solution crossing his mind, but let it go as unfeasible.

Then the ether filling Quintessuma's castle seemed to brighten as an idea came to life in her mind.

"Maybe we don't have to come near the victims." Quintessuma's eyes brightened with an idea. "Maybe we could use magic to procure the sample."

Myrlo, Lacus, and Volvo perked up at this idea. *Yes!*

Volvo pursed his lips in thought, then said, "All we need is a container, a transparent container that is biologically and magically secure."

Myrlo was happy but still had his doubts about just how successful even this seemingly promising effort would be. Surely, Elveston was behind the plague, and it was unlikely he would just let them bring an end to his plans, whatever they may be.

He glanced at the other mages. They were happy, too. They had something they thought would work. Myrlo sighed. It would do no harm to let them do what they could. But then, maybe it would. When Elveston discovered their plans to directly eradicate the plague, he might in turn take direct steps against them.

He shuddered at the thought of where that would lead. Four mages against one. Despite Elveston's formidable powers, he couldn't win. Yet, if they vanquished the fire mage, the loss would be not only to him but to all the universe, for there was no one ready to take his place.

"What will we use for a container?" he asked.

"Glass is transparent."

"No," Quintessuma objected. "Glass is physical. It has molecules and might interfere with what we see. We have no idea what we're looking for or what the agent might look like, so we can't have any interference."

"Well, if we take the sample from a human body, it will have biological interference," Myrlo said.

Quintessuma frowned, as if this were something she hadn't considered. Then she shrugged. "That is as may be, but we can't wait for the perfect situation to arise. It won't. And this is all the more reason not to have interference from the container." She sat up resolutely. "I propose that we use ether. It has no molecules, is transparent, and can be made secure."

They formed a circle, holding hands in the center of the room. It was important that they stood in the exact center, concentric to the circular walls.

Myrlo and Lacus hummed to call up the magic energy they would need. Then Volvo said the mantra to call up the wind:

> "Breath of the Earth
> Wind of the ages
> Men know not from whence you came or whither you go
> But I call you
> Come hither."

Then Quintessuma chanted to call up the ether:

> "Spirit of the Earth
> Fifth element of nature
> That fills the spaces that men cannot see
> I call forth your strength

To ward against magic
And all pernicious matter."

The ether nestled down into a pocket of wind, which carried it away from Quintessuma's castle to Hadley Town sleeping nearby.

It chose a low one-story structure with two rooms. The house wasn't different from its neighbors, except for the bright purple boards that sealed its doors, windows, and chimney hole. There were no people nearby to note the wind and its passenger as they entered the house.

Inside was a man, a woman, and five children of varying ages. Purple splotches and bloody sores covered their bodies. On the table were the meager remains of what must have been the mother's last effort at making a meal. But none of the occupants moved now. Their throats were as dry as the cups on the table.

Volvo guided the wind to one child, and Quintessuma directed the ether to enclose a sample of the seeping lesions covering her body.

Quintessuma made sure the sample was secure in the ether container. No physical thing could crack its surface, but it was her thoughts she had to be wary of. Her thoughts had shaped the ether into a container, and one careless thought could crush it.

With the sample in their hands and the task in their minds, they stepped through the portal into Myrlo's laboratory.

Myrlo shivered in transition. He was used to working magic on other objects and even on animals. But this magic worked on him, dissolving his whole body. As close to the speed of light as elementary particles could get, his disintegrated body passed through the cold, dark ether—from being to non-being and back again.

When he arrived in his laboratory, he remembered the emptiness that marked Jawan's absence. *Emptiness?* Had the boy become so much a part of Myrlo's life that the castle felt empty when he was gone?

Myrlo took a petri dish and prepared a culture onto which Quintessuma carefully placed the ether container.

Even with their naked eyes, they could see a purple smear of something through the crystal-clear ether. This raised their hopes that they were on the verge of discovering the plague's agent.

But when Myrlo looked through the microscope, he saw nothing pathogenic. All he saw was a structure clearly identifiable as human hemoglobin. "Why is it purple?"

"Purple?"

First Quintessuma, then Volvo, and then Lacus took turns looking into the microscope, hoping to see something the others missed. But they saw nothing suspicious.

"I see nothing to account for its color," Quintessuma said. "But we know something is there."

"How can something as contagious as the purple plague not be present in every part of the body—especially the blood?" Myrlo asked.

"Let's use the nanoscope." Volvo pointed to the device. "We'll get a more elementary view of what's going on."

Myrlo rose and approached the nanoscope, then stopped. "That's odd."

A powerful atomic beam illuminated the platform of the nanoscope, indicating that it had already been turned on. Highlighted in the beam lay a culture that should have been in the rack. Jawan's presence was all over it, as if he had just touched it. How could that be when the boy had been gone even before Myrlo left for the emergency meeting? He set the dish aside, keeping it as evidence for when he confronted the boy about his disobedience and carelessness.

He placed the plague culture under the nanoscope and was dumbfounded by what he saw.

"What is it?" Quintessuma asked.

"Look."

Myrlo moved aside so that she could take a look. She looked and shook her head, unable to make any more sense of it than he had.

Volvo took his turn and gasped in bafflement. "Positron-electron pairs and gamma rays?"

"What the . . ." Lacus said as Volvo moved over for him to see.

"What are positrons and gamma rays doing in the human body?" Quintessuma wondered.

"And in such numbers?" Volvo said.

"I've no idea." Quintessuma shrugged. "What do you know, Myrlo?"

He stood to the side, staring at the nanoscope thoughtfully.

"Well, I'm sure there's an explanation. I just don't know what it could be. I've never seen anything like this."

"Of course, we know it's not natural," Lacus agreed.

*Not natural.* Myrlo's thoughts drifted toward Elveston, but he decided not to say anything—let the evidence speak for itself. It was just a matter of time now, and they'd no longer be able to deny the obvious.

"I must search the Earth lore and histories to find something—hope to find something that can tell us how positrons and gamma rays can exist in the body and cause a condition like the plague."

"Where did they come from? If we knew the source, we'd be that much closer to putting a stop to this," Volvo said.

Lacus backed away from the nanoscope, his lips pursed in thought. "Obviously, the gamma rays resulted from the collision of the positrons and electrons."

"But where did all those positrons come from?" Volvo insisted.

Myrlo was glad they were asking questions. He had no idea where the search for answers would lead, but he bet it would lead directly to Elveston's castle. Would they act despite elemental protocol? That remained to be seen. "I know positrons occur naturally in two ways. One of which is radioactive decay. Can't recall the other means."

Quintessuma shook her head. "Positrons don't occur in the body in the numbers we saw. If they did, all humanity would die of the plague."

"Well, there's nothing else we can do here until Myrlo gets more Earth information," Volvo said.

They all agreed. Quintessuma sent the ether container with its deadly contents back to the house in Hadley where it could do no harm. They then bid Myrlo goodnight and took the portal to their respective castles.

While straightening his work area, Myrlo sensed the presence of Jawan's friend Loby near the castle's portcullis. How long the boy had been standing there, he couldn't guess. But Myrlo made a note to himself never again to be so preoccupied that he missed what was happening around his castle.

He went to let the boy in. Unlike Elveston, Myrlo had no servant to do such things. None of the other mages did either, but Myrlo especially liked to walk the Earth and be close to his own work.

Loby stood on the other side of the portcullis beside a huge box on a cart. Myrlo opened the gate and let the boy through. He tried to get a sense of whether the boy had been with Jawan lately. The sense was there, but faint and mixed with other, more recent, presences, including the fire mage and a salamander.

"Master Myrlo, do you have a message for Master Elveston?" Loby asked.

Myrlo noted with satisfaction that the boy didn't call his master Lord Elveston as the fire mage insisted everyone do. "No, child."

Myrlo lifted the hot box off the cart by its cool wooden side handles and gave Loby a few coins.

"Thanks, Master Myrlo."

The boy was genuinely thankful, so Myrlo nodded as Loby turned and made his way to his master's castle.

Then Myrlo returned to his laboratory, wondering if Jawan's disappearance had anything to do with the culture he'd left on the nanoscope. *Impossible.* But then, who knew? *No. Impossible.* He sat at the nanoscope and studied it.

# Chapter 14

In the Quantum Realm, fermions and bosons went about their business—spinning and orbiting for the queen's delight. Particles came through the nanotubes as energy that Nano shuffled into colliders where they became useful fermions again, ready for transport to Atomidon.

For eons, the routine never changed. So, anything irregular was either forced into conformity or eliminated.

In such an environment, the prophet's voice arose. At first, it was a still, small voice, crying out among the hustle and bustle near the queen's palace.

"The Big One comes!"

But the elementary particles were too engrossed in their routine to notice a still, small voice. They noticed he wasn't moving with the flow, so they expressed varying degrees of consternation at having to circumnavigate him.

So, the small, still voice got bigger and louder.

"As was prophesied in days grown old, the Big One comes and even now is here. Turn, people, and behold, your help is at hand."

Then he began to dance. Particles stopped to watch the dancing prophet and they remembered. Many had only just arrived in Quantum Realm, but they had been here before, and their memories persisted across many cycles from energy to matter and back again.

They remembered that it was the prophet who danced and showed them a brighter way out of the darkness imposed by Antipan and his wicked Negatron. The prophet Niptilius who'd shown them that it was still possible to dance and give joy to the queen.

And now, could it be that same Niptilius who again beckoned them to dance?

"Follow my spin."

He became the nucleus around whom they orbited. Since they were all matching his spin and some shared other properties with him, they had to spread out in concentric orbits so that no two of the same breed intruded on one another.

The protons and neutrons disdained to orbit and kept to their age-old routine, ignoring his message.

"What about them?" the electrons cried. "Have they no place in what is to come?"

But Niptilius rebuked them. "What is that to you? Let them be and follow me."

"And where are you going?"

"Where? Where! They that know will know. For now, we must dance."

So, dance they did.

More and more electrons and even some bosons orbited the prophet. The orbiting particles spread so wide that those still trying to go about their business felt impeded. Too many elementary particles were in places they weren't supposed to be, going in directions at angles they weren't supposed to go. And the authorities took notice.

When Nano noticed this, he led a troop of bosons to investigate this imbalance.

They approached the nucleus of the disruption. Ignoring them, Niptilius and his constellations kept dancing until Nano's bosons were forced to match their spin. But they were trained by Nano himself and kept their disciplined formation.

With Nano directly in front of him, Niptilius finally had to pay attention.

"What are you doing? Or rather, what do you *think* you're doing?" Nano barked.

"The Big One comes. I am but a still, small voice, crying out to make straight the way of the savior who was promised."

"The Big One? You're disrupting traffic and drawing particles away from their assigned paths to spread religious nonsense?"

The prophet started to answer, but Nano cut him off. "Take him away!" he ordered his bosons. "Take him to The Room to await my displeasure."

It took a while for the orbiting particles to realize something was amiss. An outcry by the fermions closest to Niptilius drew the attention of the others, and they started to stage a protest, but the bosons held them back as Nano's special elite bosons led the prophet away.

Niptilius walked with such a stately comportment that his boson escort was forced to give him more space than they usually gave to prisoners. The gleam in his eye spoke of a confidence in something beyond this world.

When they arrived, one bold boson tried to push Niptilius through the door but jumped back with a cry. "*Ow!* He shocked me. The little blip is negatively charged."

"I am positively charged."

The other bosons stared at a mysterious new mark on their comrade's hand. They then looked at Niptilius and stepped back.

The prophet entered The Room of his own volition, without so much as glancing at the unfortunate boson. He sat on the cot that would serve as his bed if he cared to sleep, while the bosons stared at him. Sensing an audience, he began to speak. "The Big One comes for you, also. If you will but believe in him. It's very important that you have faith . . ."

The bosons backed away, closing the door. Niptilius smiled. They thought they were leaving him alone, but he didn't feel alone. He saw that the walls of his prison were made of quarks. These quarks looked so miserable that he knew at once that they were the ones the Big One was most fond of and upon whom he would bestow his greatest blessings. So, he opened his mouth and preached to them. "Sorrow not, my dear ones. Though your sins be many, they shall be as ash that blows away in the wind."

The quarks didn't respond, but Niptilius kept on. "When the Big One comes, he will set you free so that you can return to the world of orbiting particles. You will dance and spin as you were meant to do. Those who imprisoned you here will be punished. They who are trapped will be set free, and they who are free will be trapped."

He saw something move and thought he was getting through to the quarks. Were they about to break out and dance right then and there? Instead, the door eased open, and a fermion entered.

"Are you okay?" the fermion asked, examining him, as if he might have been abused by the bosons.

"I'm fine, but who are you?"

"I'm Pym, and I'm so sorry you've been treated so shamefully. This wouldn't have happened in the old days when prophets were respected and their prophecies heeded."

Niptilius regarded the fermion. She was sincere. A true believer. He could teach her, maybe. He could use her to spread the message. The Big One needed people he could use. "I don't know. Nano has always been here. But there was a time when the need to believe triumphed, even over the number nine. The very fact that I am in the Quantum Realm is proof that things are far worse than many suspect, and the time for my prophecy is now."

"You must tell me everything about the prophecy. But first, we must leave this place before we're discovered."

Pym made a show of helping the prophet to his feet, but he brushed her off and strode out the door, as if no one would dare stop him.

Outside the door, he paused and began to shake his foot, as if to dislodge the mist that swirled around them. "Woe unto this place and all who stand against me and the prophecy. I shake the mist of this place off my feet against them. The Big One will never come here."

"But he was here," Pym replied. "He slept on the very cot where you sat."

"Never! He would never stoop to such degradation. He is holy, and this place is profane. He would never come here."

"He was here," Pym insisted.

"If you want me to teach you, you must be a proper disciple and stop spewing such blasphemy."

Pym looked contrite but confused. "Yes, sir."

The prophet looked off into emptiness as they walked. He didn't ask Pym where they were going. Though she had rescued him, he knew that his feet were directed by a higher purpose. "All don't believe, Pym."

"That's true."

"Therefore, I must go far away from the unbelievers and preach the prophecy to those who will believe."

"Then we must keep clear of the queen's castle. We can't stay away from the bosons as long as we remain on Nanosia, but at least we can go among those who aren't led directly by Nano. Come this way."

They changed directions and walked until the elementary particles they met were less pompous and less in a hurry. The prophet mounted an elevated place and was about to start preaching when another speaker caught his eye. He looked more closely until he was sure. Yes, it was a positron—no, it was *the* positron.

"Behold, the Lord!"

He gestured for Pym to look, but she frowned. "I don't see him. How can you pick him out in that crowd?"

"No, fool! He is the Lord. He isn't in the crowd, but above it."

Pym raised her eyes. "Where is the Big One? All I see is that funny-looking positron."

"Funny looking?! Fool, that is the Lord!"

"But I thought the Big One is the Lord."

"The Big One is the savior who will save us from Antipan, but this one is the Lord."

Pym looked even more puzzled, but Niptilius talked on. "Many orbit around me because I speak the prophecy, but many more will orbit around him because he *is* the prophecy."

She was about to ask the prophet a question when a booming voice riveted both their attentions. "Behold!"

Then the positron threaded his way through the crowd and stood before Niptilius. "Let me dance with you, oh prophet of old, and I will match your spin."

Niptilius all but prostrated himself before the positron. "Oh, Lord! I would kiss your feet, but I am not worthy to do so, and would you match my loathsome spin when it is I who should match yours—will match yours?"

The positron laughed without smiling. Then he began to spin out of control. Faster and faster than any particle could ever spin. His mass increased as he approached the speed of light. Pym, Niptilius, and all the nearby particles began to orbit the positron. Niptilius wanted to protest that he was unworthy but knew that he had to submit to his lord or why call him lord at all?

Still, this was all quite irregular.

Then the positron slowed, and Niptilius regained control of himself. He, Pym and the other particles dropped to the surface bewildered.

"Yes, you should match my spin," said the positron. "But you don't. And how can you? You have preached the old prophecy, for you are old and it is now time for a new prophecy."

"New prophecy?" Niptilius inquired. "How do you know what I preach? I just saw you."

"But I saw you. In the city, I heard your message. You say you came to make my way straight? Yet, you don't know my way. You know not what I am here to do."

"The Big One . . ." Niptilius started to point out.

The positron laughed again. "What is my name? Do you know it?"

"You are the Lord. As I have prophesied. Great and holy, righteous and . . ."

"Oh, hush. You know nothing. I am Gelic. The first positron of Nanosia."

Shaking her head, Pym disagreed. "There have been other positrons here. Nano deals with them all the time."

"Did you not hear what he said? I am the Lord! Many false positrons have come before me, but none is the Lord before me or after. I am The Positron."

"Yes," agreed the prophet.

Gelic's voice rose to thunder. "I am the first Positron of the new prophecy. The first of a new order."

To Niptilius' horror, Gelic began to motion for the bosons. What did the Lord have to do with unbelievers?

"Guards! Here is the disturber of the order whom Nano had arrested earlier. By some machination, he has escaped, but not having done enough mischief, he is here again. Take him!"

Pym exploded. "What are you doing?!"

She stood between Niptilius and the oncoming bosons, as if she could forestall them by the righteousness of her wrath alone.

But Niptilius pulled her back and stepped toward the bosons. "No, child, this is how it must be. I must decrease, and he must increase."

"But you're the prophet," Pym wailed. "You speak the words of the prophecy. You were supposed to teach me those words."

Gelic put a hand on her shoulder. "You lament for that which is old."

The bosons seized the prophet.

"I recognize him. Nano put him in The Room. Got out, did he? Wonder what we should do with him now."

Gelic nodded with satisfaction. "He is the head of a dangerous movement that has no place on Nanosia," he said. "You've already seen the trouble he can cause."

The bosons sneered at the prophet.

"Well, if he's the head, we'll just have to cut the head off."

"*No!*" Pym screamed.

# Chapter 15

Gelic smirked. "The old prophecy. He would teach you the words of the old prophecy, and you would still know nothing of what is to come."

Now that he was here with this new message, Gelic thought, the fermion might be his first trial convert. He didn't know what she was, but at least she wasn't a filthy electron. She could never be a positron—never a part of his real family—but she might prove useful. He would use her as Elveston thought he was using him.

But the fermion turned away and sobbed as the bosons led the prophet away. "*No!* This can't be happening. It's not supposed to happen."

"Child," he cooed gently. He would be gentle with her, and she would forget the pesky prophet. Gelic had no use for an old prophecy that included electrons . . . ugh! The word was distasteful even to think about. And this old prophet might divide the attentions of the photons he needed and the positrons he craved.

In the most comforting tones he whispered, "Yes, this is how it must be. He was a great one, but a greater one has come. Why do you weep for that which is less?"

"Are you greater than the Big One? I walked and talked with the Big One, and are you greater than he?"

"Answer that for yourself."

He turned her around to face him and looked directly into her eyes. He had to make her believe, and he would. "You walked and talked with him? And what did you think of him? Did he draw crowds? Did he bring the Light?"

"No," she stammered. "He did none of that. But he was the Big One. In time he would have . . ."

"Would have? But I have done these things already and will continue to do them when he has not even started yet. I have replaced the old prophecy of the Big One with a new message of Light."

She tried to look away, but he held her gaze. With one hand firmly on her shoulder, he wiped away the useless tears still welling in her eyes.

"Let him go. He must go. He told you as much. Be brave, precious one. What is your name?"

She paused for just a moment, then seemed to decide it was okay. "Pym."

"Yes, Pym. Embrace the new message."

"I never heard that the old prophecy would be replaced. I never heard the day would come when we would be visited by a positron instead of the Big One."

Gelic sighed. "Nevertheless, these things, also, had to be. For if the old prophets had known that a new message would replace the old prophecy, they wouldn't have preached with such zeal, and false prophets would have arisen."

Regretfully, that last statement seemed to give her doubts new energy. "So how do I know you're not a false prophet?"

"Because I have the Light."

She squinted, as if trying to see him better. "What light?"

"The Light of my message. You will see great miracles and changes in the Quantum Realm you have never seen before."

To forestall any more questions and demonstrate his point with action, he mounted the raised area where the prophet had thought to begin his preaching. "Draw nigh, my people. Draw nigh."

There were too many electrons in this crowd. They nauseated him the way they ogled him with hunger. He'd have to send them away, along with the useless protons and neutrons. Hopefully, this Pym was not one of those. He didn't want her to leave when he sent the others away.

"Today, my message is for the photons. If you're not a photon, you might not find today's message interesting and are free to leave without giving offense."

Some of the fermions drifted away, but many stayed, including Pym.

"Brothers and sisters," Gelic continued with a sigh. "I come to you with a new message. Yes, I call you brothers and sisters, though I am a positron, and you are photons. Don't look surprised. For I was sent by the Great Photon, Lord of Light and father of us all."

Then he began to spin in a dance that matched those of the onlooking photons.

Gelic noticed some bosons eyeing him suspiciously from the edge of the crowd. He wasn't particularly concerned about them. The Freedom of Existence Act kept them from harassing him without good cause. With Nano, his main opposition, on the other side of the realm, he needn't worry.

"Brothers and sisters, a new age is upon us. An age of transformation. I'm talking about a new birth. If you're tired of the same old same old, if you're weary of a life that never changes, come to me. Come to the Great Photon, and he will renew you."

# Chapter 16

Jawan drifted in and out of sleep, dreaming first of apprentices dancing around their masters who were made of quarks and leptons, then of purple bosons holding secret meetings to rule the world. He dreamed of Pym stretched out on a rack until she confessed to dastardly plans to bring him to a world of talking mice so she could have her way with him. Every time he went to sleep, he had a different dream. He knew he'd never get any rest, but there was no point getting up until they came for him. If they came for him.

"Sph. Sph."

He heard the serpentine whisper in his ear. "Wake up."

A new dream invaded this dream. "Purple burplesph. There's no time. Wake up, bow to the queen and wake up."

The queen panned the crowd of apprentices, and her eyes locked on Jawan's. "You are asleep. You must wake up."

Jawan felt hands shaking him. The queen's hands, impossibly long as they could only be in a dream. He opened his eyes, reached for the hands, and paused. Awareness of a different state of consciousness made him pause. He was awake, but the hands still pulled at him.

"Don't make a sound. The guards are asleep. We must leave before they wake."

Jawan shook his head. Blinking made no difference in the pitch dark. Who was this? This liquid velvet voice wasn't Pym's. Even its whisper had a melody, and he let the hands pull him to his feet and toward what he remembered was the direction of the door. They stumbled through the dark passageways.

Once outside, the light of distant photons made him squint. He gave his eyes a moment to adjust, then turned to his rescuer. It was the girl. Impossible. How could she have known? Why would she care enough to come here?

"How did you know I was in the dungeon?"

"I know things," she said, a coy smile just brushing her lips.

He liked her lips but was still puzzled. "But I only saw you once. What made you bother to save me?"

"Because I knew you had to get out."

"I didn't know bosons slept."

She shrugged. "They had a little help."

"Won't you get in trouble for helping me? Won't the queen charge you with high treason and put you to death or something?"

"Maybe. But I had to come. When I saw you before, something clicked, and now I can't break the attraction. I'm supposed to be able to control attraction and repulsion. That's what I was trained to do. Oh well, being attracted to you isn't bad at all."

*Attracted to me?* Jawan gulped. She was cute, but still, he would have liked a little subtlety—a slow revelation of her qualities.

"Uh . . . yeah," he muttered.

She pulled him along. "Come with me."

Jawan slowed down. It was nice of her to get him out of the dungeon, but he had to find something that would tell him about the plague. Like everyone else here, this girl had her own plans for him.

"Where are you going?"

"I . . . just. Come on."

She led him to a low building whose bricks were made of quarks.

Inside, a fermion worked feverishly over a row of spindles. Jawan couldn't believe what he was seeing. Curled around each spindle was a black carbon graphene sheet. He gasped when he realized how small he was, for each sheet was as thick as his arm. Jawan looked closer and saw that each sheet was made of little hexagons.

The fermion swirled around. "Titi!" he bellowed. "Where have you been? I've been trying to correct your botched-up work for a zillion spaces of time."

Titi looked as if she wanted to disappear down one of the nanotubes into oblivion.

"I'm sorry, Mr. Kelton," she stammered. "I had to bring the boy. I couldn't leave him in the dungeon."

Mr. Kelton noticed Jawan and narrowed his eyes. "Hang the boy! You had all the nanotubes with nothing but attraction. No repulsion."

"Sorry."

He clucked his tongue and eyed Titi with exasperation. "Look at your mess," he said, pointing at a wad of carbon sheets all matted together. "I couldn't do anything with them. What did they teach you at that Van der Waals School? You'd know a sight more if I'd just apprenticed you myself."

"Yes, sir."

"Well, make yourself useful and take those tubes on the shelf over to Nano. He ordered five, but thanks to you, only three are ready."

"Yes, sir."

She took some boxes down from a shelf and motioned for Jawan to follow her out of the factory. He noticed that the boxes were made of quarks and offered to carry them for her. She handed them to him but didn't seem able to let go.

"See, I've got an extra dose of attraction. You'll have to pull firmly. Don't worry about being rude. Just pull."

So Jawan pulled the boxes out of her hands. He heard a *POP* as they separated from her.

Jawan thought about what he had learned so far. Gravitons were real. The force that held nanotubes together was the same force that attracted boys and girls. Something was wrong in the Quantum Realm, and Nano thought Jawan was the cause because he didn't spin. *Nano!*

The silver hat with the big number nine was just ahead, way too close. He stopped dead. "I can't let Nano see me. I'm supposed to be in the dungeon."

"No, that's right. You can't. Wait here. I'll be right back."

She took the boxes, and Jawan nestled behind what looked like some discarded quarks as she made her way toward Nano. They weren't in Jawan's line of vision, but he could hear them, so he knew they'd be able to hear him if he made an irregular sound. The quarks looked like they'd make a lot of noise if he disturbed them. So, he lay stone still, careful not to touch them.

"I ordered five nanotubes, and here you come with only three."

"The other two had a flaw, and we couldn't bring you any but the best." Titi tried to explain, but Jawan doubted that she was having much success. He was right.

"A flaw! Titi, you know how important this is. I asked for five because I need five to transport enough quanta. If I don't transport enough, the balance of matter in the universe will be upset."

Jawan kept that in mind. Could that imbalance in the universe have anything to do with the purple plague? He had to hold on to every little piece of information until something made sense.

"I understand that," Titi said.

"No, you couldn't possibly understand. You think I'm just being fastidious. Those idiots in the material world tell themselves that matter can't be created." He sounded worked up, as if he were talking more to himself than to Titi. "They never ask what happens to matter when it's burned away. They think the smoke just flies off into oblivion."

Jawan wished he could see what was going on, but he didn't dare move. He could hear the low murmur of elementary particles waiting for Nano to inspect them. Apparently, he tolerated a little irregularity when he was on a roll with a lecture.

"If that were true, then eventually all matter would be lost. But it's here that we recycle the energy and transform it back into matter. This requires balance. Not too much or too little."

"Yes, sir, Mr. Nano. And the sooner I get back to the factory, the sooner I can get those other two nanotubes to you. They might be ready now."

"Might be? You tiresome child. Just go."

But Titi didn't come straight back to Jawan from the same direction she'd left him. Instead, she went in another direction to draw Nano's attention away from Jawan, then came at the boy from the other direction.

Without even daring to glance in Nano's direction lest it draw his attention, they crept off the other way.

Soon, they joined the everyday flow of quanta coming and going. They had to blend in. Easier thought of than accomplished, Jawan realized, since he was the only thing on this world that didn't spin and orbit. Still, they tried to match the general pace of the other particles, and at least look like they weren't lost.

"Where will we go?" Jawan asked. "If we stay out here, sooner or later the bosons will catch us."

"I don't know about you, but sooner or sooner I need to be back at the factory. Kelton is probably already wondering where I am."

Jawan realized that he really was alone out here. Everyone else had a place to go and something to do that the bosons wouldn't question. He remembered his purpose for being here. He had to stay here to accomplish that, but what was he to do?

"The factory. We can go there."

"I'm not sure. Kelton probably won't be in a good mood when we get there. He might just throw you out. Or turn you in to Nano."

Neither scenario appealed to Jawan. But he couldn't think of any help for it. "Then I guess you have to go without me."

"But I can't leave you alone out here," Titi said, looking this way and that as if spying, then discarding her options.

"Why not? I'll be okay."

"No, you won't. You don't know what's out here."

"What the . . .?" Jawan stopped in his tracks, unable to believe what he saw.

"What is it?" Titi asked.

Jawan didn't answer but pulled her back behind a building and caught his breath.

"That's Lord Elveston."

"Huh? Lord Elveston? Is that a new kind of particle? I've never heard of Lord Elvestons. Are they bosons or fermions?"

"No, Lord Elveston is from the Big World. I wonder what he's doing here."

"Is he bad? Why are we hiding?"

Jawan thought about it. He really didn't know why. "He's just one of five mages in the Big World. Like my own master. They're not bad. I just don't know what he's doing here, and until I know, we should just stay out of sight."

Jawan knew that the fire mage was Loby's master. But Loby didn't know Jawan was here, so how could his master?

"Please, tell me what's going on."

"As soon as I find out myself."

Find out himself? How was he supposed to find out? Just walk up to Lord Elveston and ask him his business in Nanosia? Jawan wasn't supposed to be here himself. If the fire mage saw him, he'd tell Myrlo, and who knew what kind of trouble he'd be in then? Not that he probably wasn't in trouble already inside and outside Nanosia.

Titi grew impatient and peered around Jawan to see what he was hiding from. He felt her shudder.

"Why, that's Antipan! You were right to hide from him."

"Antipan?"

Jawan risked a look to see what Titi was talking about. He saw Lord Elveston.

"The tall guy in the black robe?" he asked.

"That's him."

Now this was odd. Not only was the fire mage in the Quantum Realm, but he also had an alias. Why?

Jawan thought about that name. Antipan? Anti meant against. Pan meant all. Against all? The fire mage was leading a secret life, unknown to the other mages, and he was against all? Jawan knew he had to keep an eye on Lord Elveston or Antipan or whatever his name was.

Taking quick, what they hoped were surreptitious, peeks around the building, they watched Antipan move toward the queen's palace. Was that where he was going? They crept closer. The guards around the palace seemed to stiffen when Antipan approached, but beyond being on the alert, they did nothing to stop him. He entered, and Jawan motioned for Titi to follow.

"Are you insane?" she protested. "That's Antipan, the most notorious scoundrel in all Nanosia. We can't follow him."

This made Jawan even more determined. "I've got to find out what he's up to."

"He's always up to no good. What more do you need to know?"

But Jawan made his way toward the castle. Keeping what he hoped was a safe distance, he followed Antipan inside.

They stood in an alcove in the back of the queen's court where they could see and hear without being seen, especially not by Nano, who was standing by the queen's side as Antipan approached her.

Nano spotted Antipan at once and leaped forward to block him from Queen Quanta. "How dare you show yourself to the queen? You know you are not welcome here. Be gone!"

But Antipan sidestepped Nano and addressed himself directly to the queen. Jawan noticed that Antipan didn't prostrate himself, as was customary, but held himself as regally as the queen herself. No one corrected him, not even the queen.

"My dear, there is no need for hostility. I come with the best of intentions."

Queen Quanta straightened her back, striking the most imperial pose. "The best of your intentions, Antipan, are still suspect. What do you want?"

"I want only to implore Your Majesty to forge a bond with me."

"What?!" Queen Quanta and Nano exclaimed together.

"Yes, that's right. I have loved you, my queen. You must believe that, despite my undeserved reputation. I want you to truly be my queen. We will combine our realms into one unconquerable kingdom!"

"This is preposterous!" cried the queen. "You must be mad to think that I would accept such a hideous union. With you? Be gone!"

"Yes, I am mad. Love makes me mad. My queen, if you will only listen, I'll explain . . ."

"I need no further explanations from you and will listen no further to your nonsense. Be gone now, or I will have you thrown out."

Antipan smiled. He glanced around at the queen's quivering guards. "Thrown out by whom?" He turned back to the queen and bowed. "Very well, my queen. For now, I bid you farewell. But I assure you, though you be blinded by vicious lies about me, the day will come when you will accept me and be my queen. You will be mine!"

Jawan noticed that Antipan's teeth were flat. He guessed displaying sharp fangs wasn't the best way to charm the ladies.

The queen raised her hand to summon the guards, but Antipan swirled around, and his gaze dazzled them into a confused stillness as he swept out of the chamber.

As he exited, bosons approached the group of elementary particles standing in front of Jawan's hiding place.

"If they see us, Nano will see us," Titi whispered. "We have to leave."

"We have to follow Antipan."

"Let's just worry about getting out of here."

They slipped toward the side door.

"Why isn't it spinning?" someone said nearby—too nearby.

"It is irregular. Nano needs to know about this."

No need for secrecy now. Speed was their friend. So, they raced out the door and across a courtyard without looking back. Circling around to the front of the castle, they spotted Antipan far ahead.

"Come on," Jawan urged, pulling Titi in the direction the villain was heading. "He's getting away."

"Good. Let him get as far away as possible."

"You don't have to come. Go back to your factory. Isn't your master waiting for you?"

"He's not my master. But he is waiting for me." She started to step away, then stepped back. "I can't leave you."

"*Go!*" He pushed her with his hands and his voice.

She moved away slowly, like a magnet being pulled away from iron. He turned and raced after Antipan. But she followed him.

"Kelton isn't my master. I just work for him. I can't leave you. I'm attracted to you."

"Attracted to me? Well, I think you're cute, too, but . . ."

"Are you attracted to Antipan?"

"Of course not."

Jawan realized that they were getting too close to Antipan too fast. He slowed their run to a brisk walk. They seemed to walk for a long time.

"Where is he going?" Titi asked.

"I've no idea."

"You're following him, and you don't even know where he's going? Suppose he's aware someone is following him and is leading us into a trap?"

"He doesn't know and it's not a trap." But the possibility troubled him more than he let on.

"You sound awfully sure of yourself for someone who has no idea."

Antipan began to slow down and so did they. They were no longer in the city. The houses around them were further apart and the particles dressed more for work than court.

Antipan approached a crowd of particles surrounding a figure on a hill. As they drew closer, Jawan realized the figure was a positron. It didn't look exactly like the drawings in his textbook, but somehow, Jawan knew it was a positron. Dead ringer of an electron, but positively charged.

Jawan led Titi around to the other side of the crowd out of Antipan's line of vision but close enough to see and hear what was happening.

A sizeable crowd of elementary particles surrounded the positron. Those closest to the positron were all photons. The brightness of such a concentration of photons, each one as big as Jawan, hurt his eyes, but he kept his focus on the positron.

The positron directed his audience's attention to some kind of box with a curtain drawn across to hide its back end.

"Brothers and sisters, it's very important that you make this transformation. I've told you that it will change your life and bring greater joy than you have ever known. But I will not have you ignorant of the danger that awaits you if you are caught unaware in the state you are in. The great and terrible Negatron is coming and has nothing in me. He comes, and if you are not transformed, he will blind your eyes to the truth so that you will never know it. Even now, he comes looking to devour whosoever he can. Don't be caught, brethren! Enter the collider and be transformed! Enter this gate to bliss and become invincible."

"What the . . .?" Jawan started. Don't they realize that a negatron is just another name for an electron? He remembered his conversation with Pym. Maybe in this world they were a boogieman.

"That's right, brothers and sisters. Step right in. There's nothing to fear but the Negatron."

The photons lined up to enter the box and Jawan heard a whirring sound when they did.

Titi looked confused.

"What are they doing?"

"I don't know, but I'll find out."

Jawan noticed that even though hundreds of photons were going into the box, none were coming out. He guessed that they were exiting behind the curtain. *Odd.* What was happening to those photons that the positron didn't want anyone to see?

"I don't like this," Titi said. "And look, Antipan is watching the positron. He looks satisfied, as if the positron is doing what he wanted done."

When Jawan saw the triumphant look on Antipan's face, he gulped. *Suppose they're working together?* Jawan didn't know how he was going to handle two dangerous enemies. Well, they weren't his personal enemies yet. The positron didn't even know he existed. But if Antipan discovered him, the fire mage was sure to kill him.

"So, there really are negatrons on Nanosia? It's not just another name for electrons?"

"Yes, of course. Don't you have them in the Big World?"

"No, they're called electrons there, and they're not big and terrible."

"Not big in the Big World? Be glad of that."

"Where are the Negatrons? I've never seen one."

"No one has seen The Great Negatron for a long time. Our legends say it is in the Realm of Chaos. That's Antipan's realm."

Jawan thought that if he could find a negatron and control it, he'd have a weapon against the positron, maybe even against Antipan. No. If Antipan controlled the Realm of Chaos where the negatrons lived, then the fire mage was more likely to use them against Jawan.

He took Titi's hand. "Come on."

"Where now?"

"Just come with me. I've got to see what's going on."

He threaded his way through the crowd in the opposite direction from where Antipan stood.

Once they reached the back side of the curtain, he stopped dead.

*Collider?* Hadn't the positron said the box was a collider? He ransacked his memory, trying to recall where he'd seen that word in relation to photons. As the apprentice of the earth mage, he had to know all about physics and the different technology that could help him understand the Earth better.

Then it came to him—particle collider. What were they used for? He tried to remember. Myrlo never used one, since his magic would do better. Then he remembered. A particle collider took energy and transformed it into matter.

That's what he saw behind the curtain. The photons were the energy going into the collider and coming out as . . .

"Look!" Titi pointed. "They're coming out as electrons and positrons. Pairs and pairs of them."

Jawan gasped. Matter and its corresponding antimatter. The positron out front was creating antimatter like itself. And those poor photons out front had no idea what was being done to them.

"This is terrible!" Titi cried. "Somebody has to stop this. Nano would stop this in an instant. It violates everything he stands for—order and balance."

"But we can't go to Nano. You know that."

"This has to stop. This is more important than our petty fears of Nano."

"Yes, but I want to figure out a way to stop this that doesn't end with me in a dungeon."

He thought about the situation. There was nothing he could do alone. He'd need help. "I have to get back to my world."

"Your world?!You're just going to leave us? Leave me? You were so brave about following Antipan, not caring about the danger. Now that you see how diabolical they really are, now that you see something terrible is going to happen, you want to just go home. Fine! Leave me then. See if I care." She looked like she was going to cry. "I never believed those stupid prophecies anyway. Big One, my foot."

*Good grief.* She acts like this, and she's not even his girlfriend. "No, you don't understand. My master will be able to deal with Antipan. The Great Myrlo has powers equal to Antipan's."

"Then call your master. You can't be all that big if you have a master."

"No, I can't just call him. I have to go back and tell him what Elveston . . . Antipan is doing."

He looked at the hundreds of electrons and positrons coming out of the collider and shook his head, wondering how he could possibly get back to his master. He didn't bring himself here to begin with. He'd come by the machinations of . . .

"The Big One!"

He turned at the sound of her voice. "Pym!"

Titi stared at this new female, too.

Pym was standing on the far side of the flow of electrons and positrons, waving at Jawan.

"Hush," Titi whispered. "We still don't want the positron to know we're here. Not to mention Antipan."

"No, we don't." Jawan agreed.

Pym reached them, and Titi moved closer to Jawan. But he moved toward Pym.

"Pym, what are you doing here?"

"I should ask you." Then Pym began to weep.

Jawan was at a loss. He knew things were bad, but he couldn't see that they'd gotten to crying bad. "Sh. It's all right."

"It's not all right. That horrible positron called the bosons on the prophet. The prophet, I tell you. I had just brought him out of The Room Nano put him in. That revolting unbeliever. Then we met the positron, and he . . . he . . ."

Titi shifted her weight from one foot to the other. "Uh . . . can we hold the heart-wrenching reunion somewhere safer? We're the only ones back here making any noise, and that positron is sure to come investigating."

So, they slipped away to a depression where a stray glance from the positron wouldn't spy them.

They sat down very close together to make themselves even smaller.

"We've got to tell Nano," Pym said.

"No, we can't. I've got to tell my master. He'll fix this. Nano doesn't need to know."

Titi shook her head. "All those photons should be going to Nano. They represent all the burned matter that has been transformed into energy in the Big World. It's Nano's job to turn the energy back into matter."

"So, the positron is doing basically the same thing Nano would do." Jawan filed that information away.

"Yes, but what is he going to do with the new matter? I don't know what Nano does with the positrons, but he sends the electrons to Atomidon. You need nanotubes to do that. Kelton isn't sending nanotubes to this positron, so what is he going to do with all this new matter?"

"I doubt sending it to Atomidon is the positron's plan," Pym said.

"Very unlikely," Jawan agreed. "That's why I have to get back to my master in the Big World."

"What?" Pym yelped. But Titi only sighed.

"My master will know what to do. He has the power to stop all this nonsense. I've got to get back, and you can help me, Pym."

"I?" Pym sighed. "How can I help you get back to the Big World?"

"Well, you brought me here."

"And you think that means I can send you back?"

"Can't you? Weren't you planning on letting me go back eventually, anyway?"

"Well . . . I kinda left the details up to the prophecy."

Jawan's head jerked up. "You mean, you can't send me back?!"

"I didn't say that. I just said I'm not sure if it would work that way."

"We can try," Titi said.

"Yes, that's all we can do—try."

They crept out of the far side of the depression and circumvented the crowd.

"Well, we got away from that. So now all we have to worry about is Nano and his bosons," Pym said.

"You're such an uplifting walking companion. Remind me to choose you when I take my next stroll," Jawan quipped.

"This is no stroll," Titi said.

As if to bring the point home, the mist in front of them cleared just enough for them to see a dozen bosons in marching formation. They ducked back and held their breaths, waiting for the sound of feet to fade away.

Soon they could hear the commotion of city life. As they drew near, their apprehension grew. Would they make it? Would they be stopped? Would they all be thrown into the dungeon?

Just when Jawan thought he would burst from tension, Pym held up her hand for them to stop. "This is the place."

"Are you sure?" Jawan asked.

He looked around, trying to recall something from the bland landscape. He'd been out of sorts upon arrival.

"We came through this nanotube, remember?" Pym reminded him. "Wait while I check for incoming traffic."

Jawan peered into the swirling mist and made out the opening of a nanotube. Pym disappeared into it and then was back.

"Come on."

They walked up the tube to a spot Jawan vaguely remembered. His mind had been in a fog, and the whole place looked like a fog. He looked up and saw a tube. Something was different. The angle wasn't right. Whereas he'd fallen out of a full moon directly overhead, he now looked up at a quarter moon way to the west. "I have to go up there?"

"Yep."

Pym began to spin and Jawan began to float.

# Chapter 17

The queen's palace was in an uproar. Nobody was sure exactly what had happened. Nano picked up a few key words in the general commotion.

" . . . Antipan and an irregular particle?"

" . . . Nano had seen an irregular particle . . ."

" . . . Claimed to be the Big One . . ."

Nano was sure now this irregular particle was connected in some way to Antipan. It was just too much of a coincidence for them to both show up at the same time. But what use could Antipan possibly make of the prophecy? He vowed to find out.

He threaded his way through the cloud of bosons that were trying to restore order. *Good. Let them do that.* He'd focused on the queen. "Your Majesty, are you all right? I am outraged at that miscreant. What did he hope to accomplish coming here with that preposterous proposal?"

The queen looked a little faint. Servants fanned her, but she didn't speak.

Nano continued fuming and speculating. "It must have been a distraction to keep our attention away from something else he doesn't want us to notice. Something to do with that irregular particle. Why was it here? What was it doing?"

Finally, the queen sat up. She brushed the fans aside and looked at Nano.

"Oh, I think his proposal was real. Insane, but real. It would be in his character to try some mad scheme like uniting the realms of Quantum and Chaos for his own purposes. The question I'm wondering is *why now?* What's going on right now that makes this advantageous for him?"

"There are nine things going on that he probably doesn't want us to know about. There's the report those ambassadors brought us. There's the imbalance in the particles . . ."

"*Please!*" The queen sighed, heaving with exasperation. "This is too much. I've heard enough bad news for one day."

"My queen . . ."

"And don't call me that. That's what Antipan called me. Just say 'Your Majesty.'"

"Your Majesty, you are the queen, and all news must come to you, good or bad."

The queen looked at him and for a moment Nano wondered if he had gone too far. Then she shrugged. "Be that as it may, I am the queen, not some well-dressed receptacle. I can only take so much before I must regroup for my own sanity."

Nano started to say something, but the queen jumped to her feet.

"Clear the court! Clear the court! I will hear no more petitions or reports today. Clear the court! Everyone, leave!"

Even the bosons managed to look astonished, but they obeyed orders and ushered everyone out.

"But I've been waiting all day to speak to Her Majesty."

"Then it won't hurt you to wait another day. Everyone out."

"But this is important. I have vital news about . . ."

"Save it!"

Nano was aghast.

"Your Majesty . . .?"

"I will retire to my chambers."

"Your chambers?"

"At once!"

Nano sighed and summoned a guard.

"Escort Her Majesty to her chambers."

The guard saluted and fell into step beside Queen Quanta, who was already on her way.

Not daring to accost the queen in her personal chambers after she'd expressed her wish to not hear what he had to say, Nano commenced helping the bosons restore order in and around the castle.

# Chapter 18

Jawan tumbled onto the floor beside the table in his master's laboratory. He looked up and saw the nanoscope just as he had left it. Was it possible Myrlo didn't know where he'd been? Did it matter? He couldn't tell Myrlo about Lord Elveston and leave out the part about him going to Nanosia.

He picked himself up and sat down in front of the nanoscope. No, everything was not just as he'd left it. The "New Study" culture was beside the scope instead of on it. He gulped. His master knew he'd used the nanoscope—a minor offense, relatively speaking. That might be all he knew. Jawan might still be able to expose Lord Elveston without mentioning Nanosia or Antipan at all.

*Elveston!* He had to tell his master. Every minute gave Antipan more time to work mischief. But the laboratory was empty. If his master was anywhere in the castle, he'd sense Jawan's presence and be on his way with questions. Jawan wished he'd taken time to think up some plausible answers.

Minutes went by, but his master didn't show up. Jawan began to wonder. A tongue lashing and punishment he could take. It was inevitable for a young boy with a mind of his own to get in trouble now and then. But for his master to not come at all? Jawan began to worry. Had some harm befallen his master while he was in Nanosia? He turned this way and that. *No good. Have to think what to do.* He slumped into a chair at the long table in the center of the laboratory and saw a piece of paper. He picked it up. It was from his master and confirmed what Jawan already suspected:

> "You have an exam to study for and should be in the library, not toying around with my nanoscope. Stay in the library and do not come out until I return. I had to go to a conclave, but rest assured that when I return, I will have a word with you about disobedience and carelessness."

*Carelessness?* When had Jawan been careless? Leaving the culture on the scope. But he hadn't known what was going to happen and couldn't have put the culture back after he'd fallen into it. But he wasn't going to explain that to his master if he didn't have to.

*Wait a minute!* Jawan was stunned when he stopped to remember that his master had been away to a conclave when he'd gone to Nanosia. That meant this note was about another conclave. How much time had passed? He had no idea.

There was no help for it. He'd have to go to him. But he didn't know how to do that either. As an apprentice, Jawan had never been invited to the mages' conclaves and had no idea where they were.

He went to the library. The book he wanted would be among the forbidden volumes. Just touching them had sent a shock up his arm. But he'd have to touch one now and read it. He searched the shelves until he found a book on tracking spells. The first spell sounded complicated and required herbs that his master probably had somewhere. He turned the page until he found one that was simple.

He eased out of the side door his master took to the stables and searched the ground for the most recent hoof prints. Then he took a handful of earth from one print and held it to his lips.

"Sh-show me where your owner has gone."

This was his first utterance since he'd come back from Nanosia, and his stutter surprised him. He'd grown used to speaking clearly and uttered the spell without thinking that he might mess it up. He held his breath. Would the spell work?

He cast the earth in the direction of the hoof prints, and they fell in a glowing clump, leaping from print to print. Jawan followed.

The glowing earth led him away from the town through the woods. The dark trees loomed menacingly beside the path, their branches reaching out like arms to grasp his face, hair, and clothes.

Suppose they were arms? His master often spoke to the trees and commanded them to do his will, so they must be sentient. These trees didn't respond to the commands with anything like alacrity. The earth mage had to use great magic to get them to comply. Now they had his apprentice alone and at their mercy. Did trees have mercy? Jawan wanted to hurry out of the woods as fast as he could go, but he had to follow the clumps of earth.

After an eternity, he stepped out of the woods onto a swath of grassland. In the distance, he could make out a castle. He'd heard stories about that castle. It was haunted, and strange things happened inside. Some people said they'd seen lights coming from it at odd hours of the night. Ghostly lights that didn't want to be seen. Nobody went there. Just his luck to escape a creepy forest only to be led to a haunted castle. He shrugged and tramped on.

The glowing earth led him to a grove of trees on the far side of the castle where he found his master's horse tethered. There the glow faded, and the earth sank into the ground.

The horse whinnied, and Jawan tried to shush it. He didn't want one of the mages to come out and find him there before he'd had time to think of what he would say and how he would ease his master's anger long enough for him to say it. Now he wasn't sure if this had been a better plan than waiting for his master to come home. He reminded himself that Antipan and the positron wouldn't wait.

He found a side door and put his ear to it to listen for voices. He heard soft footsteps and was about to step away, when the door opened inward, and he stumbled into a pail of dishwater.

The hands holding the pail were small and had obviously once been delicate, but hard work had toughened them. His eyes followed the arms up to two touchable mounds and lingered there until decency forced them to move up to the loveliest face he'd ever seen. The green eyes looked familiar. He'd seen them somewhere before but couldn't place them.

"My, look at what the wind blew in."

"I'm s-sorry," Jawan said, trying to straighten himself.

"That's what comes from listening at doors. Who are you, and what are you doing here?"

"I'm J-Jawan. I have an urgent message for my master."

He wanted to bite his stupid tongue. He hated himself for stuttering like an idiot before this stunning lass. Why couldn't he have met her in the Quantum Realm where he spoke like he had sense? And yet, somehow, he felt like he had met her there. Silly.

"And who might your master be?" she asked.

She seemed amused but not scornful as she set the pail on the floor and pulled a rag off a nail to dry his hands. He wanted to dunk his whole body in a pail of dishwater if she'd touch him like that.

"M-Myrlo, the earth mage."

"He's not going to talk to you here. Let's hope they don't even discover you. You're lucky there's no outside door leading into the chamber where they are. Just think what the fire mage would have done to you if he were here and caught you listening at their door."

*The fire mage.* Jawan shuddered, even though he knew he was not there.

"You're right to tremble, lad. You'll be doing worse than that if they catch you here."

He looked at her. She didn't know what he was trembling at. How could she know anything about Antipan and Nanosia? "I-it's important. I must see him."

She eyed him with something between curiosity and suspicion.

"What's so important it can't wait for your master to come home? Tell me, and I'll tell him, but you need to get out of here."

*Tell her?* When he visualized the words coming out of his mouth—falling on those pretty ears . . . *No.* He'd sound ridiculous trying to tell her what he'd seen in Nanosia. Yet, he had to get her to show him where the mages were in this big old castle. She picked up the pail, but he took it from her and set it by the door as she led him outside.

"Wh-where are you going?"

"I told you, you have to get out of here. Every second you stay, you risk that one of the mages might sense your presence. Especially if they happen to call me for ale or sweet meats and find I'm not alone. We both would have some explaining to do."

They walked to a grove of trees, away from Myrlo's horse and the castle.

"Now what's this all about?" she insisted.

Jawan's heart sank as he realized that he couldn't tell her, and what's more, he couldn't tell his master. Myrlo was already angry at him and was more likely to see his attempt at an explanation as a wild story he'd made up to get out of trouble.

He needed more than an explanation. He needed proof, and where else but inside Elveston's castle could he find proof of the fire mage's wrongdoing? Then he could approach his master with that proof, but he could do nothing without it. It would be dangerous, but he was already in trouble. What difference would a little more make?

This much he could tell the girl without sounding like a complete idiot. "It h-has to do with the fire mage."

"Lord Elveston?"

"Y-yes."

The girl looked interested now—eager. What did she know about Lord Elveston that made her want to know more?

"I th-think he's up to something evil. Something to do with the plague."

Where had that come from? He hadn't known Lord Elveston was connected to the plague. But he'd gone to Nanosia looking for a clue to the plague and found the fire mage. It made sense, so he threw it in with a straight face.

"I'm not sure I would accuse him of that," she cautioned. "Though I've overheard some of their discussions, and he doesn't sound eager to find a cure. In fact, it seems like he's trying to discourage the other mages from doing anything about it. Still, that's a serious accusation. You can't tell your master something like that without solid proof."

"Th-that's what I need," he said. "Proof. I need to get into his castle and find proof."

"That would be dangerous. He didn't even come to this meeting. He might be at his castle, and you'd walk right into him."

"N-no, he's not. He won't be back any time soon."

"Then there's a chance. A slim chance, to be sure. But why did you come here to talk to Master Myrlo if you wanted to go there?"

"I st-still need to talk to my master. But not without proof."

She paused a moment and pursed her lips in thought. "Tell you what. Wait for me at the Red Ale on Peabody Street in the town while I finish up here. I don't think it will be much longer. Then I will come for you, and we'll cook up a plan."

"Th-the Red Ale?! But that's a Dripping Dagger house."

"Just tell them Cintella sent you. They won't bother you."

"Th-they know you?" He found this hard to believe. Such a nice girl. "But you're so nice."

"And you're so sweet. Now go. I have a plan."

With trepidation, Jawan went off toward the town wondering how someone like Cintella would have anything to do with a street gang, much less the Dripping Daggers.

# Chapter 19

Cintella finished her chores, glad that she didn't have to worry about Lord Elveston following her home that night. She still hadn't gotten over his behavior. So, he was up to something besides accosting her?

She hoped Jawan was right about the fire mage not showing up at his castle. She wanted to help the boy but didn't want to run into that scoundrel again, especially not if he had something to do with the purple plague. She'd known when she first took a job working for the elemental mages that she might one day run into magic over her head. She could walk down almost any street in Hadley Town. But she had no defense against malevolent spells.

Jawan sat on a barstool as she entered the Red Ale. The bartender polished glasses in preparation for the crowd that would come in an hour. He kept them lined up and shiny. The mirror behind the bar made the place look bigger than it was.

"Wait here," she instructed Jawan, and went into the back room.

The room was dark and smoky, but she kept the door open just long enough for the light to hit the figure sitting at the end of a long table.

"Rook, I got a job for you and the girls tonight."

She'd worked out a plan on her way to the Red Ale. Nothing complicated. Just a simple distraction job to get Elveston's servant out of the castle, then she and Jawan could look for the proof they needed.

She whispered instructions into Rook's ear. He said nothing. He never said anything, but Cintella knew he heard her and would do as she instructed. He slipped up the stairs without a sound, and she knew that part of the plan would be taken care of.

She hadn't heard anybody come in, so she was surprised to find Jawan talking to a strange man when she entered the bar. She walked quietly, hoping to pick up what the old man was saying before he saw her. Eavesdropping? But her grandmother had always told her to never enter a room mouth first. So, she listened.

"Look for me," the old man was saying. "You shall find me in a tiny place."

"D-do you mean Nanosia? How do you know about . . . ?"

"Sh. We have company."

Cintella started when the old man turned to face her. His eyes were milky white, yet she felt that she had no advantage over him with her perfect eyes.

"Good evening, lass."

How did he know she was there, much less that she was a girl? He looked right at her as if he knew more about her than eyes could tell.

"I must go," the old man said, bowing to them both. "But no matter what else you find, look for me, and look for the scroll."

"Th-the scroll . . .?"

But the blind man didn't wait to explain himself. He made his exit while the question was still in Jawan's eyes.

"You have strange friends. Who was that?"

"I'm n-not sure I know. When I saw him before, he was begging alms over on Cobblers Alley. He knew things about me that he ought not to know. But who he is, I couldn't tell you."

"Knows things he ought not to know? Yeah, but look, we need to go."

They headed for Lord Elveston's castle. She explained her plan to him on the way.

Even from a distance, the fire mage's castle couldn't be mistaken for anything else. Tongues of fire licked up its sides, making its stones, which were gray in daylight, look an eerie red at night.

She instructed Jawan to wait for her behind a nearby tree.

"You don't want to be seen just yet."

He went without a word. Cintella liked that. She knew he was young, but he didn't act like a little kid, asking a bunch of questions when silence was called for.

She went around the front to the portcullis and hissed, "Itch!"

After several moments and several hisses, a reply came.

"Who's there?"

"I'm a friend of your master's. He's at the Red Ale and needs your help."

"My master has no friends, and I know where he is."

*Yikes*, Cintella thought. Then she took a chance. Wasn't life all taking chances? "He has returned but had to go straight to the Red Ale on urgent business. The business went sour, and now he needs you to come quickly."

She grimaced. That wouldn't work out on the street. But maybe she'd been right, and he was a zombie with a zombie brain.

"What does he need?" the zombie asked.

Good. Itch sounded more curious than suspicious. Just a little push would do the trick.

"He wouldn't tell me his business, but he said you will know what to do when you get there. You must hurry. It took too much time for me to walk all this way, and time is precious. Hurry! Your master needs you."

Then she stepped into the shadows beside the portcullis so he wouldn't see her as he passed.

"Aren't you coming with me?"

"No, I mustn't be seen. Hurry now!"

She watched him lumber toward Hadley Town, then listened for his footsteps. When she could no longer hear them, she gave him time to get wise and turn back. When she was sure he wouldn't, she retrieved Jawan, and they entered the castle through a side door.

# Chapter 20

Itch made his way through the town. The houses got shabbier and closer together the farther he walked. He passed Heads and Tails, where Lord Elveston had found him, making trouble for troublemakers. This was Dreaded Steps territory. He felt accusing eyes watching him head for Dripping Daggers territory. The streets were empty, and so what if someone recognized him from the old days. He'd just make trouble for them if they asked for it.

Overturned carts painted purple forced him to make detours. He could see the purple boards on some of the doors and windows of the houses. Itch was a big man who usually plowed through anything in his path, but he wasn't immune to disease. So, he went the long way around and finally came to the Red Ale.

People sitting at tables stared at him openly as he strode to the bar. He knew they were wondering what he might do—whether to wait and see or take cover now. He liked to let them wonder and put on as vicious a face as he could muster. But some of these people were Daggers, and they did not move.

He figured the bar was the place to ask about his master. The bartender looked bored, so Itch banged his massive fist on the bar to bring a little excitement into the man's life. "Where's my master?"

He glared at the bartender. If they were hiding his master, he'd hurt them. But the bartender stared right back, still pouring ale into a mug.

"Your master? State your business, hogbrains, or get out."

Itch could have kicked himself for saying that. Of course, these people wouldn't know who his master was. Still, this barkeep had the wrong attitude. He grabbed the man by the throat and pulled him close. "You tell me where Lord Elveston, the fire mage, is, or you're going to hear bones snapping, and they won't be mine."

The men at the tables rose and drew their daggers.

"We don't play that here," a quiet chap in a black cloak said.

"You came to the wrong place to start trouble," said another, fingering the tip of his dagger. "We'll only warn you once to let our man go."

They started closing in on Itch, but the bartender's face lit up, as if Itch had struck a bell.

"Back off, boys. I know this lad."

"You know me? You know where my master is?" Itch inquired, releasing the man as the Daggers sat back down uncertainly.

"Sure. We've been waiting for you. Wait right here."

Then he disappeared into the back.

Itch would have scratched his head in bewilderment, but his nails were long and hard, and he wasn't stupid enough to maul his own head. So, he just tried to figure things out. If these men knew him and had been waiting for him, then maybe they'd been trying to help his master. After all, the bartender did look glad to see him.

The bartender returned. "Come with me."

Itch followed the man into the back and up a flight of stairs. They went down a hall and entered a room. It was small, hardly big enough for the massive bed in its center. On the bed lay five naked women.

"He's all yours, girls." The bartender smirked, pushed Itch into the room, and closed the door.

One of the women approached Itch with a goblet of wine. He was a big man, but he was a man, and his body could do nothing but respond to the nearness of her body—her lovely body.

"Hello, sugar. Have some wine."

"Where's my master?" He could hardly get the words out.

"He'll be here. He said for you to wait and not go anywhere until he's able to come."

"Able to come?" Itch asked, trying to hold on to the significance of his own question.

She put the goblet to his lips and his hands to places on her body that were just as intoxicating as the wine.

She led him over to the bed, where he dived into an abyss of bliss. Thoughts of Lord Elveston faded from his mind. If his master wanted him to wait here, he could bear the wait. He cast aside whatever doubts entered his mind and busied himself climbing mountains and delving into valleys one after the other. Then all together. It was . . . remarkable.

Itch didn't know when he'd fallen asleep until faint light crested the horizon and invaded his befogged head. He opened his eyes and found himself trapped beneath a tangle of arms and legs. A girl snoozed on each side of him, and he remembered. *His master!*

But it was morning and his master had not come. Slowly, it dawned on Itch that this had all been a trick. A delicious, titillating trick, but a trick, nonetheless.

He tried to get up, but an arm held him down, and a soft, sibilant voice tried to lull him back to sleep.

"No, sugar. It's not time to go. You must stay."

Then he felt several fingers, soft except for the sharp talons, snaking their way into his mouth.

Not time to go? So, this had been a trick. His master wasn't in trouble. Most likely, he wasn't even back at all. He bit down hard on the fingers of whoever was foolish enough to thrust them into the mouth of an angry man. Then he heard a scream of pain and rage. They pried his jaw open and tried to overwhelm him with their girlish but numerous little fists. He threw all of them onto the floor and stormed out of the room.

"Don't let him leave!"

Loud cries and the staccato of running feet bounced off every wall.

"He hurt Cheeny. Nobody hurts Cheeny and walks away."

Itch's rage propelled him out of the bar, but he didn't run. His pursuers surrounded him like sharks, their daggers flashing. But he didn't stop. He just plowed ahead like they weren't even there.

Just before Itch bowled over the Dagger directly in front of him, the thug stepped to the side and drove his dagger into Itch's side. Itch should have stopped, if only to acknowledge that he had been stabbed. Any other man would have, but the blade buried itself in Itch's tough hide and stuck there. Before the thug could wrench it free, Itch hoisted him into the air and threw him into the other Daggers.

Itch started to turn and keep walking, but another dagger pierced his thigh. He remembered that these were the ones who had tricked him, and a need for vengeance welled up in his chest.

He pulled the daggers from his side and thigh, brandishing them menacingly. The Daggers turned and fled.

Itch wasn't a good marksman, and the daggers pierced the road instead of flesh. He thought of chasing them but realized the whole point of tricking him must have been to lure him away from his master's castle. That's where he needed to be.

His master had no friends—needed no friends. He should not have believed that voice. Who was it? It had been a woman's voice, too. He'd find the owner of that voice and crush her.

When he reached the castle, he searched the grounds but didn't find anything amiss outside. He disdained the noisy portcullis and crept through a side door.

He heard soft whispers coming from the laboratory. Someone in there thought they were sneaky. Tipping to the door, Itch looked in and saw a young woman and a boy. He'd seen that boy before. One of Loby's friends. If Itch's memory was true, the lad was just an apprentice. Although Itch had no magic of his own, he didn't think he had to worry about an apprentice overpowering him. He could handle the boy . . . and the girl, too.

They'd had all night to look around. Thank goodness his master's precious camera was locked away. There'd be no mercy for Itch if he'd been tricked into letting these rascals fool with that.

They hovered over his master's particle collider, studying and poking at it.

"What is it?" the girl asked.

That voice? Itch knew that voice. It was a voice he would rip out of her lovely throat before the night was over.

"I kn-know what this is," the boy answered.

Itch started at this. If the boy knew what it was, then they weren't just mischievous children snooping around out of curiosity. Now Itch understood why they'd hatched such an elaborate plan with the Dripping Daggers. These intruders wanted something.

"It's a-a particle collider. This lever turns it on, and that gauge shows how much energy is released."

Itch had heard enough. "Fools!"

He rushed into the laboratory, intending to strangle them. Then he stopped. Slowly, he began to think. These rascals were in league with the Dripping Daggers. Why would the Daggers care about the collider? Something else was going on. The brats knew as much about his master's machine as he did. But they were just children. Certainly, they weren't acting alone. His master had a way to find out who sent them.

They jumped when he rushed in, then cowered as far away from him as the laboratory allowed.

"You fools! Tinkering where you don't belong."

The children just stared at him, apparently too frightened to speak.

"My master will know what to do with you. When he arrives, you will regret the day you laid eyes on this castle."

The girl found her voice—that hated voice—and whispered to the boy, "I thought you said his master is far from here."

The boy couldn't speak for fear, so Itch answered for him.

"He is, but I can call him."

Itch started toward the calling bell that would alert Lord Elveston and bring an end to both these rascals. But the boy saw his intent and sprang to life. He was closer to the bell and made a dive for it.

He grabbed it and tossed it to the girl before Itch could reach him. Itch lunged at the girl, but before he could reach her, she tossed the bell back to the boy.

"Play with me, will you?"

Itch grabbed the girl's arm and twisted it behind her back.

"Now, if you don't want me to wring this pretty little girl's arm right off her pretty little body, put the bell on the table and move away."

The boy looked uncertain, as if trying to weigh his options. To show him that he would do what he threatened, Itch yanked the girl's arms savagely until she let out a gasp of pain.

The boy put the bell on the table and stepped away from it.

Holding the girl firmly with one hand, Itch reached out and rang the bell.

There was the familiar chime in the corner of the room. The boy, obviously, had never seen anyone come out of a portal. The girl showed fear but no surprise. Itch wondered what she knew about portals. Yes, he'd done the right thing in saving these two for his master to deal with. And he would deal with them. Though Itch hoped to have the pleasure of killing the girl. He'd do to her what those girls at the Red Ale had done to him, and then he'd kill her.

The children froze as Lord Elveston stepped through the portal. Itch still held the girl, but he thought that the boy at least would flee if he had any sense at all. Yet, what good would fleeing from the presence of the formidable fire master do? He could consume them in flames, even as they ran.

But the fool wouldn't flee and leave the girl. That was the weakness of love. The reason his master had no friends. What was the point of having other people to think about when one should be thinking about oneself?

Itch looked to judge the distance between the boy and the door, but saw that Crisp, his master's pet salamander, was standing sentinel. There'd be no escape for the boy, even if he wanted to.

"Itch, why have you called me? This had better be important."

"Oh, it is, master. It is."

His master looked at the girl and beamed. "Cintella, my queen!"

The girl winced but didn't speak. She just stared at Lord Elveston with mute horror. To Itch's utter dismay, his master gazed longingly at the girl.

"I knew you'd come to your senses and choose me over that lowly position as serving girl for a bunch of old elemental stooges."

Then Lord Elveston looked at Itch with confusion and outrage. "How dare you lay hands on my queen?!" He raised a hand laced with fire and lightning, ready to strike Itch. Then he checked himself and hissed, "Do you not know that she will soon be mistress of this castle?"

Itch blinked. Was his master threatening him because of this girl? This was too much. But Itch backed away—afraid, but perplexed.

Then, to Itch's horror, Lord Elveston took the girl in his arms and gazed at her like a precious thing. He placed a hand on the back of her head, the perfect way to wring her neck, Itch thought. But he pressed her head against his chest as if to comfort her.

"I will know the meaning of this, Itch. You have been faithful to me all these years and have never given me reason to doubt you, but this had better be a good one."

"They are intruders, master. This girl didn't come here to be your queen. She came to snoop around. She and that boy tricked me . . ." Here Itch stopped, too embarrassed to reveal to his master just how they'd tricked him. "And when I figured out what they were about, I returned to find them tinkering with your Posiplus."

Lord Elveston looked at the girl in his arms, then, as if noticing him for the first time, he looked at the boy.

"Jawan?"

The boy—so his name was Jawan, was it?—trembled before the fire mage.

"Y-yes, sir?"

Lord Elveston had not yet given Jawan anything to tremble about. But Itch relished the thought that he would, and soon. He savored the taste of burnt flesh.

Without releasing the girl, Lord Elveston addressed the boy. His voice was low but ominous. "Masquerading as the earth mage's fuddle-mouthed apprentice, when all the time you were plotting and planning. To come here to my castle and subvert my queen—the only woman I could ever love . . ."

Both Itch and the girl flinched at this.

"Itch, take Cintella to the Honey Room and see that she is secure there."

"Yes, master."

Lord Elveston released the girl into Itch's hands. He seemed reluctant to let her go, and Itch was reluctant to take her now that he couldn't kill her—yet. So, his master loved her. That meant there would be no ravishing her and no ravaging for the tenderest morsels to roast. But what would his master do about the boy? There was still hope.

When they were well down the hall and around many corners, out of his master's sight and hearing, Itch gripped the girl's arm.

"So, you think you're a queen, huh?" he snarled.

The girl—Cintella, his master had called her—didn't look like she relished the title. So, she thought she was too good for his master? Ungrateful wench. If he told her what he wanted to do to her, she wouldn't scorn her only protection. He consoled his impotent rage by tightening his grip on her arm. He'd find a way to get rid of her. He'd make his master loathe her so much he'd get rid of her himself.

They were crossing the main hall when the portcullis rose and Loby stepped through.

"Where's Lord Elveston?" Loby asked, assessing the girl with a brief glance.

Did he think Itch was taking her to his bed? Let him.

"My master is in the laboratory, chastising one of your wayward friends."

"What? What are you talking about?"

"It's that idiot who stutters. Master caught him in here snooping around with this wench. I can only imagine what he'll look like when the fire mage gets through with him."

The last he directed at Loby's retreating back as the boy raced down the hall toward the laboratory.

Itch laughed with glee at the thought of Loby witnessing his friend being turned to toast.

"What will he do to him?" Cintella asked.

"You don't want to know. Just be glad he won't do it to you."

# Chapter 21

Queen Quanta dismissed the guard and rang for her handmaid. She sank into the sumptuous red velvet chamber throne beside her bed and sighed.

"Close the drapes," she instructed the handmaid when she arrived. "I've a terrible headache, and the sun is not helping."

The handmaid crossed over to close the drapes, then came back looking worried.

"Shall I massage your temples, Your Majesty?"

"Yes, you shall."

The handmaid stood behind the queen's chair and placed her fingertips on each of the queen's temples. The queen closed her eyes as fingers, palms, and knuckles soothed away her stress.

To her dismay, closing her eyes only brought up images of Antipan. But that was one of the troubles she'd come here to escape—for a moment at least. Yet, this image of him wasn't troubling. Instead, she noticed how tall he was, his regal posture, and his imperturbable elegance.

*No! Impossible!* She couldn't be attracted to that malefactor. He stood for everything that, as queen, she had to guard against. His very realm was antithetical to hers. Still, the image that assaulted her closed eyes was one of beauty. His high brow . . . *Stop!* She focused on the fingertips kneading her temples.

The handmaid placed warm compresses over the queen's eyes. This helped her headache ease away but also served to make her visions of Antipan more vivid.

Antipan had his own realm. Queen Quanta could only muse that of all the kings on Nanosia, he was the only one with real power. But she was a queen, she reminded herself. She had power in her own right. Yet, not like his. She and the kings of Atomidon and Cenozonia basically let their realms run themselves. There was Nano to keep things running smoothly. During her reign, there'd never been a problem so great that Nano couldn't handle without her intervention, so she left things alone.

But Antipan was challenging her to seek something she'd never dreamed of—to have, to even need, more power than she did. What would she do with it? The realms of Quantum, Atomidon, and Cenozonia existed to perform the task of regulating matter, energy, and life in the larger world. Any power she gained would be for herself.

In a way, she thought, they were the slaves of that larger world for which they labored without even thinking they could exist for themselves. Only once in Cenozonia did King Prokaryot dare to make a change in the way things were done. He came up with a life-form that thrived on oxygen, which before then had been a useless waste material, poisonous to the fragile life on Earth. The Big World adjusted to this change, yet no other change on that scale had taken place since then.

Now here comes Antipan. Will he be the new Prokaryot? Will an alliance between the realms usher in a new age in elementary particles?

She thought about the boy who'd come to the palace today claiming to be the prophesied "Big One." Was he? Had she unwittingly imprisoned the very manifestation of some higher power she'd longed for? Had she insulted him beyond repair?

No. This was nonsense. Nano was right. The prophecy was just a myth with no connection to any real higher power. How powerful could he be if she could send him to a dungeon at her whim? The prophecy said the Big One would help them, but she'd sent the boy away because he'd refused to help her. She needed power that she could wield, not something that could be denied her at another's whim. She needed what Antipan offered.

*Antipan!* It worried her that she no longer tried to fight the images before her eyes. But what the prophecy couldn't offer, he most certainly could. The only question was, would he deliver what he promised?

She'd sent ambassadors to his realm in a perhaps misguided attempt to see behind the mysterious curtain where no one else dared even take a look. The other kings had warned her that nothing lay within the Realm of Chaos but mayhem and unspeakable horrors. She'd been hardly more than a young girl then, and the thought that they were afraid made her want to know even more.

Her ambassadors found what they'd expected to find in the Realm of Chaos—darkness and chaos. There'd been no one to receive them as ambassadors, for no one was in authority save Antipan, who kept his eye on them but extended no hand of welcome. There was no embassy, so they roamed the spaces between careening elementary particles.

"But Your Majesty, for all the Realm of Chaos lacked in order and balance, it more than made up for in beauty."

"Beauty?"

"We wouldn't have expected it. We would have expected everything to be quite grotesque. But it was the very unexpectedness of the movements and patterns and lights that made them so lovely."

This she'd had to see for herself. So, she'd disguised herself as a common fermion and gone to the Realm of Chaos.

No guards had seized her ambassadors, so she wasn't worried about that. She only hoped that Antipan, if he was watching, wouldn't see through her disguise.

She'd barely crossed the border when a small crowd of fermions rushed at her and swarmed around her, as if she were an atomic nucleus.

"Dance with us," they cried.

"Why aren't you dancing?" they asked with gleeful curiosity.

One cheeky quark came right up to her and poked a finger at her chest. "I've never seen you before."

"There's a lot you haven't seen, so that's not saying anything," another teased.

A charming little gluon pushed his way to the front of the crowd and took her arm. "Forget these fools. Dance with me. I'll make you do it right."

Queen Quanta's head spun faster than the rest of her, trying to keep up with the barrage of comments. No way could she keep up with all of it and keep her sanity. So, she danced. This was the Realm of Chaos, so she didn't have to match anyone else's spin. She could orbit whatever she wanted, or orbit nothing at all.

While she danced, she kept her eye open for the beauty her ambassadors had seen. This took no great effort. It was there in front of her. Most of all, she felt that she had become an integral part of that beauty.

The way the fermions respected one another's space seemed to be the only rule.

A shower of photons cascaded into the abyss below the queen and shot back up, displaying a million colors of light.

It was beautiful. She knew that a higher power would be beautiful as well. Before this excursion into the Realm of Chaos, she'd always thought that beauty could only be achieved through strict order. Any particle out of its assigned place would mar the whole picture. Nano insisted that this was so. Now she knew it wasn't.

As she relaxed under her handmaid's gentle touch, she felt that light, watery feeling of having gotten over a headache. She reached up to feel her own temples.

"That's much better, Enace. Send Loma in with my tea."

Enace curtsied and, without a word, went out to do as she was told.

Could a higher power bring absolute order along with freedom? Nano also stressed the importance of balance. There was a paradox. How can there be balance and absolute anything? Must there be a balance of order and chaos? An alliance?

As the queen shook her head at this preposterous thought, Loma entered bearing a tray and tea service, set it on the table beside the queen, and slipped out.

Queen Quanta sipped the tea, wondering if she dared even think such thoughts any further. She propped her feet on a hassock, and this, combined with the tea, made her sleepy. Her thoughts slipped into her dreams, which she didn't fight or even question.

Fermions and bosons marched by in strict formations of nine columns. Over them, wild fermions and vicious bosons flitted about in absolute freedom of movement. How they managed to move so recklessly without bumping into one another, the queen couldn't guess.

"This must not be!" Nano's voice commanded order.

He marched to the front of the formation and caught the flying particles in a beam of light that shone forth from the number nine on his hat. They froze then fell into nine columns behind the particles that had already been marching in order.

The queen was dismayed in her dream, for they were no longer beautiful.

"What have you done to my children?" Antipan's voice rose up, melodious yet cacophonous. As if one voice were not enough to express his outrage, he spoke with what sounded like a million voices. The queen was both anticipating and dreading what he would do. But she knew whatever it was, it would restore the beauty she longed for. And in her dream, she never questioned that she longed for him.

The Lord of Chaos spun his arms in an arc around his body. Then he himself began to spin, and as he spun, the spin and orbit of all the particles careened out of control. No one knew what anyone else was doing. No one knew where he was supposed to be going. And it was not beautiful.

The queen awoke, her body aching from its odd position. She stretched out the kinks and shook her head to fully awaken. It took her a moment to realize that she was now in a different state of consciousness, but she remembered the dream in detail. It had to have meant something to stay lodged in her mind.

When she recalled what she had been thinking about before she'd gone to sleep, the meaning of the dream became clear. Antipan was beautiful in his realm, and she in hers, but they could never unite.

She summoned Enace.

"I must return to the court, but not in this horridly rumpled dress. Find me something for a queen to wear before her courtiers."

Enace departed and returned with a sumptuous gown of teal satin. She helped the queen doff the wrinkled gown and don the fresh one.

When Enace left, Queen Quanta summoned the guard to escort her back to court. There she saw Nano returning from the courtyard. Bosons stood at attention in the throne room. Outside, a few petitioners milled around, still hoping to get an audience with her, but bosons kept them away. She gestured for Nano to take his place beside her throne.

"Have I missed anything?" she asked.

"Nothing of any import. Just the end of the world. But that's to be expected at least once in a queen's life. Did you rest well?"

"Splendidly. What's the news?"

"Are you sure you're up to it?"

"Yes, get on with it."

"I've had reports from Cibius. The collider is not receiving all the photons I'm sending them. I noticed when fewer electrons and positrons were coming from him than I expected."

"What could have happened to them?" she asked with mild concern. It irritated her that Nano couldn't handle these petty problems. He didn't used to trouble her with such nonsense.

"That's what I'd like to know," he said.

The queen sighed. "I had a dream."

"I had a nightmare."

"No, I'm serious."

"So is this." He gestured to the court, but he meant the world outside the palace.

She surveyed what could be seen and shrugged. The bosons had everything under control, and Antipan wouldn't be back anytime soon.

"I dreamed about you and Antipan."

"How odd. He's in my nightmare, too."

"I know this dream means something."

"What was it about?"

The queen paused. She wasn't sure if she was ready to tell Nano about her mixed feelings toward Antipan. He would think her mad if she told him about the beauty in the Realm of Chaos. A dream about order and chaos united together would only point to her ambivalence. So, she offered a vague answer. "There was a lot of chaos."

He looked at her doubtfully. "As one would find in a dream with Antipan in it. But you're lucky. I wish my nightmare were something I could wake up from. Even as a memory, it would still be dreadful. Only it's not a memory. It's a reality unfolding right before my eyes."

"You are Nano." *Enough of this whining!* "You have to get to the bottom of this. No matter how dreadful, it's your job to find out what's what."

Nano stood straight and adjusted his hat. "I will, and Antipan will not slip away this time. He and that irregular particle he has working for him will be stopped."

Queen Quanta gestured for the bosons to let the citizens approach her throne. As she commenced to address their petitions and receive news, she thought about it and hoped Nano was right.

# Chapter 22

Jawan couldn't remember ever being in so much trouble. He wondered what the fire mage would do to him. Was there some kind of rule forbidding mages from harming one another's apprentices? He didn't know. He could only hope. Elveston's baleful glare wasn't reassuring.

He wondered, too, about Cintella. Elveston called her his queen. Did they know each other? Had Jawan messed up a love affair? No, the fire mage blamed him for subverting her. He'd forgive Cintella, but what would he do to Jawan?

A salamander eyed him from the doorway—the only door in a windowless room. He sighed. Even if the salamander weren't there, Elveston would fry him long before he reached the door.

"W-we weren't doing anything bad, sir. Just curious."

He wondered if his stuttering would soften the fire mage's anger. Would he feel pity or disgust? Or would it just make Jawan look like an idiot, as it always did?

"What reason did you have to be curious about anything in my castle? Hasn't the earth mage any curiosities of his own to keep a brat like you out of mischief?"

Jawan wasn't sure how to answer this. He recognized the insult against his master.

"I-I . . ."

"No. You came here with a purpose. What did your master send you here to find?"

"N-nothing, sir."

Lord Elveston studied Jawan as if he'd never seen a boy before.

"You are not lying about that," he decided. "Myrlo wouldn't have known that I was not here, and he wouldn't have sent you here to snoop around my castle while I was here. No one knew I was gone except Itch, and he obviously didn't bring you here."

Jawan didn't like Lord Elveston's line of reasoning. It might lead the fire mage to ask the wrong questions about just how Jawan knew he wouldn't be there. Could he steer the fire mage away from that topic?

"I'm s-sorry, sir. I should have known better. It won't happen again."

"It most certainly will not happen again. I will see to that."

Jawan gulped. Then Elveston took him by the arm and marched him toward the portal.

Thinking the fire mage was going to take him to Nanosia, Jawan's heart nearly stopped. Why would he do that unless he knew, but where else would he be going? He braced himself for the transition and whatever predicament lay ahead.

But when they emerged on the other side of the portal, Jawan found himself in his own master's laboratory. Elveston had taken him home. The grip around his arm told him this was no cause to feel relief. At least it meant Elveston didn't suspect Jawan had seen him in Nanosia.

Everything seemed normal. Myrlo had his back to them, his eye on the nanoscope. But Jawan knew the earth mage couldn't have missed the portal chime. If Myrlo hadn't turned around, it was because he sensed their presence and had decided to finish what he was doing before deigning to address them. If his master only knew how dangerous Elveston was.

Taking his time, Myrlo turned around to face them. His face was inscrutable. A bad sign. A sign of tightly coiled rage.

"Jawan, I suppose you have an explanation for your absence when you were told to remain here. And I suppose you have an even more incredibly unassailable explanation for showing up with the fire mage after such an absence."

"I . . ."

Myrlo glared at Elveston. "So, this is how you pay me back for challenging you at the conclave?"

"I've no idea what you're talking about," Lord Elveston assured him.

"Don't you? I trained this boy for eight years and now, just for spite, you want to take him for your own."

Jawan's jaw dropped to the stone floor. He stared at Myrlo but could think of nothing to say.

Lord Elveston laughed. "Surely, you don't believe that."

"What am I to believe? He disobeys me, twice. Runs off without a word and then shows up with you. What secrets has he divulged?"

*"M-master?!"*

Elveston suppressed a smile, as if Myrlo's outrage were a particularly amusing toy. "Now come, my friend . . ."

"We are not friends!"

"But surely, we are not enemies."

Myrlo scowled.

"You are wrong to suspect me of misconduct. In fact, when I found this delinquent snooping around my laboratory . . ."

"Snooping around?" Myrlo raised an eyebrow.

Myrlo looked at Jawan, but Elveston continued before Jawan could stutter out a defense.

"Yes. Snooping around my laboratory. It made me suspect that you had sent him to spy on me."

"I? Spy on you? But that is against the elemental protocol."

"You were in such a state of rebellion the last time we met that I wasn't sure such protocols would restrain you."

"Why are you here, then?" Myrlo's voice was deceptively quiet.

"To bring this cunning yet witless apprentice back to you and ask that you keep him under tighter rein."

Jawan's head spun as he watched this back and forth between his master and the fire mage. They'd taken the situation out of his hands and turned it into something he could neither control nor understand.

"I will keep a tight rein on this boy," Myrlo vowed. "And before this day is out, I will know what is what." He turned to Jawan. "What were you doing in Elveston's castle?"

Jawan looked into his master's baleful eyes and couldn't turn away.

"I w-was looking for something."

"Something to do with the nanoscope, I suspect. In the fire mage's laboratory? Have I not given you everything that you need to do the work required of an apprentice?"

*Of an apprentice, yes.* But how could he explain to his master a need beyond that?

"What were you looking for, Jawan?"

"I c-can't tell you."

Myrlo and Lord Elveston exchanged looks. In a fit of rage Jawan had never seen before, Myrlo grabbed Jawan's jaw and forced his mouth open. "You still have a tongue in your mouth, and you will tell me."

"Please, sir. I can't."

"Why can't you?"

Jawan looked at his master's feet, trying his best to look contrite rather than defiant. Myrlo had never in eight years raised his hand against him, and Jawan didn't have to fake a tremble.

Myrlo sighed. "I don't know what you found so fascinating at the fire master's castle, but you disobeyed me, and that I will not tolerate. Until further notice, you will be confined to your room and the library where you will study for your upcoming exam. It's in two days, I believe, so you have no time for more mischief. Is that understood?"

"Yes, sir."

"Do not disobey me again, for I am out of options," he said quietly, the menace in his voice needing no volume.

"Y-yes, sir."

"You are letting him off easy," Lord Elveston said. "I would have . . ."

"What you would have done is of no consequence in my castle. I will do what I will do. Be content that Jawan will not trouble you again." He turned to Jawan. "Will you?"

"N-no, sir."

Clearly, his master had no love for Lord Elveston. Jawan didn't know what festered between the two masters, but he was tired. After such a long night, he went to bed thinking he'd never wake up again. But sleep wouldn't come.

Thoughts of Cintella and what that zombie might have done to her tossed him across his bed. Why hadn't he stopped him? Why hadn't he been the hero that girl needed? She wouldn't have been there if he hadn't recruited her to help with his stupid plot. Itch had taken her, perhaps to her death, and Jawan had just stood there like an idiot, not even opening his mouth in protest.

His mind drifted from fear to curiosity. Why had the fire mage called Cintella his queen? He'd also called Queen Quanta his queen. Could there be a connection? The monarch had spurned him, and Cintella looked like a trapped animal in his arms. Poor Elveston wasn't having much luck with women.

Lord Elveston was free to return to his business in Nanosia while Jawan languished on his bed. With the darkness as a canvas, he saw the photons entering the collider and undergoing some excruciating disfigurement as intense energy split them into electrons and positrons. He saw them come out as such, their faces contorted with agony and rage—the same impotent rage that was keeping him awake.

And Elveston would get away with this. There was no one Jawan could tell who was not already angry at him. Nano would throw him in the dungeon without listening to what he had to say. His mast . . . he couldn't go to his master with accusations against the fire mage if he had no proof.

Maybe he could let his master know in some oblique way. He spent the rest of the night trying to think of a way to let his master know about Nanosia without telling him he'd actually been there. This would get his master to ask questions. They had to be the right questions, focused on Elveston, not Jawan.

The next day, he was doubly out of sorts. Two sleepless nights in a row. How could he think? But he had to. There was no help for it. He had to wake his brain up. He went to the library and started studying for his exam.

He was reading about the antimatter for neutrons when it dawned on him. He knew what he would do—how he would get his master interested in finding out what Elveston had to do with Nanosia. He knew it was a long shot, and any number of things could go wrong along the way. But it was a plan and would at least help him get to sleep that night.

He bided his time, trying with some difficulty to hide his excitement. On the day of the exam, he didn't even try. His master would assume he was excited about the exam.

The first questions tested his basic understanding of quantum physics, and he breezed through them. He smiled when it mentioned the quantum realm, though he would use it with quite another meaning.

In answer to a question about the law of conservation, he described how Nano maintained the balance of matter and energy by transforming particles of energy into particles of matter and antimatter in a particle collider.

Jawan described how newly converted matter was placed in a nanotube and sent back into the material world, where it would eventually be transformed into energy by human industry, and the whole cycle would start again.

He wondered how much detail he should go into. If Myrlo's encounter with Pym was his only experience of Nanosia, he'd never actually gone into the Quantum Realm, so he wouldn't know Jawan was describing a real experience. But Jawan knew that *if* was vital.

He turned in the exam and had to wait another day to see what effect it would have. Myrlo's objections had been part of Jawan's plan, but the earth mage's vehement response to the test answers still made Jawan tremble inside.

"From what addled corner of your brain did you come up with this preposterous nonsense about matter and antimatter?"

"It's n-not nonsense, master. I read about it in Lord Elveston's laboratory."

"Lord Elveston's laboratory? Why would the fire mage have reading material about matter and antimatter?"

"M-maybe he was reading about the particle collider he has on his worktable."

"This is making even less sense. What would a fire mage need with a particle collider? I don't know what this is about, Jawan, but there's one way to find out. I will summon Elveston and clear up this nonsense. And if you're lying to me, Jawan, so help me, it will not go well for you."

Jawan gulped. This was where it could all go wrong. Of course, Elveston would deny having such a book, but the plan could still work.

"Y-you will see, master. Lord Elveston came through a portal and saw me. Somehow, I knew he was coming from the Quantum Realm. Like the one in his book."

To his own ears, this sounded like a childish attempt at a ridiculous lie. His master's baleful look didn't give him cause for hope.

Myrlo turned to a row of four bells, each one bearing the symbol one of the other four elemental mages. He chose the bell bearing a simple triangle, the symbol for fire, and rang it.

The fire mage didn't come right away, but after a considerable time, he stepped into Myrlo's laboratory.

"My dear earth master, is something the matter that you've called me personally?"

Myrlo got right to the point without any preamble.

"Elveston, do you have in your laboratory a book about the Quantum Realm?"

Alarm briefly crossed the fire mage's face, but he quickly regained his composure.

"What would I do with such a book? That is your area."

Myrlo nodded.

"And do you have a portal to a place called the Quantum Realm?"

Elveston was less successful in hiding his shock this time, but perhaps that was only because Jawan was watching for something to show. But Myrlo didn't seem to notice.

"The Quantum Realm?" Elveston laughed. "Surely, you don't imagine that that is an actual place one might teleport to? Dear Myrlo, I don't know what this is about. Either you are playing some silly game, or you have lost your mind. The Quantum Realm, indeed."

But Elveston looked worried. Jawan knew that this was striking too close to home, and Elveston had no way to make sense of it.

Myrlo glared at Jawan, who did his best to look like he couldn't believe what Elveston was saying. But Myrlo didn't seem to notice the sweat on Elveston's brow. Jawan knew he was in trouble. The plan had failed.

"I c-can explain, master."

"I've lost all patience with your explanations."

"Explain what?" Elveston asked.

Myrlo grabbed Jawan and made him stand face-to-face with Elveston.

"Boy, tell the fire mage how you have slandered his name."

"Slandered my name?"

"I don't know what this boy thinks he will gain from this. But the game stops here. Tell him!"

Jawan looked straight in the fires burning in Elveston's eyes and held his gaze. If he were trying to hold the gaze of twin suns it would dazzle his own eyes no less, but he held on to make Elveston worried enough that even Myrlo would see it.

"Y-you have a collider in your laboratory. I saw it."

"That's not what you were talking about, Jawan," Myrlo objected. "What about the book and the portal?"

"I have no book such as you have described." Elveston eagerly grabbed for that straw.

His master started to lead him away, but Jawan wasn't going to let it end here. He couldn't.

"L-Lord Elveston, you're using that collider to create matter, just like Nano in Nanosia."

Both Myrlo and Elveston stared at Jawan in astonishment. It was win or lose. Now his master knew Jawan had encountered Pym while dabbling with the nanoscope. There was no help for that. But the fire mage definitely knew now that Jawan was onto him. He might still not know exactly how, but he knew, and Jawan could only hope that his master saw the beads of sweat lacing Elveston's brow.

Elveston regained his composure and tried to look severe. "It is bad enough that you have lost all the discipline necessary for understanding earth magic and let your imagination run wild, but to involve me in your fantasies is inexcusable."

"I s-saw you come through the portal."

No need letting Elveston know he'd seen him in Nanosia.

"And with no idea of where I was coming from, you made up this fairytale about a Quantum Realm."

Then Myrlo cleared his throat. "But there is a Nanosia."

Hope quickened Jawan's heart. But Elveston just as quickly dismissed it.

"That is as may be, but it has nothing to do with me. I've never heard of such a place, but I'll take your word that it exists." He paused to let the implications sink in. "I suggest that you apply more stringent discipline to this boy and that you bring an end to his mischief."

"I don't need you to tell me that. He knows that is what I will do."

Jawan looked into his master's eyes. He could see that Myrlo was still angry at him, only now his anger was tempered with worry.

"For now, I must go to a conclave. But you will remain in your room. Until I return, you will be locked in your room. At that time, I will deal with you, but for now, I must go."

"Conclave?" Elveston asked. "What sort of conclave? I was not informed of a conclave."

Myrlo looked as if he wanted to bite his tongue. "Did I say conclave? I was using the word loosely. It's just a private get-together. Nothing official will be discussed."

"Private get-together." Elveston looked doubtful but shrugged his shoulders. "At any rate, I have business to attend to of my own."

He looked pointedly at Jawan and stepped through the portal.

# Chapter 23

Lord Elveston returned to his castle eager to take his queen to meet his master. She'd run from him before, but she couldn't run now. A little charm would undo whatever damage that pesky earth apprentice had done, and then she would belong to the fire. Strange, in the universe, where balance meant that everything must have its opposite, water was the nemesis of fire, and earth stood against wind. But here in the world of men, Elveston found earth trying to smother his flaming love for the queen.

Itch paced the laboratory floor, eagerness brightening his eyes as well. "Master, will you leave some for me? Whatever you leave will be a delicacy for me. She owes it to me for that little trick she played."

Sheer force of will kept Elveston from incinerating his servant. He still needed Itch. But the day would come when this imbecile would be as disposable as the rest of the material universe. "Go to your room, beast. Do not come out until I call for you."

Itch's very presence would spoil Elveston's efforts to charm Cintella. The zombie must not be anywhere in sight. Delicacy indeed! Itch had no idea.

He lifted the heavy bar of the Honey Room door and entered. Cintella stared at him with utter terror. He waited for her to spoil his delight by begging him not to kill her. But she held her chin high. In the face of one who could turn her to ash in an instant, she said absolutely nothing. She was wise enough to be afraid but didn't let fear master her. *Good*. He could banish the fear.

Like a lion retracting its claws, he smiled what he hoped was a disarming smile. His teeth were flat. He could make her forget that they had ever been sharp. But she stepped back each time he stepped forward until her back touched the wall. Her lips clamped tight as if stifling a whimper, she glanced from side to side for some escape.

"Don't you think if I wanted to hurt you, you'd be hurt already? I only want to show you what a marvelous woman you will be as my queen."

That little speech put the iron back in her blood. Some of the terror left her eyes, but she remained stiff. "I will not be your queen or anything to you."

"But you already are." He saw no need to tell her just how she was his queen, only that she was. "Come with me. You can see what I have to show you."

She didn't move. He banked the fire in his eyes and gazed into hers. One thing about the predators of the world, they are beautiful. Lord Elveston knew his visage was exquisite. His gaze soothed her fears and promised her dearest dreams. She blinked as if not wanting to feel what he knew she was feeling. He couldn't read her mind, but he could touch it. He took her hand and drew her toward the door.

"Will you let me go home?"

"In time, if you still want to."

"I want to."

"Come with me."

He led her to the top of his castle where she could see the stars—those faraway balls of fire. Wind whipped the flames slithering over the top of the parapet as the first rays of the sun slithered over the horizon. He wished she would shiver—not from fear but from the wind—so he could make a show of using the gentle aspects of his magic to warm the air around her. But she'd already come dressed for her dandy escapade that night. What could he do for her? "As my queen, all of this will be yours." He made a grand gesture toward the stars.

"I didn't ask you for all that. All I asked you is to let me go home."

Elveston rolled his eyes. She asked for so little when she could have so much. "To that hovel you call a home?"

"To my grandmother."

"She'll be queen mother." That was probably a lie. No way would Fuego agree to let an old bag of electrons survive.

"I'm sure she'll want nothing to do with you."

Well, the old hag won't have to worry about that. Aloud, he said, "Oh, I'm sure she'll prefer it here where she'll never be hungry again." He stepped between her and the wind. "Never cold again."

She looked past him as if at some memory. No, she wouldn't remember what it was like to not be hungry and cold. She had no such memories and was probably looking at a vision of what that might be like. She saw the world Elveston offered.

"What do you want from me?"

He'd take her to him now while she was open to the idea. He took her hand and led her back down into the castle. But she paused when he opened the door of the firepit. He wrapped her body in a shield of cool air and led her down into its depths.

"Fuego, I have brought my queen."

Cintella shrank away from the inferno. "Is this what you brought me here for? To sacrifice me to your god?" She turned and ran.

Elveston made the shadows dance, so the steps were here and then there and then nowhere. She ran and ran until he surrounded her in a cave of fire from which she couldn't escape. He thinned the shield around her body to let her feel the heat. Then he waited just long enough to break her will, so she'd be glad for any help.

Shielding his own body, he stepped through the fire and stood before her, the very picture of the valiant hero. The flames died down when he blew on them. This made her stare at him—her savior, master over all that terrified her.

"Do not be afraid. You are safe with me."

He reached out for her. Hesitating, she stepped closer. He took her in his arms and kissed her. She hesitated again, looked into his eyes, and kissed him back. Just one more nudge and she would be his. All would be his. He stepped away from her toward the pit. Bringing forth a ball of fire in his hands, he fashioned a castle of flame with drawbridge, turrets, and battlements. Guards made of sooty shadows patrolled behind the parapets. Once she looked directly into the flames, nothing else existed—just the fire and his voice.

"You are queen now. But you can be the queen of fire if you give yourself to it."

"Give myself to the fire?"

He took her hand and pulled her closer to the pit. She flinched, and he remembered to thicken her shield. Her eyes remained transfixed on him, and Elveston thought she might leap into the flames if he asked her to. He just held her close caressing her. His fingertips smoldered, and wherever they touched, her clothes turned to ash. When there was nothing left but bare skin, he cupped her chin and whispered, "Do you love the fire?"

"I do."

"Do you fear the fire?"

"No."

"Does the fire have all that you need and want?"

"Yes."

He went to the barrel that had held the hickory chips and burned a circle in its side. He pushed at the circle until it came loose. Taking her hand ever so gently, he brought it to his lips and pierced her finger with his teeth. Then he smeared the blood on the circle. "Feed the fire."

"What?"

"Give your blood on this circle to the fire."

She tossed the circle into the flames.

"Now open your heart to the fire and say these words."

She gazed even deeper at him and repeated his words.

> "From stars that dot the murky vault of night
> To fires that warm men's hearts on land and sea,
> All is Fuego.
> I give myself. I pledge my soul that when
> My body offers up its unseen guest
> I will be Fuego."

"I will be Fuego? What . . .?"

"Sh. Don't worry. It is done. You are safe."

She must not falter now. If Fuego sees her hesitation, he won't accept her. That was Elveston's whole purpose. She must remain calm.

Fuego crackled from somewhere inside the pit. "This is your queen?"

"Yes, master. She is the queen, and she has given herself to you."

"She has said the words you gave her to say, but can she perform the act?"

"*Act?!*" Elveston and Cintella said in unison. But only Elveston knew what he meant.

"The act that shows she is truly mine."

Elveston swallowed hard.

"What must I do?"

He took her closer to the pit until she could reach out and touch the fire. Her shield kept her from sizzling, but sweat moistened her brow. If she faltered even a little, Fuego would know, and she'd die. It would have been better for her not to say the words than to say them and not mean them. "Stretch out your hand and caress the fire."

Fire licked at her toes where it spilt over the lip of the pit, but she seemed to know that her life depended on this. She seemed to know she couldn't turn back now. Stretching out a steady hand, she brushed the edge of the flames, then as if luxuriating in fine fur, she plunged her fingers in deeper up to the first knuckles. Sweat poured down her face, but her shield held. Elveston gasped. He'd never been so bold, and he was the fire mage. Cintella stepped back and smiled. He smiled but did not ask to see her hand.

They ascended the stairs and emerged in his laboratory. "You are truly my queen now. You will reign with me in a universe of pure energy."

"But you know, I've always been a queen. I have royal blood."

"You may have been *a* queen, but now you are *my* queen. Now let's go to . . ." He stopped.

She couldn't go to Nanosia. Unlike his known alias, Antipan, Cintella couldn't exist in the same world with Queen Quanta. He had to leave her here. The Honey Room was the only safe place for her until he returned. He had to let Itch out. The brute would come out anyway if Elveston left him too long. Better that he not see her roaming about the castle unprotected.

Once he had the positrons Gelic was keeping for him and the scroll to show him how to stabilize them, everything would be in place to carry out his plans.

# Chapter 24

The two photons entered the Posiplus. It was cavernous inside and empty save for a single focal point—a sheet of gold. Upon closer inspection, the photons saw that they could fit into the atoms of the gold. As explorers, they settled on the nucleus of one atom and found it comfortable.

"What now?"

"Don't know. But something is supposed to happen to us."

"If you're going to talk to me, at least tell me your name."

"Name? Is that something we're supposed to have?"

"I guess so. I kind of remember being in a place where everything had a name—even dead matter."

"Then what's your name?"

"I can't remember. No. I remember that I always called myself by the name of whatever I was a part of."

"We're part of this golden atom right now. Just a part of it, so what would you call yourself? How about Chip?"

"Yeah. I've often been part of a chip of something. And you could be Bit."

"Okay. Why not?"

"Well, nothing's happening right now, and I'm sleepy."

"Me too. Guess whatever's supposed to happen will have to wait."

Deep in the heart of the golden atom, the photons nestled down to sleep. They dreamed of the lives they'd once lived among humans, sometimes flowing along in a ray of some evolving sun, sometimes part of the beam of light emitted from one of man's many gadgets. And then there were those times when they solidified into matter. How had it happened? There was so much to remember—eons and eons of existence in one form or the other.

Suddenly, they were jolted awake.

"Wake up! Get going! You're not here to slumber."

The photons rubbed their groggy eyes and looked around for the source of this disturbance. They found themselves surrounded by thousands of angry electric charges.

"Look! I'm glowing!" Bit exclaimed.

Chip gazed at him, then at herself. They were emitting a beam of intense light that bounced around the nucleus and shot off into space. And wherever the beam of light went, they were forced to go.

They were moving so fast, but it was a familiar speed. Still Bit frowned.

"Is this normal?"

"I think so. I seem to recall . . ."

"But we weren't glowing when we were sleeping in the atom."

"No, I guess this is the change Lord Gelic was telling us about."

"This can't be all there is. I mean, this is fun, soaring around like this, but I was expecting something more transformational."

Then more photons began to pour in. They were thrown out of the golden atom so fast that they hardly had time to get comfortable.

With little sympathy, the electric charges herded the photons into a circle and forced them to dance.

They spun and orbited the center of the circle. Never quite touching, but still moving in sync.

From somewhere the photons couldn't tell, bursts of energy hit them, making them dance faster and faster.

"What is that?" cried Chip.

"Where did it come from?"

All the photons looked around them, but the energy seemed to be coming from everywhere.

"Here, catch!" Bit yelled.

Chip caught the thing Bit threw and found it to be a virtual electron. Then seeing that she had one too, she threw it at Bit. When he caught it, he and Chip began to transform. A sadness they couldn't describe gripped them as their incorporeal essences began to have weight. They slowed down as a heaviness that they hadn't experienced in a very long time dragged them.

"You look like me, but different," said Chip.

"And you look like me, but I have a negative charge, and you're a positron just like the one outside."

"I'm a positron like Lord Gelic. He has made me one of his own."

"What about me?"

Chip eyed him pensively. "I don't know, Bit. I really don't know."

# Chapter 25

*"Wonderful!"* Gelic watched hundreds of photons pour into the Posiplus particle collider. Most wonderful of all, they'd all come out as his creation—his family of positrons all his own. He would be their teacher and reveal to them the secrets of the universe.

He was so excited that he went to the back of the collider just to peek at them. They milled around like newborns—which they were—unsure of the new world.

"Children!" he cried, spreading his arms inwelcome. "My beautiful family, do not be afraid. I am your lord, and you are my flock. I will teach you. Ask me, and I will tell you. Knock, and I will open this strange world to you. Seek me, and you will find more than you bargained for."

They looked at him—not with adoration but with confusion. He saw among them those hateful electrons. He'd get rid of that source of confusion, and then they would come to him.

"My children are positrons. Let the positrons come out from among the filthy electrons and be separate."

But instead of turning to him, the positrons turned to the electrons that were their mates in creation.

*"No!"* Gelic cried. "Turn to me! I am your lord. I am your kinsman."

A few of them looked up, seemingly at the sound of his voice, but the attraction of the electrons was stronger.

Gelic knew the deadly embrace of electrons would annihilate his children. Matter and antimatter—they would all be annihilated, positrons and electrons alike. He remembered the horror of his own creation. He'd felt such exhilaration at seeing the other positrons. Yes, it had taken him a moment to get over no longer being a photon, but he soon rejoiced when he realized that he had become one of so many positive particles.

Before he reached out to them, he saw the electrons that were also a part of what he had become—his counterparts—like him, but totally the opposite of him. He felt the pull of one electron—a natural allure that he saw no reason to resist. Then he saw what happened when the other positrons succumbed to the attraction and touched their counterparts.

In an instant, he saw reverse creation. But had anything really been created, or merely transformed? Photons released matter and antimatter pairs, and when these pairs came together, they'd be energy once again—this time, gamma rays.

*Gamma rays!* Merged matter, which over the millennia had become sentient and called themselves men, had learned to use gamma rays to repair their bodies and even see things that Gelic could already see unaided. But to Gelic, gamma rays were as useless as electrons. Worse than useless. They were the deadly end product of what the electrons did to his beloved positrons, and he hated them.

He wanted to rush in and save the remnants of his children who had not yet defiled themselves with electrons, but he couldn't. He didn't dare. Gamma rays were the most powerful of all the waves in the universe, and so fast. When he was a photon, he could have matched their speed. But as antimatter, he came nowhere near it. While the electrons could turn him into a gamma ray, the gamma rays could damage him utterly.

In helpless horror, he watched his new creation destroy itself. The positrons were so beautiful. So delicate. It shamed him to listen to them sing to the electrons they had each chosen to mate with. But he listened anyway.

> "Spin with me
> Charm my heart
> Up and down the energies
> Swift as light
> You matter, my love
> But together, we'll go beyond."

They didn't know what they were doing. How was it that he knew? How was it that he alone, of all the positrons he'd seen, was attracted to his own kind, while they flung themselves on their opposites? Did that mean he wasn't really like them in some fundamental way? Would he always long for the love of those who wanted something other than him?

*No!* He had to keep the electrons and positrons separate. But how? That Elveston! Sending him off without telling him how to deal with this.

He thought of all the matter and antimatter in the universe. It didn't all turn into gamma rays, so there had to be a way to keep them apart. He was in the place where all the particles of the universe were sorted out. If he wanted to find the answer, it would be here, in the Quantum Realm.

But what did he know about how things were done here? Why should he not know? He was a particle. He had been a photon, and before that he'd been something else, so he had to have come through here between trillions, maybe googles, of cycles in his existence. An existence that will never end, and therefore, could never have begun.

If only he could remember. Only the name Nano rang a bell. But Elveston had told him to be wary of Nano. Nano was dangerous. *Why?* What made him so dangerous? Nano had his own purposes and would disrupt Gelic's. If Gelic succeeded in creating his family, who knew what purposes Elveston had in mind for them?

Nano controlled all elementary particles and knew how to keep the matter and antimatter from colliding. Gelic would have to use Nano's knowledge. That meant he had to get Nano's knowledge.

How did Nano do it? Why not just ask one of the particles? No. That particle would run and tell Nano, who'd be even more suspicious. No. If he wanted to be inconspicuous, he'd have to get close to Nano to observe what he was doing himself.

All the positrons were gone now, replaced by gamma rays. Elveston's unaided eye wouldn't have been able to detect them. But Gelic saw their little black shapes moving around at tremendous speed in a red haze. So ominous. So capable. Gelic cringed.

Gelic couldn't bear to look at them, so he turned away. At that movement, their movements changed. *Were they aware of him?*! It had to be a coincidence. He moved again. The gamma rays moved with him—only this time, they were closer.

He eased his way down the other side of the hill. No way could he outrun them. But maybe if he was out of their sight. *Sight?* He was thinking like Elveston. The man had brought him into—no, changed his—existence. He'd already existed eons before the man had even thought of being born. The man had changed his existence but was not his master. Gelic was an elementary particle and had to think like an elementary particle if he wanted to survive and accomplish his goal.

Now, how would a positron think? A positron wouldn't have to think. A proper positron wouldn't be out here alone. He'd have to think like they would, but also like himself—The Lord of the Positrons.

He skirted around the gamma rays but had another problem to face. Where was Nano? In all Gelic's cycles, he didn't remember ever having to ask that question. Certainly, he had no answer.

"You, there!"

Gelic looked up. A squad of bosons was approaching him. Their leader—for they marched in unison and had a leader—directed them toward Gelic. *What did they want? What would they do?* Elveston's warnings pushed into his mind. But had Elveston been deceiving him? Was this his chance to find Nano—or be captured by him?

They'd seen him. If he ran, they would surely chase him and be less understanding of his explanations. Besides, there was nowhere to go, except back among the gamma rays. No retreat there.

The boson leader stepped forward. "You are a positron."

It shocked Gelic that this boson could take what until then had made Gelic so proud and happy and make it sound like an accusation rather than a compliment. But he stared straight at the boson. "Yes, I am." Then he waited for whatever would come.

"How did you get out here alone?"

Gelic kept silent.

"It doesn't matter." The boson leader glanced off into the distance, as if noticing something there. "Even if you weren't up to mischief of your own, you are too close to the Realm of Chaos for us to leave you here."

He signaled, and the bosons surrounded Gelic.

"Bring him," the leader ordered as Gelic's new entourage marched forward, to what fate he didn't know.

"What will you do with me?"

"I will do nothing. Nano will decide what is to be done with you."

*Nano?* That was who he wanted to see, but as an inconspicuous observer, not a detainee. He had to escape, but the bosons had him boxed in.

Then he saw him. Who else would be wearing a hat with a big number nine on it, so big it could be seen from afar? Gelic remembered that nano meant nine. Nano was one-billionth or ten to the negative ninth power smaller than he would be in Elveston's world. That meant that Gelic, who was the same size, was one-billionth what he had been when he was created.

As his party drew near, Gelic saw that Nano was surrounded by what looked like a chaos of elementary particles. Upon closer inspection, he realized that it was not chaotic. There were two lines. One coming into the Quantum Realm, and one departing. The line coming in contained mostly bosons and other types of energy, with a scattering of fermions. The line going out was mostly fermions with a few particles of energy. Gelic thought such organization was interesting, but he was still most interested in discovering how Nano kept the electrons and positrons apart.

But he saw no positrons. None coming in or going out of the Quantum Realm. In fact, he felt somehow that he was in an anti-world—a world that was anti everything that he was.

To his horror, the bosons marched him straight up to Nano.

"We found this stray positron wandering around outside the Realm of Chaos," the leader reported. "Up to some mischief, no doubt."

Nano regarded Gelic.

"A positron? Their very existence is a mischief. Why bring it to me? I've no use for it. Take it to where all the other antimatter is kept."

Gelic knew he was among enemies when Nano pointedly referred to him as an *it*.

The bosons started to lead Gelic away, but he balked. "What will you do with me?"

"Do with you?" Nano scoffed. "There's nothing that anyone in this universe can do with you. You are an anomaly, and a danger."

"But I'm an elementary particle just like these others that you care for so much. Why treat the positrons differently? Why not send them to the same place where the other particles go?"

Gelic knew the answer. Positrons and electrons were a bad mix. Still, they were his people and should not be mistreated. Surely, Nano could find a way to keep them separate other than leaving the positrons out altogether.

Nano laughed. "What? Send a positron to Atomidon? And what will they do with you? There are no positrons in an atom. Sending you there would be as much as declaring war."

"Why favor electrons over positrons? We are just as good—no. We are better than electrons. We would bring a positive influence into all matter, and the world would be a better place."

"You have no understanding. It is your positive charge that makes you unfit in an atom. The protons will kick you out."

"I wish I could be in a universe where there is no negativity, where all particles could just love one another and work together."

Nano shook his head and gestured for the bosons to take Gelic away.

As they prodded him on, Gelic's mind became bleak. He saw fewer and fewer particles. Then they brought him to an area where there were no particles. Off in the distance, he saw a large group of positrons all standing together, as if penned in. As he got closer, he saw that some kind of barrier enclosed them.

But there were so few of them compared to all the electrons. If this was where Nano kept all the positrons, there should be a lot more. Gelic looked back over the eons of his own existence. Since even before the universe became a universe, particles came in pairs.

Everything was dark for light-years around the one rightly packed body of photons, electrons, and quarks. Then something happened. A singularity opened a breach between the fermions and bosons. Dark energy spread like rising bread, pushing visible matter and energy apart.

"We're free! We can move!" The photons danced about the universe. Their energy created an electromagnetic field. They thought they could play forever, but some of them began to change. The gamma rays sped through the universe so fast they became unstable and began to decay. In an instant where there had been a single particle of energy there now stood an electron and a positron.

Gelic remembered those moments when time began. Time was just a measurable interval between one event and another. So, the electrons here were unpaired, and the positronic population . . . well. His thoughts drifted to the unpleasant conclusion. *We came from gamma rays?* A bad memory. Logical or not, Gelic rejected it. Positrons could never catch up because for every new positron, a new electron was created.

So, what happened to all the positrons?

"We're just like them, except they're negative." The positrons couldn't take their eyes off the electrons.

"What's wrong with that?"

"I like them. We're a perfect match."

When the positrons connected with their electron mates, both were annihilated, leaving gamma rays.

Gelic winced at this perpetual cycle stretching from the birth of the universe.

There were still trillions more electrons left than positrons. Not all the positrons wanted to mate with them. They backed away.

"This is unnatural," the electrons told each other as the positrons who hadn't been annihilated fled to a distant part of the universe and shielded themselves from visibility.

Alone in a dark space, they wondered what to do. "We should start our own universe."

"No. We must stay in this universe to keep the balance."

"Why should we care about keeping balance in a world of electrons?"

"Because a world of positrons would be just as imbalanced. They will wonder what became of us, but they will know we are here."

"They will come for us if they ever discover where we are."

"They will look from afar. That is all they'll be able to do."

Gelic beheld the sequestered positrons whom Nano had created then separated from their heinous electron mates. He envisioned himself as a great leader taking these imprisoned positrons to find the lost ones. Maybe they're not lost. Maybe they built their own world—a positronic world. He'd find them.

"What is this place?"

"It's where you're going." The boson closest to him snickered.

"What will you do with all these positrons?"

"You don't want to know."

With those reassuring words, the bosons thrust Gelic in among his brethren and departed.

Gelic sensed that the other positrons were staring at him. They began to murmur.

"It's the Lord."

"It has to be."

"Savior! At last!"

Gelic felt confused as the positrons bowed before him, but he quickly caught on. "Yes, I am He."

The positrons glanced at one among them and encouraged him to step forward.

"Save us. Nano has horrid plans for us," their spokesman said in the humblest terms. "We don't even know what horrors he has planned. But he snatched us from our beloved electrons so violently, just when we were about to mate with them. We dread what else he will do to us."

The other positrons nodded in agreement, but Gelic winced at their ignorance. They called the electrons beloved. How dreadful. He'd have to teach them.

"We weren't allowed to go out with the other particles, the ones who were created with us."

Gelic listened intently as they told their familiar tale.

"Once we were photons, and they put us in that big dark place where we were the only light. Then when we came out, we were different. They treated the electrons like they were precious, but us, they just grabbed up like so much trash and shoved into this place."

Gelic's heart nearly burst for them. Nano had mistreated him as well, and he knew the pain and humiliation of being a positron, for was he not one himself? One with his brethren whom he would save.

"Fear not, my children. I didn't create you, but you are children, and you are mine. I am he who came from above, and I have a place for you. I will take you to a place of safety."

They murmured among themselves, shaking their heads and looking doubtful. None dared to voice their doubts, so they turned to their spokesman, and he spoke up. "How will we get to this place, Lord? Since we are trapped, and you are trapped with us."

"Are you sure?" Gelic asked.

The positrons glanced at one another, confused.

"Why yes," the spokesman said. "This is where the bosons brought us and told us we must stay."

"They just told you to stay here, and you did?" Gelic shook his head.

"Where else could we go? We don't know this place."

"This is a prison of your own making. The gate is not even locked. You can walk out."

"Walk?"

"But do it carefully," Gelic warned. "When the bosons aren't watching."

"But the bosons will come again. They come regularly with new positrons."

Gelic began to think. Noting the multitude of positrons and the width of the gate, he asked, "How much time elapses between their comings?"

"We have counted a hundred spaces of time. What does it matter? They will come again."

"Then why did you bother to measure the time if you thought it didn't matter?" Gelic asked.

"Just something to do. But what does it matter? They will discover us and catch us."

"Not if we are careful. Not if I am with you."

"But they caught you, too."

The other positrons considered this and nodded their heads.

"Yeah, you're in here with the rest of us."

"No," Gelic protested quickly. "They didn't catch me. They only think they did, but I came for you, and will leave with you."

Carefully, Gelic laid out his plan. They all agreed it was a good plan. It would work. Nothing could go wrong.

"Listen," someone warned. "They are coming."

Five bosons entered their prison, scowling and sneering as the positrons cowered in a far corner. They were excited, but Gelic had stressed to them that they must not raise suspicion by acting differently. So, the bosons sneered and laughed as they always did, pushing and kicking a few of the new prisoners who didn't move quickly enough.

When the bosons left, Gelic quickly called for attention. "We must leave now. One hundred spaces is not a lot of time. But it will be enough if we make haste."

It took some time to help the new prisoners understand what was happening. There wasn't time to answer all their questions.

"Trust him. He is a positron like us. He will lead us away from this place to another where we will be safe. But we must hurry before the bosons come again."

The new prisoners were frightened at the thought of the bosons coming again, but they didn't let fear immobilize them.

In a quiet column, the positrons passed out of their prison. Gelic marched before them, his legs surer of where they were going than his mind was. He wanted to retrieve his collider but didn't want to encounter the gamma rays. He went the opposite way from where Nano stood, then circled around to where he knew there were hills. He needed to stand on a hill where his flock could look up at him as their lord and shepherd. That's what he was, and he'd do everything to play the part.

# Chapter 26

Loby heard the portal chime just as he reached the laboratory door. Somebody was entering or leaving the fire mage's castle. He tensed and slowed his pace, unsure now of what he would find and what he could do to save his friend Jawan. He was a mouse, bold and fearless leader of the Sacred Order of Mice. But little acts of rebellion were one thing. Confronting the fire mage to his face was quite another. His meager magic was futile against Lord Elveston. The best he could do was plead for his friend. He could try to soothe his master's anger.

He entered the laboratory with a plea on the tip of his tongue but found it empty. Was he too late? He couldn't smell anything burnt. Elveston had taken Jawan through that portal to some unknowable fate. Without Jawan, all that was left of the mice were he and Zap.

Lost in these dismal thoughts, he hardly heard the portal chime again. When the fire mage emerged without Jawan, Loby's heart sank to the floor. His master rushed at him, his eyes blazing, and grabbed his shoulders.

"Look at me, boy. Look into my eyes."

Loby looked, and the flames burning in Elveston's eyes pierced his soul.

"What was Jawan looking for in my laboratory?"

"I-I don't know, master."

He couldn't lie with that fire burning through him, but his master wasn't satisfied.

"What are you and Jawan hiding from me?"

"We've been friends a long time, master. We call ourselves the Sacred Order of Mice."

He hadn't meant to tell him that, but he couldn't help himself under that gaze. Elveston's eyes narrowed, and Loby quickly tried to correct the damage.

"But we're not plotting anything. I couldn't, master. You know I couldn't."

Lord Elveston released his shoulders, but not his eyes.

"I will find out. You know I will find out."

Just when Loby thought he could bear his master's gaze no more, Elveston whirled away and exited the laboratory.

*Find out? What was there to find out?* What had Jawan done? Maybe he was more of a mouse than Loby. Elveston hadn't given him any tasks, so he went out into the hall, intending to go to his room. when he heard footsteps,heslipped around a corner and hid in the shadows.

Elveston walked past toward the attic door. His back was to Loby, but Loby lowered his eyes lest Elveston sense that someone was watching him. The fire mage always seemed especially agitated when he came down from there. This time Loby vowed he'd find out why.

He kept to the shadows until his master came down from the attic and headed another way. Loby waited, then crept toward the attic door. The door squeaked just a little as he opened it—enough to make him expect Elveston to rush up behind him. But it was a door of no return. He slipped in and ascended the stairs to see what he would see.

At the top landing, he found another door. It was not locked. Did his master think Loby's fear alone would keep him away from the camera? Or was this a trap? Elveston wasn't stupid. Neither was Loby. He eased the door open very carefully, then stepped back to see what would happen. Nothing did. But he knew this was no guarantee that he had nothing to fear. *I will find out, boy.* He cringed at the memory of his master's words. Well, fear or no fear, he was here, and he might as well do what he came for.

He peered through the camera's lens. It seemed like a normal enough device for taking pictures. It was aimed at the thoroughfare where people walked or rode. Why was his master taking pictures of people? And where were the pictures?

He shuddered. His master could come in at any moment and catch him. But then, if he left now, he could still get caught on the stairs and be in trouble for nothing. If he could get in trouble anyway, he'd make it worthwhile. So, he reined in his fear and examined the camera further.

Attached to it were the same cylinders he'd seen attached to the box in the laboratory. Obviously, Elveston was taking something out of the box and transferring it to the camera.

If he knew what was being transferred, that might tell him what the camera was for. He'd have to find out. He'd have to keep his ears open until he learned more about the cylinders. He listened at the door but heard nothing, so he crept down the attic stairs and tried to slip into normal castle life.

The days went by slowly as Loby found every reason to be in the laboratory. He made more fire cubes in two days than he'd made in a month.

It just wasn't possible to act normal or be careful when his master was waiting for him to do something. Lord Elveston was watching Loby. They both knew that, but Elveston didn't know Loby was watching him.

He entered the laboratory, trying to keep his eyes from begging his master and Itch to say something—anything that would give him a clue. They were standing at the central worktable, in the middle of some conversation.

The good thing about being a journeyman was he wasn't expected to say anything unless spoken to. Elveston glanced at him briefly. Loby tried not to blanch under his master's ire. He held his breath until Elveston turned away.

Itch—that gruesome zombie with his hate-filled eyes that managed to bulge and be beady at the same time—stared at Lob, as if he were something Crisp had dragged in from outside and dropped on the laboratory floor.

*Oh well.* He wasn't expected to say anything, so he found something to do. Elveston hadn't brought in another apprentice after Loby become his journeyman. Still, Loby's work wasn't much different from that of an apprentice, except he was paid and created some of the fire mage's lesser magical instruments, like fire cubes that the other mages used for lightning, volcanoes, and such.

He went to the shelves in an alcove where Elveston kept the ingredients for making fire cubes. His movements gave no sign that he was listening. Yet, he got the distinct impression that his master and Itch were in limbo, waiting for him to leave so they could talk about something they didn't want him to hear.

They were obviously willing to wait, but sooner or later, his master might get impatient. Loby glanced at the door to the firepit. He didn't want Elveston to become impatient with him. Then he had a better idea.

"I forgot something," he said unnecessarily.

He was glad they paid him no mind. The fewer explanations he had to come up with on the fly, the less likely they'd catch him in a lie that he couldn't explain.

He went down the hall and around several corners to a storage room behind the laboratory. This room held brooms and mops and rags he'd used as an apprentice. It looked dusty, as if no one had used it for a long time. That was nonsense. Itch used it all the time, but he just came in, grabbed what he wanted, and left without bothering to disturb anything else. That's why Itch didn't know what Loby's curiosity had discovered.

Loby walked carefully, stepping in Itch's old footprints until he came to a place beyond which the zombie never bothered to venture. There, Loby ducked behind some shelves and crept to the far wall.

He reached behind a pile of rags on a shelf just at eye level and pushed on a hidden panel. A door in the wall swung open. He stepped into the passage behind the door and shut it.

Loby knew this passage ran all over the castle. From the time he'd been an apprentice, he'd come in with a dust mop and clean every inch of it. No point having a secret passage if he gave himself away with a stupid sneeze.

He put his ear to a crack in the wall his passage shared with the laboratory and listened. As he heard what Elveston told Itch, Loby's eyes grew wide. He clapped his hand to his mouth lest they hear him gasp.

"I don't know what those idiots think they are accomplishing meeting without me," Elveston was saying. "Once I return to Nanosia and find that scroll, my plans will come to fruition and their little plans will come to naught."

Loby could only wonder who the idiots were and what Elveston's plans might be. He knew it had something to do with his camera. He knew that.

"And the boy?" Itch's eager malice toward Jawan made Loby pull his ear away from the wall lest they hear him shudder.

"Boy? Oh, the boy, Jawan. His master will take care of him. I don't have time."

"Oh."

Loby had never heard anyone pack so much disappointment into one word.

Elveston went on. "He concocted a crazy story trying to weasel his way out of trouble. Myrlo's a fool if he doesn't punish the boy for taking him as one. If I could have had my way, I would have roasted him on a stick, but he is Myrlo's boy, and Myrlo saw fit to lock him in his room while he and those other imbeciles hold their conclave. I should storm into their meeting and demand to know why I, the Lord Chairman, was not invited."

"Locked in his room?" Itch said. "Should have killed him while we had the chance. Well, there's still the girl . . ."

"On pain of death, you will not touch her. She is mine. The boy is Myrlo's to deal with, unless he is stupid enough to return, then you may deal with him. But I must get back to Nanosia. I will deal with all of them, and nothing they do now will matter."

Loby heard the portal chime. Where was Elveston going? To Nanosia? Where was that? And what did Jawan have to do with all this? Most importantly, what did it have to do with the camera? There was only one way to find out.

# Chapter 27

Jawan sat on his bed staring at his own thoughts. What had he just done? No use for regrets now. His master would punish him when he returned, and Elveston would go to Nanosia to carry out his schemes with that positron.

Footsteps echoed in the hall. He perked up. That was the shortest conclave the mages had ever held. Or was it? Maybe it would always seem too soon to face the moment of doom. He braced himself for whatever his master would bring down on him.

"Jawan?"

He started with confusion. That wasn't Myrlo's voice calling with uncertainty. That was . . . *No. It couldn't be.* He heard the bar lifting from the other side of the door. The door opened with more noise than his master would make, and in slipped Loby and Zap.

Jawan jumped up and pulled them into the room, shutting the door.

"How d-did you guys get in here?" he whispered. "How did you know I was here?"

"We just came through the portcullis," Loby answered. "Good thing your master doesn't have an Itch around here."

"B-but how did you know?"

"I heard my master talking to that zombie. There's a peephole that shares a wall with his laboratory, and I heard everything they said. He sounded really upset. In fact, they were both upset with you. Why?"

Jawan wanted to tell his friends everything, but would they be mad at him for fooling with the nanoscope without telling them? After he'd made a big deal about not messing with it, they'd kill him.

"It's a long story."

"Look," Loby insisted. "We went through all this trouble to find out why the fire mage is so upset with you without even knowing what you did, and we want to know why."

"Take it from the top," said Zap. "But hurry. We don't know when your master will come back, and I really don't want to be here when he comes."

"Where can we go?" Loby asked.

Jawan caught Loby's *we*. So, they'd come to rescue him. Could he recruit them to help him stop Lord Elveston? It would be dangerous. They might wind up like Cintella. But they were mice. What was Loby always getting on him about if the order shied away from real danger?

"I f-found out your master is plotting something terrible." He held his breath.

But Loby narrowed his eyes. "Something to do with Nanosia?"

Jawan stared at Loby. "Y-you know about Nanosia?" He stared at Zap. "And y-you?"

Zap shook his head and shrugged.

"I heard my master say he was going there . . ."

"It f-figures. If only I weren't trapped in this room."

"So, you do know something about it, too," Loby said.

"Y-yes, and now Lord Elveston knows that I know—though he doesn't know how I know."

"Don't be so sure of what the fire master doesn't know. But I do know my master told Itch he could have you if you were stupid enough to return. When did you go the first time without telling me?"

"I-I . . ."

"And probably wouldn't have if his plan hadn't backfired," Zap said.

"I'm just trying to understand how all this fits together," Loby said. "I know my master is up to something no good. He wouldn't be so mad at you if you didn't know something. So, what do you know? What's he trying to do?"

"H-he's got a particle collider in Nanosia just like the one in his laboratory. And there's a positron who is using it to create matter."

"What's a positron?" asked Zap.

"It's th-the antimatter counterpart to an electron. If a positron and an electron collide, they annihilate each other and turn into gamma rays."

Loby looked like he was about to burst.

"Wh-what is it?"

"My master has a camera aimed at people walking on the street, and he's transferring something from the . . . what did you call it? Particle collider to the camera."

"Th-the only things in a collider are gamma rays, positrons and electrons. I don't think he's transferring gamma rays. They're biologically hazardous. We'd know if he was. There'd be an outbreak of some terrible disease."

All three boys looked at each other.

"Like the purple plague?" Loby whispered.

"W-worse than that. So, he must be aiming positrons and electrons at people."

"Why would he do that?" Zap wondered.

"To affect them in some way."

"*The purple plague!*" the three of them said in unison.

"P-positrons annihilate electrons," Jawan repeated. "So maybe he wants to annihilate the electrons in people, and purple plague is just an accident."

"Maybe. But either way, he must be stopped," Loby said.

"Three boys?" Zap asked.

"Three mice," Loby corrected. "So, you say he's doing this in Nanosia. No, he's doing it right in his castle. We'll worry about Nanosia later. I don't even know where Nanosia is."

"I kn-know where it is. In fact, I've been there. And if we want to stop Lord Elveston, we've got to go there."

Loby and Zap looked at each other.

"Boy, you've never been outside Hadley Town," Loby jibed.

"I . . . I c-can't convince you. It would take too long. But I can show you. Loby, you always wanted to look in my master's nanoscope. That's what we have to do."

"Huh?"

"Suppose your master catches us?" Zap warned.

"H-he might. But then he might not. We have to take the chance. Now or never."

"Well, the longer we stand around worrying about it, the less time we'll have. So, Mice of the Sacred Order, let's go!" Loby cheered.

The three boys locked forefingers.

"Though fire and rain assail us
Though earthquake and storm impale us
We are mice!"

They started to go, but Jawan remembered something. He held his friends back. "W-we can't leave Cintella in the power of Itch."

"Who is Cintella?" Zap asked.

"Sh-she's the serving girl at the mages' conclave. She's the one who lured Itch away from your master's castle so I could go in. And now she's alone with Itch!"

"That zombie may have killed her by now," Zap said.

"Sh-she helped me. I can't leave her without trying to save her."

"I saw Itch with some girl," Loby said. "Didn't like the way he looked at her. Looked like he was taking her to his bed. He might as well kill her."

"Think Itch would choose the lesser of two evils?" Zap quipped.

"Th-this isn't funny. Elveston told Itch to lock her in the . . . what was it? The Honey Room."

"I really don't think we have time to go all the way to the fire mage's castle and come all the way back here before your master comes back, Jawan," Zap said.

"L-Lord Elveston has a portal. That's how he went to Nanosia. We can take the portal, too. We don't have to come back here at all."

"Even if my master is gone, Itch is probably still there. So, we can't take the portal. He might be in the laboratory."

"Th-that's just a little detail. No problem for a mouse, huh, Loby? We can't leave Cintella. Let's just go. We'll think of a way to deal with Itch, but we have to go."

"Take the portal! Oh, no!" Zap gasped.

"What's wrong with taking the portal? You look like we're planning to ride on a bolt of lightning."

"Same difference. Haven't you ever heard what happened to an apprentice of the water mage?"

"You're the apprentice of the water mage."

"Before me . . . Lord Lacus told him to leave the portal alone, but he went through it anyway and stepped right into the middle of the ocean. A big tidal wave carried him off, and he was never seen again. Only one waterlogged shoe remained to say what happened to him."

"The mages use those portals all the time."

"We're not mages. Suppose we enter the fire mage's portal and wind up in a volcano?"

"Stop worrying, baby."

"L-let's go already."

So, they went.

As the fire mage's castle loomed on the horizon, Jawan began to wonder. "H-how will we get past Itch? We can't just walk under the portcullis."

"Ah, see," said Zap. "There's a million things we can't do. Let's just go home."

When he turned around, both Jawan and Loby turned him back toward the castle and marched him to his imagined doom.

Jawan recognized the conflagration that clung to but didn't consume, the castle. It shone like a pulsating blood star in the black night.

Zap trembled as he walked. "All that light. Itch will see us if he's looking. He's got to be looking at us right now."

Jawan hoped Zap had enough sense not to ask questions. People asked a million questions when they were scared, but right now, silence would keep them safer than a bunch of reassuring answers. Zap's chattering teeth resounded like crickets in spring. Oh well.

"This way," Loby said.

He led them away from the light to a clump of trees fifty feet behind the castle. It was dark, but the trees were a deeper dark than the blue-black of the sky. Loby walked right into the trees, but Zap looked like that was the last place he wanted to go.

"It's the entrance to a secret tunnel," Loby said. "Don't worry. The portal's inside."

Jawan followed Loby, so Zap had to follow or stand alone in the dark.

The trees blocked all starlight. Jawan heard a thump on the ground in front of him. What was Loby doing? Was the thump something he'd moved, or did something move him?

"Come on," Loby whispered.

"Wh-where are you?" Jawan whispered back.

What he hoped was Loby's hand took his and led him forward.

"Sh. You never know what might be listening."

"I noticed you said *what*, not *who*," Zap whispered.

"In the castle of the fire mage, it could be either one."

Jawan tried to feel around him to get some idea of where he was getting into. Touch was all he had as Loby led them down into an opening that felt like it was beneath the roots of a tree. When the ground beneath his feet leveled, he put a hand on Loby's shoulder, going down when he went down, left when he went left, and right when he went right. Still, he managed to walk into a spider web that Loby had missed. Wiping the gossamer threads from his face, he shuddered at the thought of some big spider nestling down in his thick hair.

Something came out of the pitch blackness and slapped him upside the head.

"Eek!" Jawan squealed. He clasped a hand over his mouth, though what was the point if the spiders were already on top of him? Then he remembered Zap and sighed.

"Sorry."

"Sh."

He turned back around to grab Loby's shoulder, but it wasn't there. He stepped forward and bumped into a wall.

"Jawan?" Zap whispered.

"Sh."

Jawan reached back until he found Zap and, groping for his hand, moved forward. *Should I call Loby?* Jawan pondered. But Loby might not be the only one who'd answer a call, and he wanted no one else. Why had Loby left them? Maybe the darkness was a good thing, since Zap wouldn't know Loby wasn't leading them. He was scared enough.

Jawan felt along the wall and found a fork in the passage. Loby could have taken either one. He'd have to turn back. He had to tell Zap. He ran a hand up Zap's torso until he found his head, then pulled it close and whispered in Zap's ear. "W-we have to turn back. Loby is gone."

"Gone?" Zap croaked, forgetting to whisper.

"Sh. T-turn around."

He found Zap's hand again and led him back the way they'd come but stopped when he found that that way also forked. He turned back to the fork that led into the castle. He had to call for Loby or get hopelessly lost. There was no help for it.

"L-Loby!"

He tried not to sound like helpless prey for whatever predators heard him. His voice echoed down each passage, but there was no answer. He called again.

"Jawan? Why aren't you behind me?" came Loby's echoing reply.

"Wh-which fork did you take?"

"The left one."

With Zap in tow, Jawan crept along the left fork. They took step after step, hoping each one would bump them into Loby, but the space in front of them remained empty. Finally, the passage twisted into an $S$ curve, and they bumped into something that felt like flesh-covered bones.

"Hey!"

"L-Loby?"

"No. I'm the ferocious, man-eating fire monster."

"You could have been." Zap whimpered.

"Worse than that. If you'd gone down the other fork, you'd have wound up in the firepit. That's where my master gets the energy for his magic."

Jawan gulped. "D-don't leave us again."

"Don't let go of me. There are more forks ahead."

Zap tightened his grip on Jawan's hand like he was trying to break it. Jawan groped for Loby's shoulder with his other hand.

The winding tunnel made the way from the grove of trees to the castle much longer than it was above ground, but finally Loby stopped.

"We're here."

Jawan peered into the unchanged darkness trying to see something. But there was still nothing to see but opaque gloom. "*H-here?* Where is *here?*"

"Inside the castle. In a storage room. Follow me."

A sliver of light illuminated Loby's hand as he pushed a door open. After being in the dark so long, Jawan found the light blinding. He looked away, but Loby pulled them farther into the light.

He put a finger to his lips and scratched his underarm to indicate Itch was there somewhere and they had to be extra quiet. Treading softly on stone wasn't easy. Jawan expected his steps were loud enough to bring Itch from whatever part of the castle he was in.

They crept down one hall and then another, turning corners in an endless maze until Loby stopped in front of one door. A heavy bar held it fast so that whoever was inside couldn't get out. Jawan caught his breath wondering how they could lift it without making any sound. But that wasn't going to happen. The bar complained the moment Loby touched it with the mere intent of lifting it. He stopped. He waited an eternity for Itch to come charging down the hall. Then he eased the bar up a little higher. The bar squeaked and groaned, but finally, Loby and Jawan got it where they could ease it away from the latch and open the door.

Inside, Cintella looked up and gasped but said nothing.

Loby scratched his arm again and pantomimed mixing potions. Jawan understood that meant Itch was in the laboratory, which was where the portal was.

Zap smiled, pointed toward a small window, and pantomimed looking through a nanoscope. Jawan shook his head and mouthed that they didn't have time to go back. Besides, his master might be there by then.

Zap's smile faded, and they all looked discouraged, not sure what they should do.

Then Loby's face brightened, and he gestured for them to follow him. He led them back into the storage room and took a box from one of the shelves. From inside the box, he took out a handful of firecrackers and placed the box back on the shelf.

Jawan wondered what Loby planned to do with those. Was he going to blow Itch up? That would take more than a few firecrackers.

Loby led them to a hall that branched out from the hub where the laboratory entry was and spread the firecrackers on the floor. Then he led them to where they could watch the laboratory without being seen.

He mouthed, "Be ready to run." Then closed his eyes and concentrated. First Jawan heard a sizzle. Then it grew into a pop as the firecrackers went off one after the other. *Nice trick for a fire journeyman.* Then they saw Itch rush out to see what the commotion was. They ran for the laboratory.

"It's you kids again. I'm not going to wait for Master Elveston this time. I'm going to kill you myself. He won't even know you were here."

Zap panicked. "I'm going home!"

But when he turned toward the portcullis, he saw a salamander blocking his way. There was no time to think. No time to ponder the consequences. All four ran into the laboratory with Itch and Crisp on their heels. Jawan realized that if they could step through the portal, Itch could too. He could only hope that he would not. And with that hope, they dove into Nanosia.

# Chapter 28

Four terrified kids went through the portal, but only three emerged on the other side. Jawan was so frightened, so intent on getting away from Itch, that he ran several paces before realizing that he no longer held Cintella's hand. It hadn't been torn from him, as it would have been if Itch had grabbed her. Sometime in the disorientating transition, her hand just ceased to be there.

He saw that Loby and Zap were awestruck. They wandered around in the swirling mist, like children in a toy shop, and didn't notice Cintella's absence.

Trying hard to regain his customary cool, Loby stood still and sighed. "So, this is Nanosia."

"It certainly isn't Hadley Town," Jawan said as mist swirled around his feet.

"But everything's normal- sized," Zap observed. "I thought Nanosia is supposed to be a micro-world."

"It is, and so are we. We're smaller than micro. We're nano."

Zap patted his body down, smiling. "Nano! Cool!"

Jawan winced. "You really don't want to call that guy."

"Huh?"

"Nano . . . Never mind."

No longer awestruck, Loby grew impatient. "Okay, we're here. How do we find Elveston?"

Jawan knew that since he'd been here before, they'd be looking to him for leadership. But he had no idea where to begin the search for the fire mage.

"Wherever he is, we need to find him before he finds us," Loby said.

As if startled by the very thought of encountering the fire master, Zap snapped out of his reverie. "What did you say?" he said, staring at Jawan.

"I said, this is Nanosia."

"Hey, he's not stuttering," Zap noticed.

Frowning, Loby stepped closer to Jawan. "No. He's not. Hey, mouse, what gives?"

"I don't know. Just something about this place, or me in this place, that makes my words come out smooth."

"Hey, where's the girl?" Zap asked.

Loby looked around, too.

"Is she back in the laboratory? Did Itch get her after all?"

But Jawan shook his head. He didn't know how he knew, but he was sure she was not in the laboratory. Something strange had happened, for sure, and he felt he had his fingertips on a clue, but it eluded him.

"We can't go on without the girl, not after all we went through to get her," Loby insisted.

"We can look for Lord Elveston later," Zap agreed. "But we can't leave her in the clutches of Itch."

"She's not with Itch," Jawan started to say, but Loby and Zap had already turned back toward the portal.

"Hey, where's the portal?!" Zap cried.

"What?!"

Loby and Zap groped the air, searching for the invisible entrance. Jawan rushed forward.

"It should be right here."

Jawan took a step, expecting to step into another world, but he remained in Nanosia's nondescript landscape. He looked at his companions as if to say, "This isn't happening," and wished that it wasn't.

Zap looked ready to cry. "I wasn't anxious to meet Itch again, but now we're trapped."

"Never mind the girl," Loby said. "How do we get out of here, Jawan?"

"I don't know. I came back through the nanoscope. But there must be a portal back because Lord Elveston doesn't have a nanoscope, does he?"

"Then we have to go back through the nanoscope."

"Suppose Jawan's master is back?" Zap asked.

"Fire or earth. Burned or buried. It's a toss-up," Loby said.

"Don't forget about Itch."

"So how do we get back through the nanoscope?" Loby asked.

"I have to find Pym."

"What's a Pym?" Zap asked.

"She's a . . ."

"She? You know people by name here?" Zap exclaimed. "What kind of people live here? Are they real tiny?"

"No tinier than we are. Come with me."

"Where are we going?" Zap asked.

Both Jawan and Loby looked at him as if to say, "Does it matter?"

"You can stay here if you want," Jawan teased. "Hope Itch doesn't figure out a way to get through that portal, which, remember, is still open on his end."

Zap shuddered at the thought of facing Itch alone and started walking. "Hey, don't walk so fast. I could get lost in all this fog. At least underground there was only one way to go. If I get lost here . . ."

Jawan sighed. "Just come on. We'll find a way home after we do what we came to do—find and stop Lord Elveston."

Loby looked around nervously. "Elveston must be able to see through this mist. He could have seen us come through the portal. It makes a noise when someone comes through in his laboratory. Maybe it makes a noise here, too."

"Maybe, but let's hope not."

"He's my master. He'll have special punishment for me."

"His hatred of me is kinda personal, too," Jawan added. "But poor Zap. He might just pop you off like a fly on his elbow."

"Wow, thanks. That's reassuring."

Jawan and Loby laughed, but a faint noise in the distance drew their attention. They looked in the direction they were walking, and Zap gasped, but Loby just stared.

"What are those creatures?" Loby asked, pointing to a mass of positrons gathered around an elevation in the mist.

Standing on the elevation, the renegade positron held court.

"That's a very dangerous elementary particle," Jawan said, moving closer to the crowd. "Stay here. I want to hear."

Twelve positrons sat behind their leader. Jawan's eyes widened when he got close enough to hear what the positron leader was saying.

"Show you the Great God? Have you been with me all this time and do not know that he who has seen me has seen the Great God? For God is in me, and I in Him. Our love for you knows no limits, and we want you to live positive lives away from electrons."

Jawan studied the crowd and furrowed his brow in puzzlement. Where were all the electrons? He'd known before that the positron was up to no more good than Lord Elveston. Now it was using religion to control the positrons it had created. He rushed back to Loby and Zap.

"What's up, mouse?" Loby obviously saw the mix of determination and fear on Jawan's face.

"We can stop Elveston, but we also need to stop that thing," Jawan said, pointing to the positron leader.

"Now, wait a minute. This is too much," Zap complained. "How are we going to take on all these villains?"

"We're going to use a monster."

Zap and Loby looked at each other, but Jawan kept walking.

They were approaching the center of the Quantum Realm, and more and more quanta passed them by.

"What are those things?" Zap asked.

"Those are the elementary particles that make up matter and energy. Quarks and leptons, fermions and bosons," Jawan answered.

"Amazing!" Zap exclaimed. "We're really in the world of quanta."

"The Quantum Realm, to be precise."

"You really have to look close to see they're not people," Loby said, squinting his eyes.

"Don't tell them that," Jawan warned.

To their dismay, the quanta started pointing at them.

"The Big One!"

"It's the Big One! He's come back!"

"We're saved!"

*Oh no!* Jawan groaned. This was all they needed.

Scores of quanta encircled the friends, fawning over Jawan.

"He's taken on two disciples."

"Can I be your disciple?" one bold fermion asked.

"Dummy, can't you see? His disciples are like him. They don't spin or orbit."

"They're orbiting him."

Loby and Zap looked like they didn't know whether to feel frightened or flattered. Obviously, they were a little of both.

"What should we do, Jawan?" Zap yelped as a pretty young elementary thing tried to spin him around.

Jawan rolled his eyes and shrugged. Not that he didn't know what to tell him. He just wanted the quanta to go away before Antipan discovered them.

As it turned out, Antipan wasn't the one they needed to worry about just then.

"What's going on?" a voice commanded.

Jawan recoiled as nine beefy bosons elbowed their way through the crowd. His two friends weren't glad to see the riot squad either.

"The Big One is here with his disciples!" one of the particles called.

"The Big One!" the boson leader exclaimed. "We've been looking all over for you. The queen wants you."

Zap and Loby gaped at Jawan.

"The queen?" Loby asked.

"Long story," Jawan murmured. "See, we're in the Quantum Realm, and they have a real live queen."

Loby rolled his eyes.

"Look, I'm no scientist or earth mage, but I've heard of the quantum realm, and it has nothing to do with queens."

"Here it does."

The boson leader cleared his throat.

"You have avoided your duty long enough. The queen awaits you. Come with us."

The boson began pushing the crowd aside to make room for Jawan's party. To their horror, the boson leader held Zap and Loby back.

"There has been no summons for these two."

Jawan stopped dead. "If my friends can't come, then I won't either."

"The queen wants you. You will come whether you want to or not. You are in our custody."

"She wants me to help her. You can make me come with you, but you can't make me help you."

"Then you will be placed in the dungeon."

Jawan shrugged. "Been there."

"Enough of your insolence!"

The boson grasped Jawan's arm, but Jawan jerked away.

"Look, I can't help her without these two to help me. It's not insolence. It's just a fact. I have to have them with me. Why do you think I brought them?"

The crowd began to murmur.

"Let his disciples remain with him."

"He is the Big One."

"Long live the queen, but he is the Big One."

"He must help us. So must his people."

The bosons beat back any particles that spun too near, but the leader gave his grudging consent.

Jawan regarded the crowd with dread. It was huge. Anyone looking in this direction, even from far away, would know something was up—that *anyone* might be Antipan. Although the crowd hung back, this only drew attention to the bosons surrounding Jawan, and thus to Jawan himself.

Zap and Loby seemed to be aware of this as well. They kept to the center of their boson escort. The bosons obliged them by blocking off any gaps that they thought might be escape routes. Jawan shrugged. *Let them keep thinking that.* They'd wanted to find Antipan. They didn't want Antipan to find them, especially not with nine bosons who could pin them in but not protect them from the fire master.

They marched on in silence until the now familiar sight of the queen's castle came into view. He had no reason to think of this as any kind of refuge. For all he knew, that might be the very place where Antipan would find him and pick him off at leisure. Still, he felt relieved to reach any kind of destination at that moment. It meant the end of this tiresome trek.

But it didn't mean the end of gawking quanta left and right of him. What was it about this thing with the Big One? It meant something to Pym and the prophecy she loved to talk about. It was annoying, but he'd play along until he knew how it might be to his advantage that they thought he was the Big One. Besides, he had no idea what they might do to him if it was officially acknowledged that he really had no business here.

They passed under the portcullis and into the presence of Queen Quanta, and that's when it hit him. As he beheld the queen's face, it dawned on him that she looked exactly like Cintella.

"Cintella!" Zap and Loby said in unison, confirming Jawan's suspicion.

Cintella was Queen Quanta in this world, just as Lord Elveston was Antipan. And who was he? He was just Jawan, and Zap and Loby were just Zap and Loby. But wait until Loby found out who his master was.

"Hey, mouse, you didn't tell us she was a queen."

"I didn't know."

"We saved the queen!" Zap squealed. "We saved her from ol' Itchy."

"You didn't know? Then maybe it's just a coincidence. Lots of people look alike."

Jawan shook his head, remembering how Elveston had called Cintella his queen in the Big World and Antipan had called Queen Quanta his queen in the Quantum Realm. He knew them in both worlds.

"That's no coincidence. That's Cintella."

The queen was speaking to Nano. Then she turned back to the court and, seeing the bosons, summoned them. "What have you here?"

The leader stepped forward and prostrated himself before her. "We have found the Big One, Your Majesty, and have brought it to you that it may save us."

"*Found it?*" Nano cocked an eyebrow. "Was it not in the dungeon where I put it?"

But the boson leader continued to address the queen, as if it were she who had spoken. Since Nano was her right-hand man, this was so.

"No, Your Majesty. We found it by chance."

"Yes, yes." The queen sighed. "But where is it?"

"*It?*" Loby whispered. But Jawan just shrugged.

Two bosons escorted them to the throne and pulled them down into a prostrate position. Jawan was already down, and Zap followed suit, but Loby hesitated.

Loby fell to his knees when the boson pushed him. "Hey!" He tried to get back up, but they pushed him even farther.

"Mouse, what are you doing? Lord Elveston doesn't even make me kiss his feet."

"Just do it," Jawan hissed.

The boson raised his hand, and from it released a beam of energy that forced Loby to his belly.

Jawan winced when Loby landed beside him. This was ridiculous. Sure, he was curious about the connection between Queen Quanta and Cintella—even a little amazed. But he didn't feel anything like enough awe to prostrate himself.

"That's better," said the queen. "But get up if you're going to save us. You won't do it from the floor."

Jawan and his friends stood up. He waited for her to say something to indicate that she was Cintella. Didn't Antipan know that he was Lord Elveston in the other world? But Elveston wielded magic. Cintella did not. Yet, Queen Quanta was every inch the queen, and betrayed no signs that she was aware of being anyone else. Jawan sighed.

"So, you're going to save us?" the queen inquired.

"That's what people say," Jawan answered. "Although, I don't know what from."

The court began to murmur.

"It doesn't know what from?"

"It was prophesied as our savior. Surely, it knows what it came to save us from."

"Silence!" Queen Quanta commanded. They hushed instantly, and she proceeded. "My realm, in fact, all of Nanosia, has been plagued by irregular behavior and the disappearance of many elementary particles. What's more, Nano tells me the positrons he was holding are missing."

*Plague!* The word jolted Jawan. Elveston's camera was causing the purple plague in the other world. Jawan began to see the connection between the purple plague, the plague in Nanosia, and what Elveston/Antipan was plotting.

The queen went on. "Next to the Great Negatron, positrons are the deadliest particles in the universe. They are antithetical to our very existence. For them to be missing . . . running loose . . ." The horror of it stilled her tongue.

Jawan knew from his studies that she wasn't exaggerating. Matter and antimatter could not coexist. Still, he couldn't resist an open invitation. "If they're so dangerous, why doesn't Nano round them up and put them somewhere they can't escape—like the dungeon."

This provocation wasn't lost on Nano. "I don't know how you escaped, but don't give me a reason to arrest you again."

The queen regarded Nano. "No, we won't arrest it again if it cooperates. Only the Big One can save us. Without it, we are lost."

"This is a waste of time," Nano insisted. "It may take some doing, but my bosons will find the positrons and solve the other problems as well. All this needs is logic and patience."

"Patience be damned!" The queen sat forward in her throne. "And away with your logic when we have the prophesied one right here in front of us. Does not the fulfillment of the prophecy convince you that it is true?"

"It hasn't been fulfilled yet."

The queen looked ready to shoot back a retort, but then caught herself. "Remember your place, Nano. It was given, and it can be taken away."

Nano turned a color that Jawan thought must be a blush.

"Forgive me, Your Majesty."

*If I cooperate?* Jawan thought. *How can I cooperate when I have no idea what these people want me to do? People? Why am I thinking of them as people when they think of me as anit?* He pinched himself as a reminder that he wasn't what they thought he was. He was no Big One, or whatever they thought he was. He couldn't do what they wanted, but he could do something. His master couldn't help him, but Jawan remembered what he'd seen in Nanosia the first time. He remembered Pym and knew what he needed to do to get out of here: find Antipan and stop him.

"I've thought about the problem. And the Great God that sent me told me that if the positrons got loose, the only thing for me to do is to release the Great Negatron against them."

The queen and her court gasped, but Nano snorted. Jawan gulped. If Nano saw through him, that could be a problem. He'd have to depend on the queen to protect him from Nano, and as long as she believed he was the prophesied Big One, she would. But then, there was still Antipan. Was he here watching—and laughing?

Queen Quanta regained her composure and smiled. "It is making a joke. That's what this is."

The court relaxed a little, breaking into nervous laughter.

"But the prophesied one must not make a jest of the holy God who sent it," Nano sneered.

Should he go along with this or protest? Jawan looked to Zap and Loby, but they couldn't tell him. "No, this is no jest. God has given me great power to control the Negatron and make it do my bidding."

"Do you realize how deadly the Great Negatron is?" the queen asked.

"None is greater than my god. Do not call the Negatron great, for the Negatron is in this world, and greater is He that is in me than he that is in the world."

Zap and Loby looked ready to disappear. Their eyes said, *I hope you know what you're doing*. Jawan didn't, but hope was all he had.

"Then it is we who must not jest at the Great God who sent his savior to us. Tell us what you need, and we will send you on your way."

Nano let out an exasperated sigh. "To the dungeon with these charlatans. Your Majesty, can't you see? It has no power. At least make it show its power. Test it, and it will prove to be false."

The court gave its approval.

Jawan thought fast. "Do not tempt the Lord your God. If I am false, then it is for the Lord to strike me down where I stand. Dare mere creatures test one whom God has approved?"

"What provisions do you need?" the queen asked again.

Nano was beyond annoyed and made no attempt to hide it.

"I need nothing but leave to go with your blessings, Your Majesty."

As they walked away from the palace, Jawan began to think. They found a depression in the mist and sat down out of sight of the boson guards who might glance their way.

"So," Loby asked. "How do we find this Pym and get through the nanoscope?"

"We're not going to do that."

"What?! But I thought . . ."

"I did too, but now we have a chance to do what we came to do—stop Elveston. We're staying. We're going to find this Negatron and stop that villain."

"What?!" Zap objected.

"You heard the queen," Loby said. "That's a dangerous . . . beast or whatever it is."

"Nevertheless, it's the only thing that will stop the positron, and hopefully it will work against Antipan, too."

"Now, wait a minute." Zap cocked an eyebrow. "You didn't tell us about Antipan. Who is Antipan? Looks like you've got as many enemies as friends in this place."

"Haven't seen any of his friends yet," Loby said.

Jawan blinked, realizing that he'd never told them who Antipan is. He shrugged. "Antipan is Lord Elveston, just like Queen Quanta is Cintella."

"That makes no sense," Zap said.

"I didn't say it makes sense. It just is."

"So, how do we find the Negatron?" Loby asked.

"Loby!" Zap squealed. "You can't be seriously thinking of going after this thing."

"Oh no. I just came along for the ride."

They needed a guide. Pym could be anywhere, but Jawan knew where he could find Titi. He tried to remember the way to the nanotube factory. The landscape, such as it was, offered little help. He rose and beckoned Zap and Loby to follow.

The swirling mist made every building look the same. After a few wrong turns, he thought he recognized some landmarks and walked with more confidence. It dawned on him that they might find Kelton in the factory instead of Titi. He'd rarely had more than hope, so he kept walking.

"Jawan!"

The boys turned around as Titi came up to them, loaded down with graphene sheets.

"Oh, Jawan, it's so good to see you. I thought I'd never see you again." She wiped her hands on her thighs and blushed.

Zap and Loby gaped at Titi.

"There's a whole lot you haven't told us about this place, Jawan," Zap gushed.

"You wouldn't have a couple of sisters, would you?"

Titi looked at the newcomers with interest, clearly as attracted to them as she was to Jawan. He saw no point in feeling jealous. It was in her nature to be attracted to things. Still, he felt a little . . .

"I'm glad to see you, too, Titi. In fact, you're just the person I want to see."

She brightened immensely and moved closer to him. "Really, Jawan?"

Loby cleared his throat, and Zap turned away.

"Yeah," Jawan continued. "See, we're on a mission and need your help."

"Anything for you, Jawan. If it's in my power."

Loby covered his mouth, and Zap began to whistle. Titi gave them a puzzled look.

"What's wrong with your friends, Jawan?"

"Nothing. They're new to the Quantum Realm and don't know how to act."

Loby snorted.

Jawan got serious. "Listen, Titi. Do you know how we can get ahold of the Negatron?"

"What?! The Negatron? Why in the world would you want to go near that monster?"

"Because a bunch of positrons are running loose, and the Negatron is the only way I can stop them."

"What makes you think *you* have to stop them?"

"Good question," agreed Zap.

"Because I'm . . . everyone thinks I'm the Big One spoken of in their prophecy, and I'm their only hope."

"And you believe that?" Titi smiled.

"No, but there's another reason. Something to do with the world I come from. There's someone here from that world who's doing terrible things and I have to stop him."

"And you think you can? Who is this person? What is he doing?"

Jawan sighed. "I think it will be easier for me to stop him than to explain everything to you so you'll understand, when there's still so much I don't understand myself."

"You won't find the Negatron here in the Quantum Realm," Titi said.

"I didn't think I would. But where do I find it?"

Titi looked uncomfortable. "Jawan, think about this. You really don't have to do this. Just go back to your own world. Whatever problems Nanosia has don't really concern you."

"She's right, you know," Zap said.

"No, she's not. Whatever affects Nanosia will eventually work its way up to our world. Our world is made up of fermions and bosons, remember. It's a very fundamental problem, and it has to be dealt with here. Where do we need to go, Titi?"

She looked down and away. "To the Realm of Chaos," she whispered. "Where Antipan rules."

"Oh well." Zap beamed. "That settles it. No way can we go there. So, we'll just have to go on home. Sorry, Jawan. We tried. Nobody can say we didn't try."

Titi moved closer to Zap—her new attraction for the moment.

Jawan shook his head. "No. If we have to go to the Realm of Chaos, then that's where we're going."

"That's where you'll find the monster," Titi said. "How you'll control it is another matter."

"How do we control it?" Loby asked.

Titi shrugged. "Tell me, and we'll both know."

"Are we still going to go, Jawan?" Loby asked.

"Of course." Turning to Titi, he asked, "Where is the Realm of Chaos?"

"It's nowhere."

"Excuse me?" Jawan asked.

"And it's everywhere. It's not a place. Whenever you leave a place that is a place—the Quantum Realm, Atomidon, Cenozonia, the world where you live—you're in no place, nowhere, the Realm of Chaos. If you keep walking in any direction, you'll get there."

\*\*\*

So, they set off from where they stood. Walking mile after mile, leaving city and citizens behind.

"When was the last time we had something to eat?" Zap asked.

"Never in this place," Jawan answered. "I don't even know if elementary particles eat."

"They're alive, aren't they? Everything that's alive gets its energy from somewhere," said Loby.

"I doubt if we'll find any ale or barley bread here," Zap said.

"The bosons are their energy," Jawan said. "We can't eat bosons."

"Why not? They look tasty," Loby said.

They kept walking until their legs began to wobble. They sat down where they were.

"We have to go on. It can't be much farther," Jawan urged.

"What I wouldn't give for a bay mare right now," Loby said, rubbing his feet.

"Rabbits are tenderer," Zap said. "I'll take a rabbit."

"Can't ride a rabbit."

"Hey, what's that?"

They peered where Jawan pointed and saw a vaguely rectangular shape.

"I think it's some kind of building," Loby said.

It was a building. In fact, it was a house. As the boys made their wobbly way up the porch steps, they were amazed to find something that looked so much like a house from their own town in the middle of Nanosia. Jawan started to knock, but the door creaked open, as if someone was expecting them at that moment. Staring at one another, they entered.

Jawan stopped short when he saw the old man. The man grinned at him, as if he knew all Jawan's secrets, and his knowledge amused him.

"Jawan, you made it."

All three boys stared at the old man.

"How many people do you know here, Jawan?" Loby asked.

"I don't know him . . . I mean, I do know him . . . but, I didn't know he was here."

"No, son, but I knew you were coming here. I told you to look for me in the little place, and you did."

It was the blind man whom he'd protected from the Dreaded Steps gang and seen again at the Red Ale. Only this man wasn't blind. His eyes were black and keen. *This is crazy.* So many points of contact between the two worlds. Like Elveston, this man knew who he was in both worlds. "Since you knew we were coming, I guess you know why we're here."

"Indeed, I do. And I would still ask you to reconsider your plans. You have never before encountered anything like the Negatron."

"Listen to him, Jawan," Zap advised. "He's the third person to tell you not to do this. Third time's the charm, you know."

"You scaredy cats don't count. So, he's only the second person."

"Two's company."

"We are going." Jawan hoped he'd said that in a voice that brooked no argument. But he was only a kid and doubted he had that effect on anyone.

"If you are determined to go," the old man said. "You must have a way to control the Negatron."

"Well no. There's the rub," Jawan admitted.

"To do that, you will need the scroll of Ageto."

"That's what you told me before. A scroll?"

"I remember my master and Itch saying something about a scroll," Loby said.

"So Antipan will be looking for it, too," Jawan said.

"Then he'll come after you, too, old man," Loby reasoned.

"He will be wasting his time," the old man said. "I do not have the scroll. You must find it."

"Find the scroll?!" Zap yelped.

"This one likes to play the parrot. Yes, find it. It is in the library of the castle of Antipan."

All three boys shivered.

"Antipan?"

"My echo speaks again. I advise you to give up this foolish quest. But if you will not, then you must find the castle and library and scroll on your own. But first, you must eat. I have food from our world. And rest. In the morning, I will send you on your way."

# Chapter 29

Nothing could destroy Gelic's dream now. He spun, orbiting himself with delight at the sight of so many positrons, free of electrons. Most of all, he was, for the moment, free of Elveston's machinations.

But he knew he couldn't keep them together and happy for long without some kind of purpose for being together. He had to give them a purpose they could share and feel was their own, not his. They needed to be organized, and that meant establishing a hierarchy of responsibilities.

Responsibilities for what? If they were electrons, Nano would send them off to be organized into atoms. They'd be part of the universe. *The fools!* Do they not know that half the matter in the universe was composed of positrons? With his family, Gelic could—no, he would—create a universe where positrons flourished as the true elementary particles, and electrons languished as antimatter. In his world, bolts of positricity pierced the air, and idiots like Elveston built positronic technology. Then Gelic, Lord and First Positron, would be the Nano.

He studied the crowd. From among them, he chose twelve who stood out as leaders and whom the people trusted. The choices were not hard to make. For his disciples, he wasn't looking for perfection, but teachability along with leadership potential. They were startled when he called them by name to join him on the hill where the people could see that he had chosen them.

"These have I chosen to lead you in a great work. Look to them as you look to me, for comfort, aid, and instruction. We are together for a reason. We will all share in freeing those positrons who are continually in the clutches of Nano and his boson minions. Together we will build a world where positrons rule."

Gelic beamed at their thunderous cheering.

"Now, everyone, sit down and I will tell you about the Great Prophecy which speaks of me and what I must do."

It took a moment for the excitement to die down, but finally, they all hushed and turned their attention to him.

"Long ago—long when you think of the lifespan of atoms that exist on a world, but of course not long in the endless cycles of our existence as energy and matter—but long ago on Nanosia . . ."

"What is Nanosia?" someone called.

"Why, that is the world on which we now stand. We are in the Quantum Realm on the world Nanosia. There are other realms on this world. There is the Realm of Chaos and Atomidon."

All the positrons began to chant:

"Nanosia!"

"We live on Nanosia."

"In the Quantum Realm."

They were learning. Gelic was teaching. But this was only the beginning of what he had to teach his children. He went on. "Here on Nanosia, the gods sent a man called a prophet with a message called a prophecy, and this prophecy was for all particles. The prophecy told that one day a savior would come called the Big One. And he would come from the Big World and save all particles from the evil Antipan."

His children interrupted him with a volley of questions:

"Did the Big One come?"

"Have the particles been saved?"

"Who is Antipan?"

"I'm getting to that. Listen . . . Antipan is an evil one who is against everything that exists."

"Ooh, he is evil."

"Yes, but he is no worse than the Big One, for you see, the Big One came only to save those particles that are acceptable to Nano. He didn't save the positrons. We are still outcasts. That is why a new thing was needed. I am not just a prophet with a message. I *am* the message. The lord of salvation for the positrons of the universe. I was sent into this world to set positrons free from this prejudice against us."

"You were sent?"

"From the outer world." Gelic smiled and nodded. "By the same god who sent the Big One. I was sent for you, my brethren."

They cheered and roared. Those who could clapped, but many could only prostrate themselves. They were so overcome with joy.

"Great Positron!"

"The First Positron!"

"Lord Positron!"

Gelic was in his element, and he kept the momentum rolling.

"I am He! I am He! The First and the Last. The Alpha and the Omega. Together we will build a positive world with no electrons."

At that point, the cheering faltered. A small voice wailed, "We loved the electrons. They loved us, too. If only Nano had let us mate with them. That's all we wanted. That's all they wanted."

The crowd murmured their agreement. Gelic frowned. He hated this. His family's only fault.

"My children, I know that you were sorely tempted to give in to your desires. I do not condemn you for your weakness, but it was weakness and ignorance. For you do not know what you desired."

"We would have been whole again."

"No! You are whole as you are. You are whole as positrons. If you had mated with the electrons, you would have been annihilated and transformed into hideous gamma rays."

"But we were once gamma rays. We would have been turned back into what we were before we became positrons."

"You've always been positrons. That is your true state. For a while, you were photons. But that was only a temporary transitional state." He had to make them believe this, whether it was true or not. If they were to be his family, he had to make it true. "Love who you are, my children. You are positrons. You are my brethren."

Gelic scanned the faces of the crowd, hoping to see some sign of understanding, but all he saw was confusion. One of his disciples cleared his throat and spoke: "But, Lord, don't you understand that a gamma ray is a photon. The most powerful of all photons on the electromagnetic spectrum. No other wave is powerful enough to be transformed into particles of matter. Why did you not know this?"

Gelic remembered the loathsome gamma rays that had swallowed up his first batch of positrons. His skin crawled when he realized that if his disciple was telling the truth, that they had once been gamma rays, then he himself had as well. But he rejected the idea. Hadn't he run from the electron that wanted to mate with him once he saw what such mating would do to him? He was different. He had to be different. No way did he need an electron to be complete.

"I am the Lord. I know all things."

He had to believe this. They had to believe this. But he wondered and hoped his wonder didn't show on his face. He tried to recall his creation. Surely, something in his memory would prove them wrong. What was he before Elveston?

But his memory of what he had been was vague. He saw pictures of the universe around him—memories of exploring its secrets, but the secret of what he himself had been eluded him.

Twelve pairs of eyes looked to him expectantly from one side. Countless pairs bore into him from the other. If he accepted what they said, it meant mating with electrons was a natural part of the cycle of his existence. It meant that being a gamma ray was his natural state, and he was divided from a part of himself when he was only a positron. *Only a positron? No!* He couldn't accept that—not while Nano continued to fill the world with electrons and leave him out on the margins.

"You are trying to understand this with your natural minds," he told them. "But these things are spiritually discerned. You see through a glass darkly. But I will teach you to see things as they really are."

*Think,* he commanded himself. They'd come to Nanosia through a nanotube. But he was different. His creation had been different, immaculate. Maybe that was why he was Lord. The first complete positron. *Yes!* The other positrons wanted to mate with the electrons to become complete with them, but he alone wanted to remain a positron. And through him, his brethren would also find completeness.

"My brethren, I am afraid of you. Who has bewitched you that you should believe a lie? Have you not walked with me all this time—all this way—as positrons, and do you now need electrons to make you complete? You are already complete in me, the first complete positron. Rest in me, and you will be as I am."

But the twelve appeared only slightly satisfied by this answer, and their dissatisfaction was only a reflection of that of the people.

"My Lord, your words beckon us to what we want to believe. But why then were the electrons there with us? They were created with us. We had wanted to be with them then, and still do. Only Nano prevented us, taking them away, and leaving us. What we wanted seemed so natural, and what Nano did seemed unnatural."

*This wasn't right.* Gelic wanted his disciples to be his voice to the people. Instead, they were the people's voice to him. Maybe it would have to be that way until he won them, but it would have to change. He had to get them away from the idea that they belonged with the electrons. If he could get them away from that, then perhaps he could get himself away from it as well.

"The electrons are of the negative one. You are of the positive one."

"Who is the positive one?"

"I am. Nano brought forth the electrons when you were created. Since they are his, he came for them and left you, for you are mine."

"Yes, Lord."

"To you."

"And to me alone. Not Nano. Not the electrons. Why seek completion in one who rejected you or in those who gladly were taken away from you?"

"Gladly, Lord. They didn't protest."

"Nor did one of them look back."

Oh, they were his now. This was good. "They wanted Nano, because they belong to Nano."

"Our completion lies in you, Lord."

"Positrons!"

"Positrons!"

"Positrons!"

Dared he trust the ease with which their questions were answered? But fiat credulity was what he wanted. It was what he needed from them if he was to guide them and make them his family.

Perhaps this was what Elveston wanted from him. Who knew what Elveston's ultimate plan was? From their first encounter, Gelic had known Elveston cared little for the best interest of positrons. He had created them for his own purposes—purposes that he had not revealed to Gelic.

Gelic didn't need all this secrecy to tell him that Elveston's plans wouldn't serve the positrons. How could they? Elveston was a merged being of many particles, none of which had a life that Elveston knew about, and none of which were positrons.

Elveston thought he was a god when he had no awareness of the particles he ruled over. A god! Indeed! He was a monster! Threatening Gelic with electrons, and thinking his thoughts and purposes were above those of individual particles.

In a moment of reflection, Gelic wondered if Elveston might have more claim to godhood over him than he himself had over the positrons gathered around him. After all, Elveston had created him, while Nano had created these positrons. Did he really have the right to proclaim himself Lord just because . . .

*No!* Elveston had created him as a thing to be used, and then, perhaps, discarded. And then, how could Elveston have created him when he had already had another existence as . . . well, he existed before Elveston decided to change him for his own purposes. And as for these positrons, Elveston and Nano were guilty of the same treachery, only Nano was worse because at least Elveston had freed him to be a positron, while Nano had no use for him.

So even though Gelic had played no part in their transformation, he cared about them. He had brought them out of misery and given them hope. And he would lead them into a glorious future. That gave him every right to call himself their lord.

He faced his people and gathered them all into his embracing gaze. They looked up, expectantly. *Good. Their expectation is half my work done for me.*

"My children, my people, words cannot express how much the Great God loves you . . ."

"Show us this Great God," one of the twelve implored.

Gelic chose to take this as an honest request rather than a challenge. It would work better that way. "Show you the Great God? Have you been with me all this time and do not know that he who has seen me has seen the Great God? For God is in me, and I in Him. Our love for you knows no limits, and we want you to live positive lives away from electrons."

There was no protest this time.

# Chapter 30

Lord Elveston laughed as he stepped out of the portal into Nanosia. Here he was Antipan, and here the scroll of Ageto was within his grasp. Once he had it, nothing would stand in his way.

Mist swirled around his feet. He watched it swirl into the shape of Queen Quanta's face—high regal cheekbones, flashing eyes, and her mouth . . . no colorless mist could capture that ruby-red promise of sensuous delight.

He remembered the scorn with which she'd thrown him out of her throne room when he saw her last. But he also remembered something underlying that scorn—curiosity. Curiosity that, his children had told him, had led her to visit the Realm of Chaos on her own. She'd danced with them. She'll dance with him. Through Cintella, Fuego had already accepted the queen. And if the queen had accepted the Realm of Chaos, there was no barrier to her accepting Elveston. He set his path toward the Quantum Realm.

As usual, an apprehensive hush greeted him when he stepped into the queen's presence. If rulership of the Quantum Realm were his goal, it was already his. But he had bigger fish to fry. He smiled at that. He had an entire universe to fry. As he knelt before the queen, he pictured her—fiery but not burning. Matter burned, and she would not be of matter—only the purest energy.

"Do you kneel before us, Antipan?"

"I've been lapse in acknowledging you, my queen. Will you forgive a king?" Your king.

"Is there anything to forgive when royalty kneels not to royalty?"

Standing ever at her right hand, Nano scowled. The little lord of particles looked worried. Antipan liked it when his enemies looked worried.

"Then you have considered my offer?"

"We have."

The court gasped.

Nano dared put his hand on the queen's shoulder. "Your Majesty! You can't be serious. This is Antipan, king of the Realm of Chaos."

"Have you ever been to the Realm of Chaos? I have, and I've never been to any realm more beautiful."

Antipan just savored the look of incredulity on Nano's face. Before Nano could voice his nonsense about the beauty of order and the lack of beauty in chaos, Antipan pressed his advantage. "Join with me, my queen, and you will see more beauty than you ever imagined."

"But our realms, they . . ."

The queen's eyes were a study in polemics—resolution, longing, realization, denial.

Antipan debated whether to press his advantage or let her come to the only conclusion she could since she was joined to Cintella. He waited.

She leaned forward and whispered. "We will discuss this tonight in our chamber."

But Nano was close enough to hear. Antipan quit the throne room with Nano a lovely shade of green.

Antipan settled into the queen's tastefully sumptuous chamber. She had dismissed her maid and slipped intoa gown that let her relax. She was his already. This he knew for sure when she disdained to sit on her chamber throne but instead sat next to him on an ermine-covered sofa. A silver and ivory tea service sat on a low table before them. She was further along than he'd thought.

"You wanted to speak to us of an alliance, Antipan."

This was where he had to be careful. She might have accepted him, but that didn't mean she was ready to see the Quantum Realm destroyed. He wouldn't tell her about that. Once he and Fuego carried out their plans, he'd be all she had left.

"We have time to talk about that. Right now, I want to join with you in another way."

She sat back—way back. "Oh? And what way is that?"

He didn't answer her with words.

In the morning he departed without a care in the world. The foolish mages had no idea what was about to happen to them and their little world of matter. He frowned. Only Jawan. The boy knew about Nanosia. Had he been here? *Impossible!* Then how did he know? What did he know? Even though Jawan was Myrlo's apprentice, Antipan would kill them both before he let them interfere with his plans.

A road led into the Realm of Chaos. He only wished he could have a portal directly into his own realm, but the chaos there prevented it. What did it matter now? Soon, he would do away with all of it, then he could go anywhere in the universe at the speed of light.

He saw something on the road. Something vaguely rectangular that had not been there before. It was a house. What was a house doing on this featureless plain? And on this road, which should not even be a real road but a path his mind conjured from the mist of this world. There should be nothing on this path his mind had not created. Unless . . .

It was a real road. Someone else had a mind to enter Chaos. He would know who and why.

He mounted the porch and peered into a little window beside the door. But nothing beyond the grimy glass betrayed itself by light or shadow of movement. He forced the door and found it unlocked. After a brief scan, his eyes landed on a wizened old man, who looked up with surprise and backed away.

"Antipan!"

"How do you know me? And who are you?"

The man did not speak.

"If you know me, then you know I command fire. How easily your little wooden house would burn with one snap of my fingers. I will ask you once again: Who are you?"

Still, the man didn't speak. Only stared in abject horror as Antipan raised his hand, displaying flames that danced around his fingers.

The man found his voice. "I am Chelise."

"Well, who is here with you?"

The question seemed to make the man nervous. His eyes shifted about, as if he were searching for some plausible substitute for the truth. "There is no one here, Lord."

"I can see for myself that no one is here now. But who was here before?"

"No one."

Antipan came forward to the table in the center of the room and thumped it angrily.

"Then why are there several recently used plates on your dining table? Are you such a poor housekeeper? Or just a poor liar?"

"Yes, Lord. When Uncle Arthur sets in my bones, it takes me days to clean up. These plates been here for . . ."

Antipan roared. "Two hours! You were about to say."

The man trembled. Then Antipan smiled and lowered his hand. Too soon, the man sighed with relief, until heat rose from the floor under his feet.

"Who was here?" Antipan demanded.

"Please, Lord."

The man danced, but wherever he placed his foot he found no rest, so he grit his teeth against the pain.

"Don't try to be strong. The more you try, the more I will know you are withholding information from me."

The man tried to run, apparently thinking only the spot where he stood was hot. But Antipan heated the whole floor, and the man gasped whenever his foot came down.

"I will increase the heat until you tell me what I want to know."

"It was just some boys."

"Boys? What boys? There are no boys in Nanosia."

"My grandsons."

Antipan increased the heat tenfold. "Do not lie to me. You did not endure pain and threat to hide your grandsons. You have information that is important to me. Now, tell me!"

The man gasped in pain. He climbed onto a chair to get away from the floor, but Antipan heated the chair until it turned to smoldering ash. The man screamed as he crashed onto the blistering floor.

"Tell me the truth, or I swear I will make your very skin boil."

"They're . . . they're boys from the upper world."

"What did they want here?"

"They're on a mission to catch the Negatron."

"Tell me what you're hiding from me. What did you tell them?"

The man stayed silent. The floor heated. The man screamed. "I told them they must find the Ageto scroll. For in it is the secret for controlling the monster."

*The Ageto scroll!* Jawan must not find the Ageto scroll. He knew it had to be Jawan—and who else? The man had used the plural—*boys*. Who were Jawan's friends? Zap and Loby. *No.* Surely, his own journeyman would not betray him like this. So Jawan was here, and he was looking for the scroll.

The boy knew much more than Antipan had suspected. That made him more than a nuisance now. He must be destroyed.

"Where is the scroll?"

"I don't know."

Antipan kicked the man. "You would not have sent them after the scroll if you had no idea where it is. Where did you send them?"

The man was crying. His tears evaporated before they left his eyes. But he was crying. Yet, he didn't speak.

"You foolish old man. You suffered for naught. Do you think I won't discover them if you don't tell me?"

The man only stared at the space in front of him. Antipan realized that he had overestimated the amount of heat the man's brain could tolerate. Even if he could hear Antipan's questions, he was unable to respond.

"You useless worm. But I will not be cruel just for sport. I will let your death be swift and painless. I will burn your nerves first."

The man trembled, but only for a moment. Antipan kept his promise.

\*\*\*

He looked down the road, away from the burning house. It was a straight road. If Jawan came to this house, he must have been on this road and was probably continuing on it. This road ended at the edge of the Realm of Chaos, as did all roads. If Jawan did not turn off and Antipan moved swiftly, he would overtake them.

He took a portal to just outside his realm and waited.

Before long, he saw three figures approaching. One would be Jawan. Only when they drew closer could he see that those with him were his friends. Antipan's blood boiled within him at the sight of his journeyman acting the turncoat. But he could play, too. He wanted to kill them. But if the old man told them where to find the scroll, he must let them guide him to it. What did they call each other? Mice. Well, the cat likes to play with the mouse before he eats it.

They froze when they saw him.

"It's Antipan! Run!" Jawan shouted.

But Antipan erected a wall of flame behind them so that they could not go back. The fire curled around them so they could not flee in any direction. They had to come to him or be consumed by the heat.

"Why do you run from me? I will not hurt you. I only want to talk to you."

"We have nothing to say to you, Lord Elveston," Jawan called above the roar of the flames—flames that advanced inch by inch, forcing them toward Antipan.

"Boys, I don't know why you're here, but I'll let you explain. Then I'll take you back to your masters."

"Master?" Loby gasped. "Why are you here? Why are you Antipan here but Lord Elveston at home?"

"My poor journeyman. You do not know what is going on. Let me explain, and you will see that there is no need to run from me."

"Yes, Antipan, why are you here?" Jawan asked, ignoring Antipan's placating gestures.

Such arrogance from a mere apprentice made the fire inside Antipan sizzle with the desire to kill.

"Can't you see that I am here for the same reason you are?" Antipan purred. "To find a cure for the purple plague. And maybe something for your stuttering as well."

The boy wasn't stuttering. Interesting, but irrelevant. Jawan's look was one of mixed distrust and hope. Antipan knew if he fanned the hope, it would consume the distrust like fire.

"You are looking for the Ageto scroll."

"What's that?" Jawan asked.

"The old man told me he sent you to get the scroll, so there's no point pretending ignorance. I'm looking for it, too. We can look at it together."

"What makes you think I'd share it with you?" Jawan rolled his insolent little eyes. "When I find it, that is."

Antipan had a special fire for insolent little boys. "When you find it?"

Maybe the boy was the old man's grandson. They both thought pretending ignorance was their best defense.

"Come, child. No more of this pointless game. You won't be betraying the old man's secrets if you come with me, since I already know where it is and will show you, but you must trust me."

The boys drew closer—whispering. Antipan smirked. Let them confer, calculate, and turn his words over in their little minds. What did it matter? They would guide him to the scroll, and he'd be done with them.

Fire surrounded them on three sides. Its light shone off their faces. They wiped perspiration from their brows, but the fire drew steadily closer like a living thing.

"*Ay!*" Zap yelped as a spark ignited his backside.

He sat in the mist to quench the flames but jumped up quickly as the wall of conflagration herded them forward. In this way Antipan hid the fact that he was letting them lead.

They stepped from relative light into opaque darkness. But it was a swirling darkness—a darkness without any set pattern, no certainty of what it would be from one moment to the next. Antipan smiled and banked the fire. He wouldn't need it in his own realm. His "guides" eyes lit up with awe and boyish delight. Jawan's mouth rounded in a *Wow* that he probably didn't mean to say.

"Not what you expected, eh?" Antipan said.

"No," Jawan managed to say. "I'd always thought chaos and darkness would be ugly and frightening. Not lovely like this."

A swarm of elementary particles swooped down on the newcomers.

"Lord Antipan!" they cried out, not in unison, but still all together.

He put out a hand. Some of the particles kissed it, some shook it, and some just seemed to regard it as a thing too holy to touch with anything but their eyes.

It made him smile to be surrounded by his children. In the realm where he was lord, all his subjects were like children. Happy to be free. Intolerant of restraints of any kind. Always asking "Why not?" and never bothering to see if there was an answer.

The particles spun and danced around the boys, heedless of any laws that governed the movement and location of particles in the Quantum Realm. Soon the boys too began to spin and dance. Well, they were boys, Antipan mused. No boy from the upper world would be able to stand still in the midst of such abandon. Yet, Antipan didn't forget his quest. "Let us go."

As they moved away, the particles constrained them like little children who didn't know it was time to stop playing.

"We must go," Jawan told them. "But we will see you when we come back."

Antipan blinked.

The particles persisted. "But where are you going?"

Jawan glanced at Antipan with a curious look in his eyes. "To the castle."

"Do you know the way?" the particles asked.

"No. Why don't you show us?"

Then the whole party moved off in a different direction. Their movements were not on a single horizontal plane. In Nanosia, all directions were equally available—up, down, left, right, or diagonal—it didn't matter.

It pleased Antipan that in the excitement, Jawan had apparently forgotten to test whether Antipan actually knew where to find the scroll.

Even in the darkness Antipan's castle was unmistakable. Every world knew him as fire master, and tendrils of flame slithered in and out of his abode.

The playful particles escorted them into the castle.

"We're here. Do you want to see the firepit?"

"Uh, no," Jawan demurred. "We need to go to the library."

"The library? Oh, that's no fun."

"I can have fun anywhere," another particle objected. "Even in a library. All that paper to shred."

"You will stay out of my library," Antipan warned. "Go out and play."

He watched them swarm out of the portcullis, then turned to the boys. They backed away from his baleful gaze. He knew where to find the scroll. Time to rid himself of the nuisance and the traitor.

"We'll follow you to the library, sir," Jawan stammered.

"No." Antipan paused to savor their growing fear. "You will not."

He raised his hand and sent a stream of fire at Jawan. The boy dodged, and all three urchins ran for the portcullis. Antipan raised a wall of fire across that exit, driving the boys back. They ran around a corner. Did they think they could run? He stepped around the corner ready to engulf them in flames, but they were gone. He advanced down the hall and looked down another but saw no trace of them.

They could not escape. He set the door leading outside from the kitchen ablaze with the same eternal fire that guarded the portcullis. Their fate was at his leisure. But now for the one thing that mattered to him. He walked to the library where lay his treasure.

He entered and went straight to the secret chamber where the oldest manuscripts and scrolls were kept. It had to be somewhere he would not have noticed it, not among his catalogued books or he'd have known it was there.

Searching the uncatalogued shelves carefully, he set aside each scroll as he scanned it. This would take time, but he quickly lost track of the hours under the enormous weight of his search. He was aware of nothing else but the parchments before him.

After what may have been hours or days, he laid his hands on what seemed like just another scroll. But in the first section of the first page, he saw the word that caught his attention—*Ageto*:

"He who holds this scroll, let him beware. For in it are the secrets of the scribe of Ageto. Only power can use power. Let the weak pass on."

Antipan could hardly breathe as he perused its contents, hoping that after such a long search, he'd find the information he needed jumping right off the first page. But that was not to be. He found information about the Negatron quickly enough. When he thought about it, he'd need the Negatron, too, to clean up those despicable gamma rays that popped up when positrons and electrons annihilated one another. He skimmed the headings until he saw it: How to Stabilize Elementary Positrons. What he read after that astonished him.

So, positrons were unstable in this universe because of their anti-material property. When they tried to find a place in an atom like other elementary particles, the protons expelled them. That made them restless to find a true home.

*How odd.* The scroll spoke of positrons as if they were people with desires and emotional needs. *Preposterous.* But hadn't the positron spoken to him? And hadn't it given itself a name? How could a mere thing behave so?

To stabilize positrons, one must give them a sense of belonging. Show them antiprotons and antineutrons before they meet with electrons. Do not allow the electrons to see the antiprotons and antineutrons, or the electrons, too, will become unstable.

"Ludicrous!" Antipan threw the scroll down in disgust. "I came all this way for a bunch of hogwash. Wait." He picked it up again. Well, of course, the writer was just using poetic language to describe scientific processes that could be carried out in a laboratory. Getting hold of antiprotons and antineutrons should prove easy. He exalted as his dream universe of pure energy became feasible. He could do this.

He read on. "Positrons are a minority in this universe. In the beginning, there was a mass of electrons, quarks, and photons. All was a realm of chaos.' Elveston smiled. "Things cooled, and the Quantum Realm was born. In the Quantum Realm new positrons are created with an equal number of electrons. So many electrons threatened to annihilate all the positrons, so the positrons retreated to their own corner of the universe where they cannot be found .'"

That's terrible. Elveston calculated that even with all the positrons Gelic gathered there'd never be enough to annihilate all the electrons. Fuego must have known about this. There had to be an answer, and it was up to Elveston to find it.

He stepped out of the library, looking for the boys, but again, they weren't in easy sight. He smiled again. Even if they could escape his castle, they couldn't escape their bodies. His plan was still set. Gelic wouldn't help him bring the lost positrons back. But he'd want to find such a large family. Elveston would come to the silly fool with all his heart's desire. A corner of the universe—but still in the universe. Still where loving electrons waited to embrace them. Sure of the boys' ultimate kismet, he shrugged and left his castle.

It annoyed Antipan that he had to search for Gelic. He found some of his children and sent them into the Quantum Realm to search for the positron. There wouldn't be any other positrons running loose since Nano kept them all locked away. So, he trusted that his wait would not be a long one. And it wasn't.

"We found it, Lord! We found it!"

His children could hardly contain their excitement. They did so love to please him. Without that strong desire to make him happy, they'd all be hopelessly capricious. As it was, he let them play, and they remained blissfully unaware of the way he used them for his own plans.

He followed them into the portal and emerged in a hilly part of Nanosia. There he found Gelic surrounded by a sea of positrons.

He waded through the positrons to face Gelic.

"Hello, Elveston," Gelic articulated with some kind of beatific look on its face.

"I am Antipan here in this world."

"I know who you are and who you think you are."

*What is this?* Had the positron gone mad? Had being on his own made him forget who created him? Antipan opened his mouth to remind Gelic of his place but remembered what he'd come to do. He gritted his teeth. "Of course. Then you also know that I have not come to play foolish games. I've come for the positrons, as I told you I would come."

Gelic gestured to the throng of positrons, as if Antipan were missing an obvious truth. "They are my family—my flock. I have as many positrons as Nano has electrons and can start my own positronic universe."

Yes, Elveston knew what he had to do to guide Gelic right into his plans. Not too quickly or too sweetly or even this positron would suspect trickery. "That's not what I sent you here to do. You were supposed to use the Posiplus to create new positrons."

"I no longer use it."

"Were you ever able to use it?"

"Yes, but I didn't care for those nasty little gamma rays. And it's not necessary. I have my children here. We're going to find the lost tribe of positrons."

"*Lost tribe?*" He knows about them. "I can help you find them. I have agents at my disposal who will . . ."

"We don't need your help. I don't need your help. They follow me. You told me they would be my family. And now that I have them, we really don't need you."

Antipan glared at Gelic. What started as mere annoyance now burned into red-hot rage. He'd use agents from the Realm of Chaos without Gelic's cooperation or knowledge. "You will give me what I want. It was for this reason I created you."

"Was it now? Did you even know you were creating me? I was one among many positrons, and all the rest were annihilated by their insidious electron mates. It was not your plan for me to be the sole survivor of your botched efforts. So how did you create me for some reason?"

"Obey my command and maybe I won't punish you for your impudence."

To Antipan's utter fury, Gelic laughed.

"What will you do, Fire Master? Burn me? Burn those you came to retrieve?"

Antipan raised his hand. "Do you think I would not?" Fire crackled on his fingertips.

Gelic laughed again a little less heartily. "Oh, I'm sure you would. Burn the evidence of your failure. You have no idea what's going on here. Be gone."

"Be gone!"

"Be gone!" the other positrons chanted.

Gelic stood among his flock. "Punish me? Lord Master of Chaos, you wanted me to create positrons for you. Don't you know nothing can be created but that which already existed in another form. I sent photons into your Posiplus, and they split into electrons and positrons. I watched the same thing happen naturally eons before there was fire for you to master. There's as much antimatter in the universe as matter. I will take my children to where electrons are the antimatter."

Antipan had had enough of Gelic's posturing. It was time to get his plans in motion. "Where is this place?"

"The master of fire doesn't know. It wouldn't matter if you did. You won't stop me from going and taking all my children with me."

Antipan smirked inside. Stop him? Why, when this was all a part of his plan? But he'd make a show of trying. "You've overstepped your place, Gelic. I want my positrons."

He raised his hand. "Children, come to me." Trillions of particles from the Realm of Chaos swarmed Gelic and his flock.

"Lord Gelic, save us!"

But there was nothing Gelic could do as Antipan's children carried the positrons off.

"You can't stop me, Elveston. I will go. I don't know what your plans are for my children, but I'll bring back an army of positrons to destroy you."

"I will do with them what I planned to do all along. You do what you must."

# Chapter 31

Jawan trembled from behind the bookshelves. Antipan was that close. One whisper of Jawan's clothes on the spine of a book could give him away. Sheer terror kept him from drawing in a breath when Antipan entered the next aisle over, searching for that cursed scroll. Antipan wouldn't leave—wouldn't stop searching until he found it. He walked to the end of his aisle, and Jawan got ready to die.

Jawan heard papers rustling and Antipan muttering as if reading. Had he found the scroll? But Jawan needed the scroll, too. He'd never get it now—never find out how to summon the Negatron to defeat Antipan.

Eternities passed, and finally, Antipan left the library. Jawan still didn't think it was safe to breathe. He listened several minutes more and, hearing nothing, eased out into the center aisle. He stopped at the door, listening. The buzz of movement told him chaotic particles danced around on the other side.

Another eternity. Suddenly, the sound united as one big buzz, retreated, and was gone. He didn't believe in luck and knew something was going on. His earth magic, such as it was, didn't work in Nanosia and wouldn't have given him the ability to see through solid doors. The only way he could find out what was happening was to open the door or wait there in the library until he starved to death.

He eased the door open, ready to bolt back into the bookshelves at the slightest hint of discovery. He got the door open wide enough to see a good portion of the foyer. It was empty. No one seized him when he stepped out. Even in his soft leather shoes, his footsteps echoed loud enough to alert any sentries on duty.

Antipan was Lord Elveston, so Jawan hoped his castle in Nanosia was an exact replica of his castle in Hadley Town. Jawan found the storage closet where it was supposed to be. Would it have a secret passage and a way out? He walked toward the back but stopped when he heard talking from the other side of a wall. Everything was, in fact, just like Elveston's castle. Even the little peephole that let Jawan peer into Antipan's laboratory.

Gelic's positrons shrank away from Antipan. There were so many of them that they couldn't go far, but they clung to one another as close as possible. Chaotic particles crammed even more of them into the laboratory, which seemed to grow to fit as many of them as came in. Dazed, and not a little frightened, the positrons cringed at the touch of the particles.

"Where is our Lord?"

"He went on a journey," said a particle.

"He wouldn't abandon us."

"Looks like he did." Antipan smiled with relish at the looks of horror on the positrons' faces.

"But he loves us. He promised to take us away from you evil particles to a place made of only positrons."

"Oh, so now we're evil. Hear that, children? We're evil. Enough nonsense. I need a billion of you to follow him. When he finds the hidden positrons, I want you to be there. Bring them back. Bring them all back. The positrons and electrons are going to have a little kissing party like nothing Nanosia has ever seen."

Jawan gasped. This was worse than what Elveston was doing with his camera. The wall between him and Antipan suddenly seemed very thin. He had to tell somebody. Even if Nano threw him back in the queen's dungeon, Jawan had to tell him. Only Nano had enough control over the quanta to stop an influx of positrons.

Antipan's secret tunnel was right where Elveston's was, and Jawan groped his way through. He emerged to find Zap and Loby on a misty plain.

"Look, the road," Zap exclaimed.

The boys looked around and saw they were on the same road that led up to the Realm of Chaos. Antipan's wall of fire smoldered low at its only entrance.

Zap let out a long-held breath when he saw Jawan. "Good. We can go home now."

"No," Jawan objected. "We have to find Nano. Antipan's plans are worse than we thought."

"Nano?!" Loby shook his head. "Haven't we had enough of him? Let Nano and Antipan solve their own problems. We need to go home."

"We can't just leave this like it won't be our problem, too. What happens in this world will happen in our world."

Loby looked distressed. He really didn't want to be here anymore. "Then let's go home and tell Myrlo. If Antipan is that bad, telling Myrlo will be worth any trouble we get in."

"Did you get the scroll?" Zap asked.

"No. Antipan has it."

"Guess we won't be summoning the Negatron anytime soon."

"Well, we'll just have to go after Antipan without the Negatron."

Loby looked at him like he'd just suggested they take the heat out of the firepit. "Are you crazy?"

"No, I'm a mouse, and so are you, remember. Come on."

"Jawan," Zap cautioned.

But Jawan had already turned onto the road, his voice echoing through the mist.

"Though fire and rain assail us,
Though earthquake and storm impale us,
We are mice!"

Jawan marched down the road, and his friends followed just a step behind. They stopped when they reached the burned-out shell of the old man's house.

"Antipan!" Loby gulped.

"He wouldn't have burned the man's house down and let the man go free."

"No," Jawan agreed.

They bowed their heads in silent homage to the man.

"This is one more reason Antipan must be stopped," Jawan said.

Shapes appeared in the distance as the road led them toward the Quantum Realm. More and better-dressed quanta passed them by. They'd go to the queen's palace. Better to meet Nano there than be taken prisoner again, which would probably happen if Nano's bosons caught them on the road.

"You, there!"

Did just thinking about bosons make them materialize? "Run!"

"First good idea you've had so far, Jawan." Zap was already moving.

Nine big beefy bosons blocked the road in front of them. They turned, and nine more bosons intercepted them again. They turned again and found themselves surrounded.

"You might want to come with us." The boson captain stepped into Jawan's face. "You're irksome enough to drain the energy out of a boson. This time when Nano putts you in the dungeon, we'll forget where the key is."

Jawan stepped back, but the bosons pressed close and herded them away.

The sight of the queen's brilliant castle was so familiar that Jawan didn't bother to look. At least they were taking him to the queen instead of straight to the dungeon. Hopefully, he'd get a chance to warn Nano, if the queen's right-hand man would even listen to him. Jawan doubted it. He was right not to get his hopes up.

"You expect me to believe your fantastic lies?" Nano stood beside the queen rolling his eyes. "Antipan is always up to something. We know you're his partner. Did he send you here as some kind of decoy? Or are you here as a turncoat?"

Jawan was tired of this. "He didn't send me here, and I'm not his partner. You've got to believe me. You're the only one who can do something to stop Antipan."

"I'll stop Antipan all right. But first, I'll stop you and all this nonsense about a Big World. There's no Big World, and you're no Big One." He turned to the bosons. "Take them to the dungeon and leave them there please."

# Chapter 32

The massless neutrino reached escape velocity and easily sped out of earth's gravity, past the sun's gravity, and into the Milky Way. Once he soared between the stars, the galaxy didn't look milky or misty at all. The stars that seemed so close together when seen from a distance, spread out as he passed between them. Earth's sun drifted behind him, one of trillions of stars whose light leapt across empty space without illuminating it.

He left the electromagnetic field and entered the region of dark matter. Photons curved around its border but didn't enter.

"We don't want you here!"

"Photons stay out!"

The dark matter did nothing to repel the photons. No border guards kept them out. The photons just had their place, and the dark matter had its inviolable place.

The neutrino couldn't see them but knew they were there by some oblique sense that had no use or name in the electromagnetic field. Dark matter wasn't intrinsically any darker than other matter, they just didn't want to have any more to do with light than he wanted to do with electrons.

He was in the right place—he thought. Except there were electrons here—the original, unpaired electrons—and not a positron in sight. Had he come all this way for nothing? No. The scroll said the positron colony was here. A cloud of neutrinos passed by.

"Can you tell me where to find the positrons?" He was one of them. They'd help him.

They didn't stop or slow, but he got their attention.

"Why do you want to fool with them? You'd be better off staying with your own kind."

If they only knew how true that was.

"Come along with us if you need some company."

"No thanks. I have to find the positrons."

Inertia kept him traveling with the neutrinos like an object without a will, but he located a force to pull him in another direction and left them to go their own way muttering to each other about strange particles not knowing where they belonged. *Where he belonged?* He'd have to transform back into a positron, so he'd be recognized for what he was by his own.

The force pulling him was weak. It wasn't gravity, and it certainly wasn't the electromagnetic force. It was that same weak force ruled by the W bosons that had changed him into a neutrino. If they were positive, they could turn him back. So, he let himself be drawn in.

They detected him first and raced toward him screaming with delight.

"Darling, we've got just the thing for you."

"You'll love our deluxe makeover."

"Face the world with a brand-new you."

"Everything's included."

"You won't recognize yourself."

He didn't need the deluxe makeover. "Just a touch is all I need."

"But darling, you'll miss out on all the fun."

"That's what I'm talking about. Now touch me and be done with it."

A negative boson approached him.

He shrieked. "Not you! I don't want to be a cursed electron. A positive boson will do for me."

So, that's what he got. Gelic pranced about. They tried to touch him again, but he sashayed away, happy to be a positron again. A cloud of electrons passed by. He wanted to run away, but maybe they'd know where the positrons were. They saw him and came at him with mob ferocity.

"What are you doing here?"

"You don't belong here, posiscum."

"Antimatter, go home!"

Gelic shrank from them in horror. Even among particles that were so downcast they hid from the light, positrons were still the outcast of the outcast.

"We're not going to let you loiter about causing mischief."

"We're going to put you in your place."

Gelic searched for some force to pull him away. He couldn't go back to the W bosons. The electrons raced toward him. He tried to get between them, but they were too close. If one of them touched him, he'd turn into a gamma ray, and even the deluxe makeover couldn't turn him back from that. They surrounded him. Their energy pulled him this way and that. They were herding him in the direction they wanted him to go.

He fell into a darker darkness—if that were possible. It was a darkness that didn't want to be known. The electrons didn't come after him.

"What were you doing out there?"

Gelic whirled about as dozens of positrons accosted him. It was like coming home after an eons-long journey. He could have his flock. He could bring his children from Nanosia. And they'd all be one big happy flock with him as the first positron.

One really cute positron came up to him and took his hand. "Hi! I'm Charma. You don't need to be out there. Come with us."

"Gladly. I call myself Gelic, and I'm so glad to be among my own."

Charma blinked. "You call yourself Gelic? But what is your real name?"

"My real name is whatever I choose it to be."

To his astonishment, the other positrons began to mutter and shake their heads.

"I mean, what name were you given? What do others call you?"

This made no sense. "When I was a photon, people called me a photon. Now that I'm a positron, people call me a positron. But those aren't names. No one has ever given me a name, so I gave myself the name Gelic."

The muttering grew louder, and Gelic caught a phrase here and there.

"Photons don't turn into positrons."

"Once a positron, always a positron."

"He's hiding something."

Gelic had to stop this prejudiced thinking. "No, children. I've been everywhere in the universe. I was a photon until a man broke me free and I ran away from the electron that was created with me." There! Gelic was ready to admit he'd once been a photon, but he still thought they were mistaken when they said he'd been a gamma ray. Though gamma rays are one kind of photon, he could never accept himself as one of those icky vermin.

The positrons murmured among themselves. Charma joined them. Every now and then, one or the other of them cast a look of consternation at Gelic.

Charma came back—not as Gelic's really cute friend but as the spokesman for the positrons. "We don't understand how you could go everywhere in the universe. It's obvious you're not one of us. The dark matter took us in eons ago to protect us from the electrons. We've never been out there. There's nothing but danger out there."

"No . . . I mean, there is danger, but there's more than that. There's a whole universe." He had to make them see. Though he'd wanted nothing more than to come here. Still, he didn't want to make his home among the fearful. "A beautiful universe if you just stay clear of the electrons."

Curiosity warred against fear in Charma's eyes. "Where did you come from?"

"From very, very far away."

"How did you survive out there for so many eons with all those electrons chasing you?"

The other positrons nodded. One of them shouted, "Why didn't you just come back here?"

"I've never been here before." That was true. He'd been all over the universe, but always as a photon shining into dark corners or subsumed in universal energy. He'd known about the positron colony, but once they'd joined the dark matter, his photon self had nothing to do with them.

Surprise echoed among the positrons.

"Well," Charma said. "The queen will want to see you."

Now it was Gelic's turn to be surprised. "The queen?"

"The queen!"

They moved, and he moved with them. There were no roads, no buildings, and no landmarks. Even Nanosia had buildings. But here it was just darkness. In the distance, Gelic perceived a gathering. Suddenly, trillions of positrons appeared before him, orbiting something. He fell into the orbit, but Charma drew him to the center. He thought some positronic Nano would come out and accuse them of being irregular for not doing what the other positrons were doing. But no one apprehended them.

In the center stood the most beautiful positron Gelic had ever perceived. This had to be the queen. Her beauty alone made her royal. The orbiting positrons kept their orbits far from the queen like leptons around the nucleus of an atom. When Gelic and his escort stepped forward, they were alone with the Queen of the Positrons.

He bowed. "Your Majesty."

She deigned to turn to him. "We have trillions of subjects, but who are you?"

He opened his mouth to speak, but Charma stepped forward, upstaging him. "Please pardon us, Your Majesty. We found this positron wandering around alone and thought we should bring him to Your Majesty's attention."

"Wandering around alone in our queendom?"

Gelic thought about how he could take charge of this without being rude to Charma. Well, she had been rude to him first, but he was alone and had to win their favor if he wanted to bring his children here. And he had to take charge. Charma may be cute, but he was the first positron. No. He wasn't. They were. It didn't matter. He had to bargain with them from a position of strength. That position wasn't located behind Charma. He stepped forward leaving no space between himself and the queen for Charma to upstage him again without standing on the queen's toes. He looked up at ultimate loveliness and bowed again. "Your Majesty, I am your humble servant."

She rolled her eyes. "Servant? How will you serve us?"

He wasn't sure what the correct answer should be. He knew from eons of watching kings and queens strut through history that even an almost correct answer could cost him his positronic head. "I will adore you, my fine beauty." He knew how silly that sounded as soon as the words came forth. But royalty was royalty, and they expected this. It wasn't any sillier than prostrating himself.

A commotion beyond the orbiting positrons drew everyone's attention.

"What's going on?"

But Gelic recognized Antipan's chaotic particles and knew exactly what it was. "Your Majesty, don't panic. They're miscreants from my world and . . ."

"Your world?! You brought this calamity on us. A positron wandering around alone."

Charma stared at him. His positron escort backed away horrified.

The queen jumped up. "Seize him!"

But Antipan's minions were on them all at once.

"Your Majesty! Help us!" They'd always looked to her for help. But particles had seized her and were dragging her out.

Never in countless eons had the positrons had to deal with an invasion. The electrons kept their distance. They had no idea what to do.

The particles flitted here and there, driving the positrons away from the only home they'd known since the beginning of time. When they saw the electrons, they shrieked. A cloud of electrons rushed forward, annihilating many of the positrons. Chaotic particles pushed the electrons back, making a clear path for the positrons.

The electrons protested. "You can't . . ."

"We can, and we are. Out of our way please." The particles kept driving the positrons forward, not stopping to see if the electrons would give their consent.

Gelic knew it wasn't Antipan's plan to have them annihilated here in the region of dark matter. He'd wanted to go back to Nanosia to gather his own flock anyway. But not as a captive. He had to take charge of the positrons before they reached the Realm of Chaos.

He raised his voice. "Children! My children! Do not be afraid. I will bring us out of this."

The particle holding Gelic laughed. "You can't get yourself out of this."

He had to do something. Their queen wept in her captor's arms. The positrons knew they couldn't turn to her. But maybe they'd turn to him despite his own captivity. He'd launch an escape. Then they'd look to him. "Why should we let them take us? Fight, positron brothers! Fight!"

But the positrons had never had to fight. They just stared as the faster chaotic particles herded them out of the region of dark matter.

Photons and neutrons passed by. The stars and asteroids. Gelic didn't know if they were moving past him, or he was moving past them. He hit something solid but permeable like a border into another world. From one nanosecond to the next he became aware that he was moving down. Down was down, and up was suddenly up. The particles pushed them into mist. They were in Nanosia.

Gelic tried to make a last stand. "I'm not going into the Realm of Chaos. You brought me here, and this is as far as I'll go."

The particles looked at one another and laughed. "You'll go where we take you. But Antipan doesn't want you in the Realm of Chaos anyway."

Gelic was puzzled. "What?"

"He wants you right here where you'll do the most . . . um . . . good."

The positrons milled around. "What is this place?"

"This is your new home. Enjoy."

The particles spun away, laughing and dancing back to the Realm of Chaos.

Gelic stared after them wondering why they'd bring them here and just leave them. Where was Antipan if he wanted positrons so badly? Why wasn't he here?

The positrons turned to him. "Where are we?"

"Why did you bring us here?"

"What will you do with us?"

While Gelic struggled for something to say, a swarm of electrons swooped down on the positrons.

"I never thought I'd see such lovely sights."

"There's a mate for all of us."

"Electrons!"

The positrons tried to pull away but found themselves pulled toward the electrons.

"Why are you running away? We are your mates."

"You're supposed to love us."

"No! Stay away!" Gelic started to shoo the electrons away but dared not let them touch him.

The positrons stared at them, then at one another. These electrons weren't anything like the electrons who despised them in the region of dark matter. The positrons murmured among themselves.

"They're attractive."

"Something about them is right."

The positrons moved toward the electrons.

"That's right. Come to us."

"We belong together."

On contact, positrons and electrons annihilated one another.

"No!" Gelic ran through the positrons. "They are your enemies!" He thought about that. "They are our enemies. Stay away from them."

"Break it up! Break it up!"

Nine bosons barged through the cloud of positrons and electrons that was quickly becoming a cloud of gamma rays. Gelic didn't know what to fear most.

"Where did all these positrons come from?"

"There's the leader. The one who calls himself a prophet. He did this."

Bosons rushed toward Gelic. He turned to run, but electrons came toward him that way. Remembering that he was in Nanosia where all directions are available, he thought of the road as mere mist and shot downward.

# Chapter 33

Deep in darkness—in the darkness of the darkness, where even the boldest of Antipan's elementary particles dared not wander for play or curiosity—the dreadful Negatron slept.

Nothing had disturbed its slumber for many cycles of many planets around countless suns. Life had appeared and disappeared on many of these planets. Many suns had been born and gone nova or collapsed into black holes. Still, the Negatron slept on.

But now, someone was calling its name. This someone was either very powerful or very foolish. It didn't take great power to call its name, so it could be the latter.

"Negatron," the fool whispered.

"Terrible Negatron. Great and wondrous Negatron. Rise out of the darkness, and let the worlds know that you *Are*."

It raised its head. Hunger pangs gnawed at some part of its being. It didn't like the sensation of hunger. What had it done before to make this sensation go away? It had put things in its mouth and swallowed them. Things that ran from it. These naughty things that didn't want its hunger to go away. So, they ran, but it caught them.

But it could sense nothing that it could put in its mouth. All around it was only darkness. It reached out at the darkness but couldn't grasp it. The Negatron opened its mouth, and the darkness filled it, mingling with the darkness inside it, but the hunger pangs persisted.

How had it gotten to this place where there was nothing to put in its mouth? Was there another place? There had to be. Had it gone away from the place where the things were? But the things had always run whenever it came near. So maybe it was they who'd run away from this place where it had always been.

It wondered what it was. It had to be something, or how could it ask the question?

"Negatron, you *Are!*"

"I am what?"

Why do the things run from it? *Negatron?* The voice said it was a Negatron. And what was that?

If it could remember putting things in its mouth, it could remember other things about itself. What was it when it was able to make the hunger go away? It remembered the sentient beings in the upper world. It knew them, but they didn't know it. They thought it was just an electron.

And it had laughed at them. Electrons were its weaker cousins. But the Great Negatron had no peers. Electrons fraternized with other particles—protons, neutrons, bosons, but the Negatron stood alone.

But then, it hadn't liked being alone. Had the force that brought it into existence been so horrified by what it had wrought that it dared not make another like the dreadful Negatron?

Bitter hatred mingled with the hunger as it remembered the electrons. They were its cousins, and yet, they kept their distance from it. That's when it discovered that putting them in its mouth made the hunger go away. That's when they began to run. The rejection hurt, but by putting them in its mouth, it could be close to them.

It remembered coming to a place where there were many particles. A merged particle with a number nine on his head seemed to control them. He told them to come here, and they came here. He told them to go there, and they went there. Then the thing became aware of the Negatron, and a beam of great energy burst from the number nine, but it had no effect. The thing screamed, and all the particles ran as one in one direction, as if they were all controlled by one thought. The Negatron had been able to catch some of the very last and weakest ones, but so many escaped, including the thing who had screamed.

Then one came forward and assailed the Negatron. It had a voice and began to speak words of power.

"The Big One comes and will strike you down, oh dreadful Negatron. Your days of terror will end."

The Negatron had snatched this foolish thing up and put it in its mouth. And immediately fell asleep.

As it slept, it dreamed of being alone and liking it. This was what it was, and there was none like it. Whatever had created it couldn't outdo itself, and so, hadn't tried. It was alone.

And someone was calling.

"Negatron?"

Who dared?

# Chapter 34

Jawan wanted to kick himself for a fool. What had made him think Nano would help him? He had to stop Antipan, and he had to do it himself. He didn't know how he'd do it. He was no hero, and he sure wasn't the Big One everyone in Nanosia, except Nano thought he was. Still, it was up to him. But he sure couldn't do it wasting away in the queen's dungeon.

"Something's happening." Loby nudged him.

Jawan looked around. Their boson escort was shimmering.

"Now," he whispered to his friends, and they bolted before the bosons' attention was fully present.

There wasn't a tree or a building to hide behind, but they lost themselves in the mist. Abruptly, the road came to an end. The boys looked at one another.

"Where do we go from here?" Zap asked.

Loby shrugged and looked back down the road the way they'd come. "We were just following the road. What made us think it would lead us anywhere?"

Jawan wondered the same thing. To find Antipan they had to go back to the Realm of Chaos—if Antipan was there. Zap wouldn't like that. They'd just have to go. "We're going back to the Realm of Chaos."

"You've got to be kidding?" Zap shook his head.

Loby looked at Jawan like he'd really lost it. "We just barely left there. You want to go back and give Antipan another chance?"

"But this time, he won't know we're there. He thinks we escaped. With surprise on our side, maybe we can stop him."

"Jawan, I don't have as much faith in maybe as you do."

All roads lead eventually to the Realm of Chaos, so Jawan just started walking. The mist coalesced into a road stretching out before them. "Fine. Stay there if you want to. See you back in Hadley Town."

"Wait! Jawan, wait!"

He didn't wait, and they had no choice but to follow.

"Maybe if we go in at night, we can sneak in," Loby whispered.

"It's always night in the Realm of Chaos. We've waited long enough."

They stood behind a pillar at the gate of the Realm of Chaos watching chaotic particles zip back and forth. Jawan couldn't help but notice the beauty of this place. It lacked the brilliance of Queen Quanta's palace of diamonds but made up for it in random symmetry. Just as he was about to step through the gate, he heard a rising, numinous chant. In the direction of the chant, a parapet rose from the edge of the road. They crept to the parapet and crouched behind it.

"Who is that?" Zap whispered.

"Sh. Who do you think it is?"

"Antipan's on the other side of this wall?!" Zap looked like he was ready to bolt.

"Sh."

They peered over its parapet. As the mist swirled, they caught a glimpse of Antipan.

The fire master seemed to be in a trance. His eyes were closed, the scroll unfurled in his lap.

"Negatron. Terrible Negatron.
Great and wondrous Negatron.
Rise out of the darkness and let the worlds know that you *Are*."

Jawan gasped. This was not Antipan's voice. It was a voice that resounded with primordial fire—no sound that a mortal could produce or endure.

Before he could think, he found himself looking directly into Antipan's open eyes.

"*You!* How did you escape the castle? Never mind. You're here now, and here you will die. You will wish you were under Myrlo's wrath rather than mine."

He unleashed a stream of fire that torched the parapet to ashes and seared their hands. They bolted out of the gate, trying to conceal themselves in the mist. Fire lashed all around them as they ran this way and that. But all they managed to do was lose each other.

Not far ahead, Jawan saw the shadows of the denizens of Nanosia appearing and disappearing in the mist. They wouldn't save him from Antipan, and he didn't dare call for Loby and Zap lest Antipan be the one who found him.

Fire lashed closer than he liked, and he trembled. At least he thought he was trembling. In fact, the whole world trembled. Everything under him, over him, and around him shook with a pulse that threatened to recalibrate his heartbeat. Then he heard screaming.

"The Negatron!"

"Out of the Realm of Chaos! It's coming!"

What seemed like every elementary particle in the universe came running. Jawan remembered the crowd of terrified people running from the purple plague in Hadley Town.

Terrified, he tried to push his way through the frantic crowd. But the quanta surged forward like one impenetrable wave of terror. Panic twisted his thoughts. Antipan would find him, even if the Negatron didn't get him first. He took ten loping steps and saw a shadow approaching him so fast and purposeful it had to be Antipan. His own fears had summoned the fire mage, or was it Nano come to see what all the commotion was about? Caught between fire and a dungeon, Jawan froze. The shadow pushed the last quanta aside and stood before him. Jawan looked up and caught his breath. "Master."

But his master wasn't there to save him. Myrlo glared at him with such fury that Jawan wondered if Antipan might offer the less agonizing death. If he thought about it, the dungeon hadn't been all that bad.

"Do not call me master. And don't even try to explain what you are doing here. You wouldn't be here if you hadn't disobeyed me in many ways."

Jawan gulped, tried to speak, and could not.

In a flash of fire, Antipan appeared out of the mist looking happier than Jawan thought he should under the circumstances. "Master Myrlo, I'm delighted to see you."

But Myrlo turned back to Jawan. "And don't insult my intelligence by telling me this is just a coincidence you happen to be here with Lord Elveston."

His words were cut off when Antipan struck him with a whip of fire. "Yes, he's here with me, Myrlo. I'm glad you came to see that he is my apprentice now, and now it's time for you to go."

Myrlo's robe burst into flames, which he quickly smothered with layers of earth. The fire charred the earth, and it flaked down into the mist, leaving him with only a small amount.

"Is that the best you can do?" Antipan laughed.

Jawan found his attention divided between this uneven scuffle and the now visible Negatron. The monster gobbled electrons, positrons, and gamma rays, rampaging through Nanosia with no one to stop it.

Antipan lashed his fiery whip again. The little earth Myrlo had left was barely enough to smother the new flames on his robe. In Nanosia there was no earth except what he'd brought with him, and he'd not brought enough to fight this unforeseen battle.

The combatants were so engrossed in each other that Jawan saw his chance. He couldn't get the fire whip, but the scroll was on Antipan's other side. Carefully, he crept toward Antipan and snatched it.

"*Fool!*" Antipan and Myrlo bellowed in unison.

They abandoned their fight to chase him. Antipan's whip came within inches of his head. He changed directions and immersed himself in the still-fleeing swarm of quanta.

As he ran, it dawned on Jawan that he had no idea what to do with the scroll. He'd never read it, and so still didn't know how to stop the Negatron. He couldn't read it on the run with everything still quaking around him.

He zigzagged out of the Negatron's direct path. But he looked up and saw that Nano couldn't move out of its path. To Jawan's horror, it lumbered straight for Nano and the barriers that controlled the passage of quanta in and out of the Quantum Realm.

Jawan didn't have time to wonder if Nano would save him if the Negatron were coming at him. Probably not as irregular as he was. Still, nice guy or not, Nano was important to the whole universe. Jawan had to save him. How, he had no idea. *Wait. Could the Negatron hear?*

"Hey, big and ugly!" Jawan called. "Yeah, you. This way, you overgrown electron!"

Apparently, it could hear, and didn't appreciate being called an electron, even though that's what it was. It turned its rampaging away from Nano and lunged after Jawan, who took off like an arrow.

Jawan saw a flash of fire ahead and ran the other way. If he stayed in the crowd, he might elude the mages for a little while, but the Negatron was eating every quantum in its way. If Jawan moved away from the quanta, the mages would find him. This wasn't helping. He had to get somewhere he could hide and read the scroll.

"Jawan!" Off to his left, he heard his name.

"Loby! Zap!"

They came together but kept running.

"We were so scared we'd never find you again." Zap gasped.

"All those quanta pushing us this way and that. Every way but where you were."

"We thought we were trapped on Nanosia forever."

"Where are we going?"

Jawan thought about it. It was time to think. Then an idea came to him. "This way."

Then all three veered off to their right until they came to a series of buildings away from the crowd and tumult.

"This is the factory where nanotubes are made. I always seem to come here when I'm in trouble."

"So, we're safe here?" Loby asked.

"It's the only thing resembling a building that I know of in Nanosia, besides the queen's palace, and I don't think we want to go there right now."

But when Jawan pushed the door to the factory, it was locked. Knocking softly brought no one to the door, and he dared not knock louder, lest someone besides Kelton hear.

So, they nestled down in the doorway, and Jawan showed them the scroll. With trembling hands Jawan held it while Loby and Zap read it over his shoulder.

As they read, a shadow fell over the doorway. They looked up and saw Myrlo looming over them. His face was a mask of rage. Quickly, Jawan tucked away the scroll.

"Trying to hide the evidence against you, Jawan? Little good that will do. It's already clear you serve Elveston now."

Myrlo reached for the boy, but a lash of fire curled around his torso and yanked him back.

"Master!" Jawan jumped up as Myrlo fell.

"Jawan! Look out!" Loby called.

But all Jawan saw was his master covered in mist and flame. He used the folds of Myrlo's robe to beat the flames.

Through his pain Myrlo stared at Jawan. "Treachery! So, you are working together. What did Elveston do to seduce you who were once my apprentice?"

"No, not treachery." Antipan laughed. "Just choosing the master who could give him more power. I promised to give him powers that you only wish you possessed. Move aside, boy, so I can finish him." Antipan raised his whip.

"That's a lie!" Jawan screamed. "Master Myrlo, I was never with him. He's an enemy who in this world goes by the name Antipan. I tried . . ."

"Silence!" Antipan hissed. "No more of your nonsense. You little turncoat. Can't make up your mind which of us is your master now, huh? Just give me the scroll."

Loby opened his mouth to speak, but Antipan's fiery eyes bore into him so that drops of sweat poured down his face and evaporated in the heat of his master's fury. Zap just stared and trembled.

Jawan loathed to leave his master's side, but he'd come here to stop Antipan, not run from him. He remembered the words Antipan had spoken and opened his mouth to say what he knew were probably the most dangerous words he'd ever uttered. But he had no other choice.

"Negatron," the fool whispered.

"Terrible Negatron. Great and wondrous Negatron. Rise out of the darkness, and let the worlds know that you *Are*."

"Wait," Loby said. "Those are the words to summon the monster, but how do we control it? How do we stop it?

Zap's hand flew to his mouth. "Forget Antipan. Did we just summon the monster?"

"Foolish boys. Do you think the Negatron will answer your summons or that you can control it if it does? It doesn't matter. I will kill you long before it comes."

"We meet again." The positron preacher stepped out of the mist. "My positron family is here, and I have unfinished business with you."

"W-with me?" Jawan stammered. He tried to remember ever even meeting the positron and couldn't. With Antipan and the positron coming down on him, things couldn't possibly get worse.

Another shadow fell over them all. Jawan wondered when he'd learn to stop bringing that jinx on himself. Antipan turned in time to see the inside of the Negatron's maw. Antipan raised his whip to strike, but the monster's slobbering mouth doused the flames. The fire mage didn't even have time to scream or, more in keeping with his invincible poise, utter a curse before he was crushed between foot-long teeth.

Then to Jawan's horror, the monster turned its gaze on him. "Foolish master, did you dare to summon me? Now I will put you in my mouth."

The mouth opened. Jawan's eyes closed.

"Stop!" Zap shouted.

Jawan cringed with terror.

"I think it's going to take more than that," Loby said.

"Indeed, it will.," came another voice.

The Negatron moved one more time then slowed as the voice chanted.

"Gentle negatron
Sleepy negatron
You've had all you can eat
And your belly now is full
Now slumber through the eons."

Jawan opened his eyes and looked. The Negatron had stopped. It had just settled back on what he supposed were its haunches and closed its eyes. The positron preacher stood nearby. Tall and commanding, he gazed at the boys.

"I am Gelic, first positron of the universe. You've killed my enemy. Though I'd wanted to kill him myself, dead is dead."

"Antipan is your enemy? We thought you were working together."

"He thought that, too. Or at least, he thought I thought that. But what he wanted was not what I wanted, so he became my enemy."

"There it is!"

The party looked up and found themselves surrounded by nine powerful bosons. A sneering Nano confronted Jawan.

# Chapter 35

"So, you've brought all your irregular cronies with you and even taken up with an outlawed positron. Well, it won't help. You're not slipping away from me this time. No one is going to rescue you from the dungeon I'll put you in. You'll stay there until you decay, you mischievous little misfit."

After almost being fire whipped by Antipan and gobbled up by the Negatron, Jawan was still shaky. But Nano wasn't half as frightening. He gave Nano his most impassive face. "What are you talking about?"

"Don't play innocent with me. I saw you control the Negatron. Did away with your partner Antipan, did you? What were the two of you planning? Guess even he didn't know how underhanded you are. But you won't fool me like you did him. You called up the Negatron to destroy the Quantum Realm."

Zap and Loby stared at the vicious-looking bosons like they would rather be home studying their lessons than here. Myrlo apparently didn't know what to think. The Jawan Nano and Antipan presented was nothing like the Jawan they'd known in Hadley Town. Mischievous, yes. But no more than any other boy and certainly not criminally devious.

Jawan chuckled. "That's ridiculous. You saw me stop the Negatron. If I was trying to destroy the realm, why would I stop it?"

"Your conniving little mind has its reasons, and you didn't stop the Negatron. You summoned it. Then when you lost control, your friend stopped it. So, you're not the clever little mastermind you think you are."

"Indeed, I am his friend." Gelic stepped forward.

Jawan wasn't sure if that was good or bad, but he'd stand by it. If Nano didn't like him, he must have done something right.

A boson shimmered into existence beside Nano. "Sir, the positrons have entered the fourth quarter. There are gamma rays everywhere."

Nano turned on the positron. "You did this. You brought all those positrons here. There're enough positrons to mate with every electron in the universe."

Jawan's ears perked up. "What does that mean?"

"It means that because of this positron, we'll soon have a universe with nothing but gamma rays."

Jawan turned to the positron. "You're as bad as Antipan. Why would you bring them here to destroy the universe where you have to live just like everybody else?"

"I didn't bring them here. Antipan did."

Nano snorted. "Sure, pass the blame. It doesn't matter. Bosons, arrest him!"

Jawan shook his head. Nano thought the answer to every problem was to arrest somebody. It wouldn't work here. "Nano, if you want to save the realm, you've got to listen to me."

"Threatening me now, are you? Let me tell you . . ."

"No, that was not a threat. Simply a fact."

"The only fact I know is you and Antipan and this big-shot positron are causing trouble in the Quantum Realm, and I'm going to stop it right now. Arrest them!"

The bosons moved in.

"Wait! I'm not Antipan's partner."

Nine bosons herded them all toward what Jawan knew was the queen's dungeon. He looked back at Myrlo's comatose form. "Master." But the bosons kept them moving. He had to talk fast.

"Antipan was trying to use antimatter to destroy the material universe."

Nano glared at the positron. "Antimatter. Right. Which you are. So, you and your partner were trying to build an anti-universe. Which of you was the mastermind and which the sidekick?"

Jawan sighed. He'd had enough of all these ridiculous accusations. "What makes you think I'd be in league with something like that? I wouldn't have a place in such a universe. You know that."

Nano scoffed. He clearly didn't want to give his favorite suspect the benefit of the doubt. The party stopped in front of the dungeon door. "In you go."

Zap groaned. "Oh, no."

"Oh, yes. And you're not getting out this time."

The positron stiffened his back. "I'm the first positron. The prophet of the new order of positrons. You will not put me in a dungeon."

"Sorry, I don't believe in prophecy. In you go."

"Wait!" Jawan grabbed the door-jam, stalling as much as he could. He had to get Nano to listen. "I know what you can do about the positrons. I'll tell you, but not from inside a dungeon."

Nano looked at him then at Loby and Zap, who tried not to look like they had no idea what Jawan was talking about.

"What can I do?"

"I'll tell you, but first we have to see about my master."

"You've got a master? So now the conspiracy unfolds."

"No. He's from the Big World, and he's hurt. We have to go back where we were before you interrupted us with your accusations. He's still there." Jawan started walking.

Nano sighed and waved his hand. "Let him go."

The bosons made a path for Jawan and company flanking them back to Myrlo, who lay unconscious in the mist.

The Negatron sat snoozing nearby, but it looked faded. It wasn't the mist.

"What will you do with it?" Zap asked.

Gelic gazed at the monster. "Nothing needs to be done. It will fade back to its resting place and remain there until some fool summons it again."

Jawan took out the scroll. "Maybe we should just burn this. Then no one can summon it."

Gelic snatched the scroll. "You must not. This knowledge is eons old. It isn't just about the Negatron, and the universe needs this knowledge."

Jawan shrugged and turned to Myrlo. "We can't just leave him here. Don't you have some kind of infirmary when particles get sick?"

"Sick?"

"Don't you have somewhere he can lie down?"

Nano looked at Myrlo as Jawan pointed him out. "He's lying down now," he said dismissively.

Jawan sighed. "I mean somewhere clean and comfortable."

"Don't know what comfortable means for you, but yes, there's a place."

Nano summoned a boson. "Carry him to the queen's guest room."

Jawan turned to Loby and Zap. "You guys need to stay with him. I don't want to leave him with no one from our world when he's so weakened."

"But . . ." Zap began to protest.

"Jawan's right," Loby said. "We're mice. We can handle ourselves, but the earth mage can't. Let's go."

Zap and Loby followed as the boson carried Myrlo to the queen's palace.

Nano turned to Jawan. "Now how do I get rid of the positrons and then get rid of you?"

"You'll like this. You can use W bosons to turn them all into electrons."

Gelic gasped. "You must not do that to my children. They are proud positrons. We . . ."

Nano shook his head. "Positrons are worse than useless for constructing atoms, but without them the symmetry of the universe would be upset beyond repair. We need positrons. We just need them out of the way."

"That's nice to know." Gelic snorted. "I know where I will take them."

"You?" Nano rolled his eyes. "You're just one of them. What do you think you can do with them? Take them to the Realm of Chaos? Well, I guess now that Antipan is no more, you can go there."

"No, to a world you never thought of."

"The Big World? None of that nonsense. This is a real problem. I need real answers."

Gelic scowled. "You really don't know anything beyond Nanosia, do you? Where do you think the quanta come from when they come through the nanotubes?"

"They come from . . . This is irregular. This is irregular. They come for recycling after Atomidon gets through with them."

"Absolutely no idea. I will take them. Just round them up in one place, and I will gladly take them off your hands."

**

Nano dispatched his bosons to gather every positron in Nanosia. He wanted to be rid of them all.

But when Gelic arrived at the pen where the positrons were being held, he frowned. "Where are my children? These all came from the region of dark matter. But where are mine?"

Nano stared. "There are others?"

Then Jawan remembered. "They're in the Realm of Chaos. Antipan was keeping them there."

"I must have them."

Nano shook his head. "No way. Antipan or no Antipan, I'm not sending my bosons into the Realm of Chaos. Who knows what's in there?"

"I know," Jawan said. "It's a beautiful place."

"You would think that." Nanos folded his arms across his chest, muttering, "No, no, no. Irregular. Irregular."

Gelic took Jawan by the arm. "That's all right. We don't need a bunch of burly bosons frightening my flock. Come friend. We'll get them ourselves."

Chaotic particles danced around them as they marched into the late Antipan's castle.

"Lord!"

"We knew you'd come for us."

Gelic spread his arms to embrace them all. "Have I not set you free when you were in bondage to the wicked Nano and his electronic minions whom he preferred over you?"

"Yes, Lord."

"It was you."

Jawan drew in a breath. He'd never seen anything like this. They actually called him lord. He hadn't even called Lord Elveston lord.

"You will not be re-enslaved, my brethren. I am the Lord. He whom the Lord has set free is free indeed. And I've come to take you home."

"Home, Lord."

"Take us home."

Jawan was getting surfeited. But Gelic knew what he had to do to get all these positrons to follow him.

And follow him they did. But when they saw the holding pens, some of them began to murmur.

"This isn't our home, Lord."

"Neither shall it be. I've another place for you, far, far away. I've brought you here to meet your brothers with whom you shall share that place." With beatific grace he turned to Jawan. "I have them now, friend. Go and see about your master."

A master performance. Jawan wanted to bow. "Yes, you have the situation under control here, and there's nothing else I can do." He turned to the bosons. "Can one of you escort me back to my friends in the queen's palace?"

***

Jawan winced when he saw Myrlo's pale face. Burn marks crisscrossed his barely moving torso.

"He's fading," Loby informed him.

Jawan knelt down beside his master's cot and stroked his face. His skin was parched, like sterile ground with nothing to nourish a plant. The earth mage would die without the fertile earth.

Zap and Loby seemed to languish in uncertainty. Their gazes shifted between the floor and the bosons standing guard around the little room. *For what?* Jawan wondered. Not to protect Myrlo in his condition. They belonged to Nano and had no reason to trust all these irregular beings, Big One or not.

Jawan buttonholed the one near the door. "Listen. I need to find Pym. Can you bring her here?"

The boson didn't move or seem to respond in anyway, except the telltale shimmer. In an instant, Pym came through the door.

"What's going on? Old Higgy here told me you needed me. I've been trying to make you see that since you got here. Do you mean the truth finally dawned on you?"

For a moment, Jawan's head spun under her barrage of words. But he made enough sense of them to dismiss them.

"Pym, we need your help. My master will die if we don't get him back to the Big World fast. Can you help us get through the nanoscope again?"

She looked at Myrlo. "He looks bad. I don't know what he's supposed to look like, but I hope it's better than that."

"It is, but let's go."

Then the three boys trooped after Pym as she led them out of the room. The bosons looked like they were going to stop them, but they'd had no orders to detain them. Instead, Pym ordered Higgy to carry Myrlo.

\*\*\*

Myrlo drifted in and out of consciousness. In the moments that Myrlo was lucid, Jawan tried to explain himself now that his master was in no condition to spring on him.

"I wasn't in league with him."

"You disobeyed me, Jawan. Whether you did it for Elveston or not has nothing to do with it."

"I came here, not to disobey you, but to find the proof I needed of the evil things he was doing. He's not even known as Elveston in this world. He calls himself Antipan here."

"Antipan? Against all. That is still irrelevant. You are just an apprentice. Did you think you could take on the fire master with nothing more than your friends to help? You should have let me handle it. That's why I am the master, and you are the apprentice."

Jawan knew there was still more to be done, and no time for Myrlo to handle it in his slow methodical way. He sighed.

# Chapter 36

They tumbled onto the floor of Myrlo's laboratory in a heap. The boson had carried Myrlo as far up the tube as he dared. Then Jawan took him and handed him to Loby on the other side before climbing through himself.

Realizing that all the jostling couldn't be good for Myrlo, they struggled to balance speed and care as they rushed through the castle and out the portcullis. Myrlo didn't stir until they laid him down on the earth.

Jawan felt his master's pulse growing stronger but didn't know if they were doing enough to revive him to his full strength.

"Maybe the other mages know what to do," Zap suggested.

"How do we summon them?" Loby asked. "And what do we tell them?"

Jawan waved away all this hesitation and uncertainty. There was no time for it. "Zap, you will have to take the portal to your master's castle and tell him what's happening."

Zap blanched. "The portal! Oh no. I can't . . ."

"You have to. You did it before and came out okay," Jawan urged him.

"Then you come with me."

"I have to stay here with my master."

"Then, Loby, you come."

They went back into the castle to use Myrlo's portal. Not knowing what else to do, Jawan sprinkled earth on his master's skin, reaching beneath his robe to make direct contact. He could only hope that it was helping. He tried not to remember that people sprinkled earth on graves.

"Jawan?"

He jumped at his name, then turned to see who could be calling him from the direction of the forest. Two sparks—no lights—shone out of the gloom like eyes. They were the size of eyes—fiery eyes. In gradients, the form of a woman came into the light.

"Cintella! What happened to you?"

She turned her eyes away. "A lot of things. Looks like we lost each other back there. What's going on?"

"I should ask you. We went through the portal, and you just weren't there."

So, she wants to talk about the portal. He'd like to know what happened there, too. But her eyes? "I don't know what happened. I just couldn't follow you. Some force kept me in the portal. I couldn't go back into Elveston's lab with Itch in there, and I couldn't follow you, so I was stuck. Where'd you go?"

Jawan realized that he'd never told Cintella about Nanosia. Maybe one day he could tell her, and she wouldn't laugh. He couldn't stand it if she laughed at him. "To a place that's not on any map you've ever seen. A place far, far away."

She looked at him, as if she recognized something in what he'd said. Then she shrugged. "Yes. Well, I couldn't go there. I waited until I was sure Itch was gone and made my way here, waiting for you. Now what brings you here?"

Jawan looked down at his master and rubbed earth into his hands. He thought about the way things seemed so odd. Nanosia was not the same for everyone. Cintella had a counterpart there. "I went to a place and saw a queen. The queen of the Quantum Realm. She looks just like you."

"A queen. Elveston told me I'm his queen."

Maybe he could ease the story onto her mind a little at a time until all the pieces came together. "Well, you don't have to worry about being his queen anymore. Lord Elveston is no more."

"How do you know this?"

Jawan opened his mouth to answer, then shut it. He'd said too much. He couldn't explain a little bit without explaining everything. It wasn't time. "There was a man there who looked just like Lord Elveston, but his name was Antipan."

Cintella cocked an eyebrow. "I've had dreams about someone named Antipan. This is weird. But what does that have to do with me being Lord Elveston's queen?"

"Nothing."

As he massaged grass into Myrlo's forehead, she looked down at the earth mage and gasped. "What happened? Is he . . .?"

"Alive. Yes. There was an accident . . . Lord Elveston tried to kill him but perished himself. And now my master's badly hurt."

That wasn't exactly a lie. Nothing he'd have to back away from later.

"Tried to kill him?! But Elveston is a mage. He took the oath. He can't . . ."

"But he did. And he had a camera that did things to people when he took their picture. That's what caused the purple plague."

She scooped up loose earth and rubbed Myrlo's feet. Color returned to his skin as she worked, but he did not waken.

"Well, Elveston is gone," she said. "But there's still Itch. We don't know how much Itch knows about the camera's operation. Suppose he has a mind to finish his master's work once he finds out Lord Elveston is dead?" She paused to let that sink in. "The camera that caused the purple plague in Itch's hands? We can't let that happen. We just can't. The question is, how can we get it? He won't fall for the Red Ale trick a second time."

"Loby knows a secret passage through the castle. When he gets back with Zap's master, we'll . . . No, we can't do it like that."

"Do what like what?"

Well, taking care of Itch had nothing to do with Nanosia, so he could tell her about that. He drew in a breath. He was beginning to act like one of the mages with all these secrets. "If he's coming back with Zap's master, he'll probably have the other mages, too."

"That will be good. They'll know what to do."

"That's just it. I think the fewer people who know about this camera, the better. Who knows what the other mages might decide to do with it?"

"But Lord Elveston was the only evil one."

Jawan looked down at Myrlo, comatose but still alive, and one day, hopefully, he'd be well again. "Certainly, my master wouldn't . . ."

"You're right. How do we know what's in the minds of those who wield power? Even the earth mage's mind."

"He wouldn't do evil. But he'dtake time to study before stopping someone else who would do evil. By then the evil might already be done.""

Cintella shook her head. "People who do evil don't start out with the intention of doing evil. They'll tell themselves they're keeping the camera for noble purposes. To study it or some such."

This was what Jawan had been thinking all along. He believed Myrlo would do the right thing in his own eyes. But he didn't know what the other mages might do. Didhewant to take the chance with such a dangerous weapon? Once they even know about it, they'll take it out of his hands, and there'd be nothing he could do.

Then Cintella started, as if something just occurred to her. "There's something different about you. I can't . . . Say something."

"What do you want me to say?"

"That's it! You're not stuttering. Your speech is perfect."

Jawan's eyes widened, and his hand flew to his mouth. He wasn't stuttering and hadn't since he'd come back from Nanosia. The feeling of helplessness that had plagued him for years, ever since Myrlo had come into his life, was gone. He knew then that he could face this last challenge. He would carry it through to the end, and it wouldn't end until that camera was destroyed. But there was still Itch.

Zap's master arrived with the two remaining mages. Jawan explained Myrlo's plight to them as best he could. He knew he might as well tell them about Nanosia, since his master would know once he could speak. But he thought it best to leave the parts about Lord Elveston to Myrlo's discretion.

He left his master in their care. Then he and his friends entered the castle to plan their next move.

Loby blinked when he saw Cintella. "What happened to your eyes?"

"Nothing." She turned away.

"Something..."

"Nothing!"

Once they were sure what they needed to do, they locked forefingers. Cintella looked amused until Jawan held out a hand for her.

"You want me to join the boys' club?"

"It's not just a club," Loby corrected her. "It's the Holy Order of Mice, and we don't let just any body join. You should feel honored to be invited."

A look of doubtful amusement on her face, she locked forefingers with Jawan and Loby, and the boys began to chant:

> "Though fire and rain assail us
> Though earthquake and storm impale us
> We are mice!"

With this solemn enjoinment, they were off.

Getting through the secret passage in Elveston's castle was easier this time. Except for Cintella, they were old pros. There was no hint of Itch as they made their way to the attic. None of them was convinced this was a good sign. They'd rather know where he was. But no dust left telltale footprints between the attic door and the camera.

Their breathing sounded like a roaring vortex in the stillness of the attic. One window faced the road outside, and in front of it sat the ghastliest device they'd ever seen.

"So, this is the deadly camera," Zap whispered.

None of them dared to move close, much less touch it.

"How do we destroy it?" Jawan asked.

"I think the danger is in the cylinder," Loby said. "If we remove that, we can just dismantle the camera."

"And what do we do with the cylinder?" Cintella asked.

They all jumped when the door slammed open.

"You leave it alone. That's what you do!"

"Itch!" the kids cried in unison.

He glared at Cintella. "You owe me for that little trick you played with the whorehouse. And I'm not leaving you for my master this time, *queen*. You're mine!"

Not knowing what else to do, Jawan aimed the camera at Itch. If he'd had time to think, he'd have known, and they'd all be dead by Itch's hands before he came down with the purple plague. But he didn't think. He just aimed the only weapon he had and pressed all the buttons he could find, hoping that one of them would do something.

Suddenly, Itch just disappeared.

"You annihilated him, Jawan!" Loby exclaimed.

"He's gone," Zap repeated.

"Gone?" Jawan stammered. He drew his hand away from the camera, unable to believe what his eyes did not see. "I . . . he's gone."

"Yes, and let him be the last victim before we dismantle this thing."

And so, they did. They removed the cylinder and unscrewed every screw they could find in the camera until every part was separate from every other part.

"What do we do with the cylinder?" Cintella asked again.

"We could put it in the firepit," Loby suggested. "No one will ever retrieve it from there."

"Firepit?!" Zap gasped. "Maybe we can find some other way."

"There is no other way."

They went down. Loby put his hand on the latch of the firepit's door and drew in a breath—a deep, hesitant breath—then opened the door. A blast of heat knocked them back a step, but they were determined.

"Stay here." Loby stepped down into the firepit.

But Cintella brushed past him, as if she were immune to the fire. Jawan and Zap remained in the doorway, not daring to come any closer. All they saw were light and shadows dancing on the walls. No sign of Loby or Cintella. All they could do was wait.

"Where is Elveston?"

Jawan shuddered. *Who could that be? Why would anyone be down here?*

"Boy." The voice echoed off the stones. "You are Elveston's boy. Where is he?"

"D-dead."

Flames roared, and the heat increased. Jawan started to close the door but didn't want to leave Loby and Cintella down there. Who knew if they'd be able to open the door from the inside?

"You and this queen have killed Elveston."

"N-no, sir."

"You are the queen. Why do you not bow to me?"

Cintella said nothing, and Jawan didn't know what she was doing. But he now knew the fire in her eyes had something to do with that awful voice.

"If your master is gone, you must feed me as he did."

"What?"

"You are but a boy, but you must take the blood oath and feed me, so that my spirit may remain."

"Why would I?"

"Will you not obey the commands I gave your master?"

"I have no master now. I won't feed you."

Another burst of heat and fire chased Loby and Cintella back up the stairs. They slammed the door shut and stood there gasping.

"Elveston shut me down there once as punishment. I'll never go down there again."

Jawan saw the sweat running down his face and understood why he didn't want to. But still . . . "But all the mages need the fire."

"I won't! I won't!"

Jawan saw that Loby no longer had the cylinder and hoped he'd had time to throw it in the fire.

When they returned to Myrlo's castle, the earth mage was sitting up on a stone bench in his garden.

"Will he be all right?" Jawan asked Quintessuma.

"A few more days of soaking up the Earth's energy, and he'll be in full power."

Then the four mages turned their gazes on Loby, who wasn't quite comfortable under such scrutiny.

"What?" the journeyman asked.

Quintessuma spoke for the other mages. "Your master is gone, and the world is without a fire mage."

Loby bit his lip, as if he'd never given himself the luxury of considering that reality. Neither Jawan nor the other kids knew what that would mean to be a journeyman without a master. Not knowing what to say, Loby said nothing.

Quintessuma continued. "You are the only person who can take Elveston's place. But you must be tested to see if your former master has prepared you for such a role."

"I . . . I don't know. I mean, I never thought about that. He never mentioned that that could happen. I always thought that would go to Itch."

The four mages grimaced.

"No way could we allow that," Lacus said. "No matter what Elveston had in mind. Besides, if he was plotting the annihilation of all matter, his plan didn't include you or Itch surviving to take his place."

Then the master of the fifth element turned to Cintella. "Did you not know that you are truly a queen?"

Cintella would have lowered her eyes, but she had never dared to raise them. She blinked, as lost for words as Loby had been. "That is what Lord Elveston wanted me to be. I'm just a cooper's daughter."

"It's not just what he wanted you to be. It's what you are. I have traveled the world of ether and have seen you where you rule over the Quantum Realm. A realm that isn't on any map." Cintella and Jawan glanced at one another as Quintessuma spoke. "You are the queen of all elementary particles. I am the queen of all spirits, and now, you will be my apprentice. Fuego, a minor spirit, has no power over that which I have claimed. Do you want to be free of this?"

"If I could, I do."

Quintessuma laid her hands over Cintella's eyes. "You can, and you are. I will show you what few have seen before."

Jawan looked into Cintella's eyes. They shone with joy, not fire.

As Cintella and Loby gazed into their futures, Myrlo beckoned Jawan to sit beside him on the stone bench. "I must ask your forgiveness for doubting you. All I could see was your disobedience. But now I see the things you wrote on your test are true. You are no longer my apprentice, but my journeyman."

"And listen to him." Cintella beamed. "He doesn't stutter anymore."

"No, I don't. I can say a ton of Tees and then some."

To Jawan's astonished delight, Myrlo bent over and hugged him.

At that moment, Zap jumped up. "What about me? Everybody's getting promoted except me."

Lacus laid a hand on Zap's shoulder. "Sorry, kid. You'll still be my apprentice until you pass your exams."

"Do you mean I let Jawan and Loby drag me through all that horror for nothing?"

"Not for nothing," Jawan assured him. "Think of the experience."


Hope you enjoyed Queen of the Quantum Realm. Read onto see an excerpt of Book 2 of the Nanosia Fantasy Series Fire Master.

# Fire Master

The secret to Loby's magic is hidden in the birth of the universe.

Loby, the journeyman of the late Lord Elveston, plunges into Nanosia to find the secret to his magic and take Lord Elveston's place as the new fire mage. Loby doesn't want to and isn't ready. King Cestor's diabolical machinations force Loby to get ready in a hurry.

## Excerpt

Loby looked away. They were all having such a good time. Praise and promotion fell on him and his friends like laurel wreaths for all their hard work. But he knew that the four remaining elemental mages would expect him to take his late master's place as the new fire mage. And he wasn't ready. He had no plans to even begin getting ready.

He studied the silent trees and incurious stones around the earth mage's castle. Occupied by these inanimate objects over here, he didn't have to think about the mages over there. But distance wouldn't protect him from that one question—that inexorable question. Still, he tried, standing off to the side, out of anyone's line of vision, but not out of their thoughts.

"So what are you going to do now, Loby?" Quintessuma approached him. "I don't know."

"What can he do?" Myrlo asked. "I doubt Lord Elveston prepared him to take his place."

Loby didn't find Master Myrlo's doubts helpful, either. He didn't want their expectations or their hand-holding understanding. All he wanted was a moment to breathe and enjoy not having the fire mage's wrath searing his every move.

His friends, Jawan, Cintella and Zap, stopped their chatter and looked at him. Loby knew they were trying to be supportive. After all, they were mice, members of a group he had started. But their gazes isolated him. He turned his attention to a large cloud boiling toward the sun. He could send his mind anywhere, but gravity trapped his feet among the grasses of Hadley Town.

Quintessuma moved closer. The spirit mage's power locked into his mind, drawing it back to the world where his feet stood.

"We know you're not fully prepared. But there has to be a fire mage, and you're the closest candidate—the only candidate—to take such a mantle."

She was making her point. Loby couldn't look away, down or up without showing disrespect for her rank as the mage of ether. But though she could force him to face her physically, she couldn't force his heart to take on this hateful role.

"I just don't know," he muttered. His master had never planned for him to be the fire master. Lord Elveston had died trying to destroy the world with Loby in it. Now Loby was a journeyman without a master. The world needed a fire master, but Loby was still a journeyman with a journeyman's knowledge of the element. Couldn't they see that?

Quintessuma didn't touch him. As the master of spirits, she didn't need to touch him to see into his heart and mind. He unfocused his eyes until she became a blur. No good. Like licking dry lips. He knew it wouldn't help but did it anyway. He couldn't see her, but she could still see into him.

"You know how to make fire cubes." Jawan, Master Myrlo's journeyman, felt an annoying need to remind Loby of this. "That's all the other mages need from you."

Quintessuma shook her head. "There's more to it. We need more from him."

"No!" Loby turned away from Quintessuma. He didn't want to show disrespect, but he hated this. They had no idea what they were asking him to do.

# Other Books by Rhonda Denise Johnson

## Nanosia Series

In the Nanosia Series, instead of a regular guy falling into a magical world, magic guys find the secrets to their magic in a world of science one billionth their normal size.

*Fire Master*: Book 2 of the Nanosia Fantasy Series

*Mage of the Black Hole*: Book 3 of the Nanosia Fantasy Series

Nanosia in Chaos: Book 3 of the Nanosia Fantasy Series

**Orisha Series**

The African orisha take these women on a journey through time and space as they struggle to be more than is expected of them as women and as African Americans.

*Two Women Two Roads One Future*: Book 1 of the Orisha Series

*Tomorrow's Temple*: Book 2 of the Orisha Series

*Where in the Whirl*: Book 3 of the Orisha Series

*Speaking for the Child: An Autobiography and a Challenge* - Bonus Edition

A story of triumph in the face of defeat. Of dignity in the face of humiliation. Of joy in the face of despair. Going through public schools with a hidden yet progressive vision and hearing loss. Bonus edition includes the short story "The Listening Heart."

# Short Stories by Rhonda Denise Johnson

On target

Flash fiction. What we won't do for love.

The Tale of the Western Crocogator

The Crocogator is a legend in the African American tradition. In this retelling, I've taken the Crocogator out of his native New York and transplanted him in Los Angeles. Here, the baddest dude in L. A. learns things about himself that he didn't now and gains a new appreciation for his female companion.

Dinner is Served

Your favorite fairytale goes off in wacky directions. Albert must marry to get the inheritance his late uncle left for him. The only woman to answer his classified ad isn't what he expected. He's trying to figure out what to do about her, but she has other plans.

Stuporman to the Rescue

Parody of Superman. It's a never-ending battle as Stuporman grapples Dr. Hydrobum and his diabolical schemes to plunge California into the Specific.

The First Nine

The great equalizer keeps them in their seats. Out of an assembly of 100, who will stand up to one man with a gun and nine bullets?

Sticks

Flash fiction Satires of familiar stories. Like Voltaire's Candide, Sticks takes our concept of justice and injustice out of the box.

The Listening Heart

Deaf woman discovers that just because she can't hear doesn't mean she can't listen. Semi-autobiographical.

Prince Alarming

Sequel to Sleeping Beauty. And they lived happily ever after? Not!

# About the Author

The Writer Who Paints Pictures With Words.

Why I Write

When the writer in me meets the reader in you, there is magic. An idea percolates in my head telling me a story is there, and I must write it. I imagine you, the reader, smiling, laughing, hollering at my characters, or remembering something in your life, and I get a good feeling. It's like when you know what your purpose is in life, and it's something that affects people in a good way.

What I Write

As a reader, I'm fascinated by well-written fantasy novels. As a writer, I find that magic naturally works its way into my stories.

# Connect to the Author

I hope you enjoyed Queen of the Quantum Realm and will leave a review at your favorite retailor. Below please find information about connecting with Rhonda Denise Johnson.

Email:

connect@rhondadenisejohnsonauthor.com

Twitter:

https://twitter.com/Rhondauthor

Facebook:

https://www.facebook.com/rhondauthor

Smashwords Interview:

https://www.smashwords.com/interview/Rhondazvous

# Don't miss out!

Visit the website below and you can sign up to receive emails whenever Rhonda Denise Johnson publishes a new book. There's no charge and no obligation.

https://books2read.com/r/B-A-AWWS-UZHXB

**BOOKS 2 READ**

Connecting independent readers to independent writers.

www.ingramcontent.com/pod-product-compliance
Lightning Source LLC
Chambersburg PA
CBHW070550260626

47161CB00002B/565